MADISON SQUARE MURDERS

MEMENTO MORI: BOOK ONE

C.S. POE

This is a work of fiction. Names, characters, places, and incidents either are the product of the author's imagination or are used fictitiously, and any resemblance to actual persons, living or dead, business establishments, events, or locales is entirely coincidental.

Madison Square Murders
Copyright © 2021 by C.S. Poe

Published by Emporium Press
https://www.cspoe.com
contact@cspoe.com

Cover Art by Reese Dante
Cover content is for illustrative purposes only and any person depicted on the cover is a model.

Edited by Tricia Kristufek
Copyedited by Andrea Zimmerman
Proofread by Lyrical Lines

Published 2021.
Printed in the United States of America

Trade Paperback ISBN: 978-1-952133-35-0
Digital eBook ISBN: 978-1-952133-34-3

For Greg.

Hugs, kisses, and I probably owe you a Coke.

MEMENTO MORI
Remember that you must die.

CHAPTER ONE

It was Monday, March 30, 8:22 a.m., and there was a body in a crate.

Correction: a skeleton in a crate.

Detective Everett Larkin raised his free hand and glanced at his watch.

And it was actually 8:23.

"I looked, and behold a pale horse," called Detective Ray O'Halloran over the silver-and-slate-colored rain drowning Madison Square Park and the uniformed officers unlucky enough to be tasked with cordoning off the lawn north of Shake Shack. "And his name that sat on him was Death."

Larkin released a breath, the wispy plume of air immediately lost to the same wind and rain that had uprooted the crabapple tree he stood beside, its gnarled roots reaching in vain toward the sky and thousands of pink blossoms carpeting the sodden ground like a flower girl at a wedding had gone buck wild. A makeshift tent had been erected over the hole and unearthed wooden box tangled in the tree's remaining embedded roots. A lone detective with the Crime Scene Unit, his white PPE bodysuit soaking wet and muddy, was taking photographs.

"Hear that, Grim?" O'Halloran asked as he stepped up beside Larkin.

"I drive a black Audi," Larkin answered in a modulated tone. It was an old joke. He wasn't flustered by it anymore. He hadn't taken his gaze off the unusual crime scene before him.

O'Halloran snorted and slapped Larkin on the back like a frat boy with something to prove.

Larkin stumbled forward. The current of rain pouring off his umbrella went down the back of his suit jacket, and one wingtip oxford in a two-tone green skidded along the grass before he stepped into a puddle past his ankle.

O'Halloran, the Irish fuck, started laughing.

Larkin raised his soaking wet foot. He glanced at O'Halloran—big in all the ways that lent bullies the self-assurance of it being perfectly fine to pick fights with someone shorter, more slender in build, even if Larkin was a thirty-five-year-old man with ten years on the force, and O'Halloran with even more. *Some boys never grow up*, Larkin thought as he briefly studied the older man's ruddy complexion, mussed strawberry-blond hair, and shit-eating grin.

"Why am I here," Larkin asked, his voice still calm, flat, and lacking the upward inflection found in English when asking a question.

Cupping a meaty hand around his mouth, O'Halloran barked over the storm, "Millett!"

The CSU detective turned, and Larkin involuntarily began cataloguing details. He was tall—six feet at least—though his shapeless PPE offered little else by way of physical details. His brown hair—honey, caramel—*why were subcategories of hair color always the names of foods?* Larkin wondered—was plastered across his forehead. He was classically handsome, sort of like a hardboiled PI brought to life from the pages of an old pulp novel. And like those gritty investigators, this CSU detective was about as disgruntled and didn't bother hiding it.

Millett put his camera in a case, secured the lid, yanked off his glove with a quick *snap*, and approached the edge of the tent. He offered a hand to Larkin and said, "Neil Millett, CSU."

O'Halloran spoke before Larkin could open his mouth. "Millett, this is the Grim Reaper."

Millett flashed O'Halloran an irritated expression.

Larkin squared his shoulders, shook Millett's hand, and corrected, "Everett Larkin."

"Isn't that what I said?" O'Halloran interjected with feigned innocence.

"Cold Case Squad," Larkin added.

"Cold Case?" Millett echoed. "They let you guys outside?"

"I believe the department is ethically obligated to allow us to see the sun once a quarter," Larkin said, although the joke was delivered so dryly, it came across as gravely serious.

But a smile crossed Millett's face as he gestured to the washed-out park. "You picked a good day."

A sudden clap of thunder sounded overhead, so powerful that it seemed to reverberate in Larkin's chest like a rhythm, a beat, stuck on repeat in the back of his mind like the irritating melody of a child's windup toy. He tightened his grip on the handle of his umbrella. "Why am I here," he asked, once again directing the question to O'Halloran.

"Isn't this what you do, Grim?" O'Halloran countered. "Knock down the door to Homicide, treat us like a bunch of rookies holding our dicks in both hands, steal our cases, then take credit for closing them?"

"We're on the same team," Larkin said.

"The fuck we are." O'Halloran was smiling, but his mouth was a razor's edge. "That's why your squad gets the funding, the press conferences. Hell, I bet your lieutenant got a chub just seeing my number on the caller ID this morning."

"Chill out, O'Halloran—" Millett began.

"Shut the fuck up and go bag and tag some goddamn dirt, faggot."

Larkin's vision blurred, like an optometrist switching lenses on a phoropter.

Better, one?

He snapped his umbrella shut, held it in both hands as he spun so as to be face-to-face with O'Halloran, and slammed the length of the impromptu weapon against O'Halloran's sternum. The older detective dropped his own umbrella out of reflex, stumbled backward into the rain, and landed flat on his ass in a puddle the size of a small lake.

Better, two?

Larkin stepped under the tent and turned to stare at O'Halloran as he adjusted the cuff link on his shirt.

"What the fuck?" O'Halloran roared.

"He must have slipped," Larkin concluded in his same even tone. And when thunder boomed a second time, he clenched his jaw so hard that he thought, briefly, he might crack a molar.

Millett was humming in agreement as the rumbles died down. They both watched O'Halloran climb to his feet, now soaking wet and plastered with pink blossoms. "You trip or something, O'Halloran?" Millett called over the rain.

"Fuck you!" O'Halloran snapped.

With no inflection in his tone, Larkin asked, "Is this case mine now."

O'Halloran picked up his umbrella. "A hundred-year-old fucking skeleton in a fucking box buried in the fucking park? Yeah, it's yours, Grim. With blessings from all of us in Homicide. Fuck both you homos."

"Drive safe," Larkin said before O'Halloran stomped across the park, making for the yellow crime scene tape. He glanced up at Millett, whose cheekbones were still bright with color. "I'd like to be updated on the situation," he prompted.

Millett met Larkin's unblinking gaze, and then the flush on his face deepened. He quickly about-faced and returned to the hole, saying over his shoulder, "O'Halloran's blowing smoke up your ass about the hundred-year-old thing. No way of knowing that with just a cursory once-over."

Larkin had stopped fiddling with his cuff link at some point and realized he had begun worrying the silver band on his finger. He dropped his hand. Released a breath. "John or Jane."

Millett had retrieved his camera before looking back. "I'm not the ME."

"Bear with me," Larkin said. "I'm used to having the pertinent details already established by the time I take over."

That made Millett—well, he didn't smile, but his shoulders relaxed a bit. "Between us?"

Larkin agreed.

"Assuming the pelvis belongs to the skull—John Doe."

"Narrow pubic arch, then."

"That's right," Millett answered. "I'd even venture a step further and guess he was at least in his twenties at time of death, but the ME will have the final say on that."

"Based on."

"Wisdom teeth were erupted." Millett motioned Larkin forward, and when they stood shoulder-to-shoulder, looking down at the partially visible skeleton through the wooden crate's broken lid, Millett said, "I've seen a lot of bizarre deaths in this city… but a body in a box, cracked open like a time capsule, is a first. What about you?"

"What about me."

"Seen anything like this in your workload?"

"There is nothing comparable in Cold Cases, no." Larkin felt Millett staring and looked up at the other detective.

"That's some seriously resounding absolution."

"Yes."

Millett narrowed his eyes. "An ex of mine liked to remind me: New York is nearly four hundred years old. That's a lot of murder."

9,022 cases, Larkin wanted to correct. He was only concerned with the recorded murders that had gone unsolved. The everyday victims. The ones whose names never made the newsprint. The ones people didn't want to know about. And that number was 9,022. Their dreams, their fears, first loves and first heartbreaks—everything that had once made them human, all now consolidated into a tidy pile of DD5 forms with the same notation made year after year until the lead Homicide detective officially deemed the case a loser: *No progress to report.*

That's when the lost cause was punted to Larkin's desk. And in a city of nine million, Everett Larkin stood alone, unmoored. The only one who hadn't forgotten—*couldn't* forget—those 9,022 lost souls. Their case numbers were a memento mori by which he mourned. Each day was an anniversary of another victim awaiting justice, and *yes, Detective Millett*, Larkin wanted to say, *I know every single one*.

"When you take samples—" Larkin paused when he caught sight of a man standing near the yellow tape, looking out of place. "—please take some of the crate too."

"You're going to have to fight the department to pay for that test."

"Take the sample." Larkin detached from Millett. He flicked his wrist in a quick, come-hither motion to the older man, who pointed to himself in confirmation, spoke to a nearby uniformed officer, and then was allowed under the tape. "Detective Everett Larkin, Cold Case Squad," he said as the stranger hurried to join him under the tent.

"Harry Regmore, Parks and Recreation. I, uh, I called in the—erm...."

"Body."

"Yeah." Harry adjusted the brim of his torn-to-hell Mets ballcap. A pair of UV safety glasses were perched on top.

Larkin was already cataloguing everything about Harry Regmore in that uncontrollable, compulsive manner that had, at least in part, turned his burden into the foundation of what made Larkin a good cop. Harry was middle-aged and built like an ox, with dark, dark eyes in a face that hadn't seen enough protection from the sun. He wore a flannel shirt in what Larkin decided to refer to as Lumberjack Red, Levi's with some black staining strictly below the knees, and boots— steel-toed, most likely. Harry's eyes cut toward Millett on Larkin's left, and he swallowed hard. He retrieved a pair of dirty, well-used gloves from his back pocket, unfolded and refolded them, then returned them to the pocket.

Larkin said, "Death makes some people nervous."

Harry chuckled a little. "I've seen death before, detective. Grew up in the Bronx in the '70s."

"Then why are you anxious."

"Huh? No. It's just early, you know? Only had one cup of coffee, and then this whole—"

"Don't lie."

Harry pulled his gaze away from the scene and asked, "You're not gonna run a drug test, are you?"

Larkin didn't answer. He'd been a detective for seven

of his ten years on the force, and found that when it came to interviews or interrogations, silence was one of the best and most underutilized tools. Because most people? They wanted to talk. Humans were social creatures. They craved communication. If Larkin didn't provide an outlet, whoever sat opposite would often do whatever was necessary to get Larkin to engage. Sometimes that meant offering a sliver of information, a vital clue that would bring life back to a cold case. Sometimes it meant snitching to make a deal. And sometimes, if they weren't very bright, they'd implicate themselves.

Of course, there were some people who simply had nothing to say. Larkin had both a good cop and bad cop routine for those sorts—the former being deducing a mutual connection and offering a piece of himself to establish trust, the latter being his stare. He'd been told it was like looking death in the eye, but unlike the old saying, Larkin was never the one to blink first.

Harry, it turned out, was the talkative sort. "I was smokin' some yesterday, that's all." He looked back to the hole as Millett's camera shutter *snap*, *snap*, *snap*ped. "But then this storm hit… the tree's a public safety hazard, you know? I have to remove it."

"I don't care that you smoked weed on your day off."

A puff of cold air surrounded Harry's mouth as he exhaled.

"How old is this crabapple."

Harry shrugged. "I'm just here to remove it," he said again. But after another short stretch of silence, Harry reached into his other back pocket and removed a wallet. His big fingers pawed through a collection of business cards before he found the one he wanted. "Give Mable a call, over at Parks and Rec. She oversees most of what goes on at Madison. She could probably tell you about the crabapple tree, if you actually wanted to know."

Larkin studied the card before slipping it into his pocket. "When did you arrive at the park."

"What time is it now?"

Larkin tugged back the sleeve of his suit coat. "8:33."

"Most people would say eight thirty."

"I'm not most people."

"Right. Okay. Six thirty, I guess. I saw the tree from the road, so I parked and came to check it out. Some jogger—in this storm, the fuckin' douche—came from that way, and we both saw them bones in the box," Harry explained, pointing toward the hole Millett was once again waist-deep in. "I called 911 because I'm not about to fuck with that."

"Where did the jogger go."

Another shrug. "I don't know. He left, I guess."

"Where do you live, Mr. Regmore," Larkin inquired.

"Sorry?"

"Do you still live in the Bronx."

Harry adjusted his cap again. "Are you asking? Yeah, I do. Concourse."

"How did you see the downed tree from the road when you live nearly ten miles away in a different borough."

"I'd been at my cousin's. Used to be, we'd get a little stoned, eat about four roast beef sandwiches each, with onions and gravy and mozzarella, and spend the entire night coming up with answers to all of life's questions. Now, I smoke a joint and pass the fuck out. I was heading back to the Bronx."

"You were taking Madison uptown."

"That's right."

"Instead of the FDR."

"They was saying on the radio there was some collision. Because of the rain. I was gonna avoid it."

Larkin said, "You are, of course, lying, Mr. Regmore."

"I don't understand."

"You specified you were going back uptown. So your starting point was somewhere south of the Flatiron," Larkin explained, making a quick motion to the angular building barely visible through the fog and rain from where it loomed on Twenty-Third Street. "The Battery is the southernmost point of Manhattan and gives us a radius of about three miles, which, even taking surface streets, could get you to the park within ten to twenty minutes, no matter where your starting point was. But that implies you awoke and immediately jumped in your vehicle, and while you do stink of weed and day-old clothes, Mr. Regmore, you look as if you've taken a moment to freshen up, and, of course, gathered your shoes, wallet, keys, phone.

"That is not to say you weren't concerned about making it back home to properly shower and get ready for the day, but even avoiding the FDR, you could reach Concourse in under an hour with some savvy driving. You claim to have been living here since the '70s, to have been visiting your cousin for a number of years now, so you would be familiar with the ideal routes. Which means you could have gotten a bit more sleep and not left before the sun was up."

"Well, I—"

"Now, see, in order for me to be here," Larkin continued, "dispatch would send a patrol car. Average response, from call to travel time, is about eight minutes. Patrol would then request Homicide. O'Halloran phoned my lieutenant before he'd even arrived—you wouldn't know that of course, but I do. You see, he's very fair-skinned and his nose hadn't quite gotten red from the cold, so he hadn't been here more than a minute or two prior to my arrival. In fact, CSU likely beat him to the scene, which is quite typical of his behavior, but I digress. My lieutenant phoned me at 7:55, but seeing as I was already dressed and on my way out the door, it was quite easy to segue downtown. I arrived at—" Larkin checked his watch again, merely for a touch of dramatic effect. "—8:21. Are you certain you were here at 6:30."

Harry blinked once or twice, looked toward the hole and the crate again, then said, "I guess it was probably closer to seven. Look, man, they got me on a special project at work this week. I was supposed to get in early. But I was running late because of the fuckin' skunk weed my cousin buys. If I said I got wrapped up in all *this* shit a little earlier, it'd look like I wasn't scrambling, you know?"

Larkin narrowed his eyes. "Are you certain it was 7:00."

"Oh, for fuck's sake." Harry removed an iPhone from his flannel shirt in Lumberjack Red, swiped, and said, "I called 911 at 7:06."

"Thank you, Mr. Regmore."

"Can I go now? The patrol cops had me waiting this whole time."

"Did you touch anything."

"What?" Harry gave an overt expression of shock. "Hell no. I was waitin' under the Shake Shack roof until youse all started showing up."

Larkin dismissed Harry and watched him walk toward the park gates, where he was swallowed whole by the storm.

Millett said, his voice puncturing the steady *pat, pat, pat* of rain on the tarp overhead, "I bet the in-laws love that human polygraph trick come Thanksgiving, huh?"

Larkin shoved his left hand into his trouser pocket and stared.

Millett looked away first. He crouched in the hole, disappearing briefly from view, then straightened and offered up a plastic evidence bag. "This was near John Doe's feet. I don't think it was visible when Cheech called it in."

Larkin accepted the bag and spun it around. Inside was

a face.

Specifically, a bronze casting of a face. It was an impressive piece of artistry—adult male with a chin cleft and horribly crooked nose that suggested whoever the model had been had once found himself on the losing end of a brawl. His cheeks were slack and eyes closed—a study in sleep. It took an additional moment of examination for Larkin to deduce why something about the face was *off*, only to realize the artist hadn't thought to include eyebrows or eyelashes.

"Are you acquainted with Detective Doyle?" Millett asked, staring at Larkin from within the hole.

"No," Larkin murmured. He turned the mask over again and studied the negative space where it could perhaps be worn, should the unique dimensions match the wearer.

"Forensic artist. Down at 1PP."

Larkin glanced at Millett and raised one eyebrow.

"You might want to give him a call."

"Why." Larkin's questions were rarely, if ever, delivered with the necessary inflection found in English. He knew it bothered people—*bothered Noah*—but to control it required a more conscious effort at slowing the perpetual spinning of his Rolodex brain. It required him to be wholly present to current conversations and events, and that came with a host of problems Larkin worked to actively avoid. So the end result was a deadened and uninterested tone taken with most people, even if Larkin didn't mean to come across as such.

"Because art is his forte," Millett was saying, pointing at the bag, "and, I wish this wasn't something I knew, but *that* is a death mask."

CHAPTER TWO

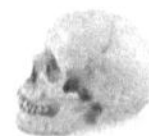

Larkin sat in his sedan on the corner of Twenty-Third and Madison, his left foot still wet, windshield wipers set to high, and an outgoing call ringing in his ear. Thunder crashed overhead, and Larkin squeezed his eyes shut. A shudder coursed through his body and he gripped the steering wheel with one hand, so tight that the material audibly protested. As the thunder's rumble dragged on like some ancient God had awoken from slumber and was now starving for sacrifices, Larkin focused his hearing on the wipers, breathing on their beats.

Gerr-zzk, gerr-zzk, gerr-zzk.

"This is Mable. Hello? *Hello?*"

Larkin jerked to attention and said into his cell, "Ms. McClennan, my name is Everett Larkin. I'm a detective with the NYPD's Cold Case Squad."

"I'm about to run into a meeting."

"I'm calling specifically—"

"*Shit.* About the body in the box over at Madison?"

"That's correct. I'd like to schedule a time to meet with you."

"Detective, my inbox is blowing up, my phone won't stop ringing. I don't know how the body ended up buried in the park, and frankly, it's not my job to figure it out—it's yours," Mable explained in a gravelly, smoker's voice. "That's why you folks get the big bucks from the city, anyway. I'm in full damage control right now, and I don't have time to say 'I don't know' six ways to Sunday."

Larkin said coolly, as if he'd not been snapped at by an administrator clearly jonesing for a nicotine break, "I have a few questions about the crabapple tree that was uprooted."

"Jesus Christ," she whispered. "Fine. Eleven."

Larkin picked up her business card from the cup holder he'd set it in and recited the address, which Mable confirmed before hanging up. He immediately added the appointment to his phone's calendar, set a reminder, then glanced at the evidence bag on the passenger seat—the bronze of the mask dull and unremarkable in the gray morning light. Larkin wanted to know whether the artwork intentionally lacked any dazzle, in the way that counterfeiters would dye paper with black tea to look weathered and aged, or if it really was old. And how old was old, exactly? Millett hadn't known anything beyond his claim that it was a death mask—a tradition that had found a resurgence during the Victorian era, apparently. But that in no way meant it was actually from a previous century. If it were, did it match the cranial features of John Doe, or was it an item simply buried with him? Had it been tradition to leave the mask with the deceased? Were they always made of bronze? If it were a replica—that is, modern—for God's sake, *why* was it there at all?

Larkin specialized in death and worked in the medium of murder, but this? This was a ritual of death that was unknown to him, and if he wanted *something* he could chase while waiting on the ME to provide him tangible evidence, Larkin needed an artist to answer his questions. He made a call to One Police Plaza, the headquarters of the NYPD and colloquially known as 1PP, and requested Detective Doyle, per Millett's suggestion. More often than not, Larkin worked alone. His squad consisted of only ten detectives, and they had to spread as much of the 9,022 cases between them as humanly possible. Nonetheless, he was accustomed to requesting aid when necessary, and accepting it in whichever form it came: confidential informants, local authorities when cases required he travel out-of-state—Larkin even had a few connections at the FBI, despite the animosity between the feds and the city. So Larkin figured working with a fellow detective, and one thankfully unassociated with the brutes in Homicide, would be a relatively painless experience.

After several rings, voicemail picked up. A deep, smoky, and unhurried voice said, "Detective Ira Doyle, Forensic Artists. Please leave a message."

Beep.

Larkin checked his watch. "This is Detective Everett Larkin, Cold Case Squad. The time is 9:07. I've taken on a case where I find myself in need of an expert on the subject of bronze face masks—what might possibly be a death mask, although this is speculation—and your name was suggested to me." The sky flashed a brilliant white before thunder cracked so loud, it was as if the Earth were splitting in two. Larkin jumped, swallowed a lump that might have been his heart in his throat, and hastily added, "I can be reached at this cell number, or my desk at Precinct 19."

Larkin disconnected, tucked the phone into his pocket, covered his face with one hand, and began to cry. A few wet sobs, a few strangled gasps, and then he cleared his throat and raised his head. He twisted the rearview mirror and checked his appearance: ash-blond hair parted on the side, clean-shaven, splotches of red in his otherwise pale complexion, and light, light gray eyes. A face poetic in its tragedy, a contemporary psychopomp regulated to a scale of monochrome.

—a crown of dandelions, the crackle of open flames, that first kiss, both of them shaking and tasting like sugar and alcohol and the sepulcher of innocence—

Memories bled like watercolors left in rain. A gradient of daffodil—no, *gold*—to slate, mud, *death*.

Larkin dried his cheeks and tugged the silver band off his finger. He slipped it in his trouser pocket, put the sedan into Drive, and pulled into uptown traffic.

Larkin had made the decision to return home and pick up dry shoes before returning to the precinct, which then turned into an entire wardrobe alteration, because red derbies couldn't replace green oxfords without taking into consideration all other facets of his apparel. Larkin hiked the steps of Precinct 19 on Sixty-Seventh, between Third and Lexington, wearing a dark charcoal suit, black tie, gold and gray and black checkered pocket square, and the aforementioned derbies. It was still raining, but the worst of the storm—*thunder and lightning*—seemed to be on its way to Jersey.

"Spooky Larkin!"

Larkin stopped and looked to his right at the rolling doors of FDNY's Ladder 16. The police and fire departments of New York had held grudges toward one another since… probably their founding in the 1800s, and although Larkin had never been a military man, he suspected the rivalry was something akin to Army versus Navy. Whether by design or mistake, their two houses had ended up next door on the Upper East Side, and in the five years he'd been a detective at this precinct, it'd proven to be an… *interesting* experience.

And while the cops had long ago nicknamed him *Grim*, about a year into working at this precinct, the FDNY had settled on *Spooky Larkin*.

Either way, he couldn't win.

"What."

A firefighter stood in the driveway between their buildings, some heavy-looking gear in either hand. The rain didn't seem to concern him. "Heard you knocked a Homicide boy on his ass."

"Where'd you hear that."

He shrugged one shoulder. "You know how radio transmissions are."

Larkin rolled his eyes, clasped the evidence bag between his chest and arm, pulled shut his umbrella, and stepped through the door flanked on either side by the green lanterns marking the occupancy of police. Larkin moved through reception, the soles of his shoes squeaking against the linoleum floor. He took the stairs to the second floor, where the Cold Case detectives shared a bullpen fashioned with drab, mass-produced furniture that could have belonged in any office across America. The overheads were bank fluorescents that hadn't been replaced since the '90s, and someone had brewed engine oil for coffee in the breakroom, the smell mingling with the damp air and concocting a miasma that could only be described as *Monday*. On the far left were several offices, including Lieutenant Connor's, two interview rooms, and a third that once might have been for interviews but was now full of media, both current and obsolete, the shitty desk with a wobbly leg that no amount of Post-it pads seemed to level, and computer chairs with no support left due to a decade of asses flattening the cushions. Detectives fondly referred to this room as the *Fuck It*.

Sitting at Larkin's desk—in his chair, no less—was a stranger. Larkin's memory—like a Rolodex he could flip through to find any subject, any conversation, any name—began automatically searching for this man's face. Not a cop who worked at Precinct 19, not a CI, nor was he any lawyer or administrator from a past case. Of this, Larkin was quite certain, because he wouldn't—*couldn't*—forget.

The stranger had the lean build of someone who took care of himself, with height that was all arms and legs. He was slouched in the chair, arms crossed behind his head, long legs stretched out, and feet anchored to the floor as he idly spun side to side. Brown tweed trousers, shirt sleeves rolled back, tie loosened, with a matching rumpled suit coat and a large, flat bag on the floor beside the casters. His dark brown hair, like a Hershey bar (there's that food again, Larkin noted), was messy in a way Larkin suspected was done on purpose, and it was apparent, judging by the man's five o'clock shadow at— Larkin checked his watch—9:44, he wasn't one for adhering to dress code.

Larkin placed his umbrella in a stand near the stairs, walked across the bullpen, then said, "Excuse me."

The man swiveled, looked up, then straightened his posture in an easygoing manner. "Everett Larkin?"

"That's correct. Who're you." Then Larkin snapped his mouth shut, spun the mental Rolodex again, and replayed that deep purr from the voicemail earlier. "Detective Doyle," he answered himself.

Doyle got to his feet, his movements like a ballet in the way his casualness still managed to be graceful. He stood a head taller than Larkin and offered a big smile when Larkin took a step back in order to meet his gaze. "Ira Doyle. It's a pleasure." He offered a hand.

Larkin shook it, cataloguing the size of Doyle's hand in his own, his grip, temperature, the callus on Doyle's ring finger that confirmed he held a pencil quite often in a dynamic quadrupod stance. "Why the house call."

Doyle had crow's feet around his brown eyes. "I was in the area, actually."

"No, you weren't."

Doyle raised one thick eyebrow and asked with a tone that suggested nothing but amusement, "Oh?"

"No. There's no practical reason for you to be on the Upper East Side," Larkin explained. "So how'd you get here… I see no umbrella. Your hair has product in it that appears undisturbed. You're also wearing a white shirt that's dry."

"I have a coat."

"Yes, it's on the floor. If it had gotten wet, you'd have draped it over the back of the chair." Larkin continued, "The Uptown 6 is a straight shot from 1PP, but during the morning rush, you'd be lucky to arrive in under thirty minutes, and I only phoned thirty-eight minutes ago. It is unlikely, given the attitude you display in your posture, that you raced out the door the moment you listened to my message. This means you didn't take the subway because, one, you're not wet from the walk, two, your hand wasn't cold when we shook, and three, you simply wouldn't have had the time."

Doyle slid his hands into his trouser pockets. His entire face lit up—and Larkin wasn't particularly fond of this idiom, but it would work for the moment—like a Christmas tree.

"So you drove," Larkin concluded without missing a beat. "Taking the FDR could get you here in twenty minutes. And this option would avail you additional time to get your act together. I didn't recognize the blue Honda Civic parked on the street, but I assume it's yours because the seat was pushed back quite far, enough that I took notice of it, and you *are* tall."

"Six four," Doyle confirmed. "And you've called me lazy twice when we've only just met."

"No. You're projecting. Based on your need to shave, disheveled appearance, and overall posture, which combined suggests a disinterest in the job, I have logically deduced you would need additional time to gather your belongings before making your way uptown."

Still smiling with his entire face—no, his entire body—

Doyle asked, "Are you aware you don't speak with an intonation when asking questions?"

"Yes."

Doyle chuckled, and the sound settled around them like smoke on water. "I've heard about you."

"Watercooler talk."

"What else would it be? They call you the personification of death." Doyle bent, collected his suit coat and big bag, and dropped them into a molded plastic chair situated beside the empty neighboring desk, then rested his backside on Larkin's desk and crossed his arms.

Larkin took a seat. He aggressively avoided eye contact while placing the bronze mask opposite of Doyle and jostling the computer mouse. "The death rate in New York City is 6.4 per 1,000 population."

"There it is."

Larkin grunted.

"But now that we've met, you strike me as more Holmesian."

"Please get off my desk."

Doyle twisted at the waist so he was staring at Larkin, who pointedly refused to look away from his screen. "I really was in the area."

"A forensic artist leaving his downtown office." Larkin made certain to not phrase his words into an actual *question* this time. He was quite aware of his odd speech patterns without complete strangers publicly pointing them out.

"Field sketch," Doyle confirmed. "I listened to my voicemail afterward. 9:07, wasn't it? I'd just missed your call. I checked in with the senior artist, then drove over here."

"This is the Cold Case Squad," Larkin stated, finally casting Doyle a quick, sideways glance. "I assure you, the rush was unnecessary."

"But you've piqued my interest," Doyle answered. "A death mask."

"Conjecture."

"Maybe. How about you let me see it?"

"How about you get off my desk."

Doyle slowly pushed off the furniture, turned, and planted his big hand on the desktop. He held his tie against his chest with his other hand and leaned down. Doyle's cologne penetrated Larkin's personal bubble like an arrow of masculinity—woodsy, spicy, heady, *dangerous*. It left him reeling, as if he'd been punched in the head. KO'd by neroli and base notes of sandalwood and cardamon.

Larkin looked up.

Doyle's eyes were brown with flecks of gold, like those bags of pyrite chips sold to children in tourist shops. He said, without any malice to his tone, "I think we've gotten off on the wrong foot."

A detective seated at the desk in front of Larkin's snorted and looked over his shoulder, holding a phone to one ear. "No way, kid," he said, addressing Doyle, who, by Larkin's estimate, was in his late-thirties and by no means a child. "Grim's just *that* fucking welcoming."

Larkin flicked a stony stare in the direction of Detective Jim Porter, a short, stocky, middle-aged man who had an unfortunate case of extreme receding hairline. Larkin narrowed his eyes, waited until Porter took a fucking hint and minded his own business, then returned his attention to Doyle.

Doyle hadn't looked away.

"What are your qualifications," Larkin asked.

Slowly straightening, Doyle reached into his back pocket, retrieved a wallet, then displayed his shield.

"Your artistic qualifications," Larkin corrected. "I've

seen enough objectively bad police sketches to know being accepted into a prominent unit doesn't necessarily mean it was based on merit."

That easy smile flirted across Doyle's face again. He tucked his wallet away. "The same can be said about Cold Cases, don't you think?"

Larkin's mouth twitched as he considered one or two of the detectives who'd *somehow* been promoted to his squad. "I suppose."

"BFA in illustration from SVA," Doyle answered. "MA in History of Art and Archeology from NYU."

"The second degree sounds scholarly."

"Lofty aspirations of a cushy museum job—but I was led astray by the siren's song of less pay, long hours, bad coffee, and bureaucratic bullshit. I think it was the uniforms." That smile again, before Doyle added, "I look good in blue."

Larkin considered Ira Doyle. It was true that the Forensic Artists Unit consisted of only three detectives and it was a team basically impossible to finagle your way into without considerable skill or considerable connections—hence his curiosity into Doyle's background so as to deduce which of the two got him the job. Because if Larkin was going to employ the assistance of others on one of his cases, no matter how minor in the grand scheme of things, he wanted only the best. He did not have the time nor patience to second-guess the authority of others in their select fields. And while he didn't know where on the academics scale those two schools qualified for their respective degrees, the fact that Doyle was a traditionally trained artist with additional schooling in art history....

Spinning in his chair, Larkin picked up the evidence bag and offered it. "This morning's storm uprooted a crabapple tree at Madison Square Park. An employee of Parks and Recreation phoned 911 at 7:06 to report a wooden crate had been unearthed. Inside was a skeleton."

"Male?" Doyle asked as he accepted the plastic bag and studied the bronze face.

"Unofficially. And adult, based on erupted wisdom teeth. But we can't assume the likeness of that mask is of the victim."

Doyle didn't answer right away. He set the mask on the desktop, went to what upon third glance appeared to be a portfolio bag, and retrieved a ruler from the outer pocket. Doyle dug out a notepad from his suit coat, flipped to a blank page, then nabbed a pen from the cup on Larkin's desk. He began measuring various features of the face and jotting down what Larkin could only surmise to be the dimensions. "Why is it that a case not even three hours old has been handed over to you?"

"Homicide didn't want to be saddled with a loser." Larkin leaned forward and tilted his head in order to study Doyle's expression. Doyle appeared intrigued by the presented mystery, but was cool, even casual about it. Interested in the way that people were interested in Buzzfeed's Top Twenty Hot Summer Beach Reads. Something that was fun but ultimately forgotten.

Except, no… that wasn't quite right. Because Doyle's eyes were bright and laser-focused, like he was doing a sudoku puzzle and was the sort of man who committed to completing the entire 9x9 square, come hell or high water.

"Sudoku," Larkin stated.

"Karaoke." Doyle looked sideways. "Sorry, I thought we were calling out random Japanese loan words." He smiled with his entire face again. "You want to roll your eyes so bad."

"No, I don't."

"Yes, you do. You keep looking at the ceiling."

"There's a water mark. It might be from the storm."

Doyle snorted. He put the borrowed pen between his teeth and turned the mask over to study the negative space.

"That's my pen."

Doyle held it out.

This time, Larkin did roll his eyes. "Keep it."

"What about sudoku?" Doyle asked before putting the pen in his mouth again.

"Nothing." Larkin's phone dinged from his pocket—an appointment reminder. "Tell me about this mask. I need to leave for a meeting soon."

"Where to?" Doyle asked around the pen.

Larkin had removed his phone to check the notice. "Parks and Recreation."

Doyle glanced at Larkin for a second time. He removed the pen and asked, "You suspect the employee who called it in?"

"Of course not."

"Of course not," Doyle echoed.

"When a hole is dug in a city park, it's expressly for the purpose of removing a tree or planting a tree. I want to know when the crabapple was planted."

"Huh. That's smart," Doyle said.

"It's common sense."

Doyle hissed and dramatically clutched his chest. "*Ouch.*"

Larkin ignored the playful jab and added, "Test results from the crate—hardwood, softwood, lacquered, pressure-treated, etcetera—as well as your professional ruling on that mask will narrow my scope of focus a great deal."

"A murder from the 1980s is approached differently than if it were the 1880s," Doyle concluded.

"Your example is problematic, but yes." Then Larkin shifted in the chair, wheels skating across the uneven floor.

"Is that mask from the 1880s?" He heard the lilt in his voice tip upward, just a little, in admitted curiosity as to what Doyle saw that he did not.

"Do you have a magnet?"

"Pardon."

"A magnet," Doyle repeated.

Larkin glanced at his desk: computer monitor, keyboard, mouse, pen cup, sans the one that'd been in Doyle's mouth, and a high stack of brown accordion files in varying degrees of thickness and wear—his active cold cases. Each file was a Lost Boy, unclaimed by their nannies and forgotten by their families, brought to Neverland so Peter Pan wouldn't be alone.

If only it were so romantic.

Larkin pushed the chair back and got to his feet. He walked across the length of the bullpen and entered the breakroom off to the right. The stink of burned coffee hit him like a wall, but then Larkin picked up a second, sweeter scent underneath. He zeroed in on the box on the countertop.

Krispy Kreme.

Detective Miyamoto had been here. She, in her own words, had PMS-induced cravings for sweets that were so intense, she alone could keep her dentist gainfully employed until menopause. And when that sugar crash came, she'd buy a dozen full-size donuts—*"Icing and cream-filled, do you think I'm fucking playing?"*—and after polishing off about half the box, Miyamoto would leave the rest in the break room for whoever else was on the clock.

Larkin approached the counter, lifted one side of the lid, and peeked inside. He smiled, pulled the cardboard top open the rest of the way, and removed a napkin that Miyamoto had scribbled *Larkin* on with a ballpoint. Underneath was half a donut: yellow frosting, confetti sprinkles, and cake batter filling oozing from one side. Larkin took it, then swiped a magnet off the front of the fridge that wasn't holding a flyer about departmental sports teams or the warning from Lieutenant Connor: *Ulmer—I swear to God, if you touch my lox, I'm sticking my boot up your ass*. He then returned to the bullpen.

Doyle looked up. "That doesn't look like a magnet."

Larkin instinctively angled his body, as if he were ready to defend his donut against a tackle and scuffle maneuver. In his other hand, he raised the magnet, realized he'd grabbed one in the shape of a cat's backside, butthole and all, (some beat cop thought they were funny as hell), and tossed it.

Doyle caught it one-handed—*show-off*, Larkin thought—and then laughed as he studied it. "Cute."

"Detective Doyle finds cat anuses cute," Larkin commented. He carefully tore his donut in two, shoved one wedge in his mouth, then sucked the cream filling off his thumb. Doyle was staring at him when he glanced up from the task at hand.

"Patron saint of June 5, are you?"

"I don't know what that means."

Doyle's smile was back, although it seemed to never be gone for long. "It's only the holiest of holidays for cops— National Donut Day."

"There's no such thing."

"There sure as fuck is," Doyle replied. "Krispy Kreme?"

Larkin glanced at the remaining chunk of processed sugar in his hand, then nodded.

"June 5," Doyle reiterated. "You thank me then. Do you know the difference between a life mask and death mask?"

"If this is intended to be a trick question, the names give away the answer," Larkin said before eating the rest of his donut.

"You're cute," Doyle stated. "In a stick-up-the-ass, sees

the world in black-and-white with a severely disadvantaged sense of humor sort of way."

"That's inappropriate."

"Life masks were made with wax or plaster laid over the individual's face, allowed to harden, then removed in sections. From that negative, artists could recreate a positive face with all the detailed characteristics unique to the sitter: wrinkles, scars, nose and ear sizes—you get my point. From there, the mask could be utilized after the fact to sculpt busts or paint portraits. Washington and Lincoln sat for life masks."

The donut had left Larkin's fingertips sticky, and he rubbed his thumb absently against the pads of his index and pointer while stating, "That's not a life mask, though."

Doyle's eyes crinkled a little, and those flecks of gold seemed to spark, like….

—white sunshine skittering across the shattered surface of a lake—

"Why do you say that?"

"I don't know. I'm not an artist," Larkin answered.

"Are you familiar with the phrase memento mori?"

"It's Latin—remember that you must die."

Doyle nodded. He fiddled with the magnet still in his hand. "A tangible reminder of our own mortality. It's a study in death."

Larkin considered this for a moment, then said, "That's an interesting word choice."

"Which?"

"Study. As a noun, it has half a dozen different meanings, including: a piece of artwork."

"It can also imply an investigation," Doyle countered.

There was a sudden but subtle shift in the energy around them, something quantifiable but its calculation for measurement foreign to Larkin. It passed between them in a second. Like a loss of gravity, the crackle of electricity in the air before a storm, the tingle of blood rushing back into a limb after sleeping on it wrong, stuck in a loop of spins while waltzing.

It was there, and then it was gone.

But the look on Doyle's face—he'd felt it too.

A partnership in art and investigation. A study in death.

Raising a thick eyebrow and holding the mask out to Larkin, Doyle asked again, his tone a touch more somber, "Why do you say it's not a life mask?"

Larkin took a breath and then closed the distance between them. He accepted the mask and carefully studied the subject's expression a second time. Eyes closed, facial muscles relaxed, a suggestion of a smile, as if in the subject's final moment, all of the universe's unknowns were revealed to him and he found the truth to be… a relief. "After death, if the body is kept in a reclined pose, the muscles of the face naturally follow the pull of gravity and create the illusion of a smile."

"Sounds very Poe."

"He preferred the imagery of worms feasting on human remains."

"Nice," Doyle said with a decidedly dry tone.

"Am I correct."

"About Poe? You've clearly read more—oh, the mask, yes."

Larkin handed it back and asked, "Why the magnet."

"Before postmortem photography became readily available during the Victorian era, influential figures in society had their likeness cast after death. This memento mori was either left in its plaster form, or sometimes reproduced in bronze." And with that, Doyle placed the magnet to the mask's forehead, and the cat butt stuck, even through the plastic evidence bag.

Larkin raised his eyes and met Doyle's. "Bronze isn't magnetic."

"This is cast iron," Doyle agreed. "Painted to look like aged bronze." He plucked the magnet free. "So to answer your question, no, this death mask is not from the nineteenth century. However, the artist appears to have gone to great lengths to replicate authentic death masks of the period."

"Why be mindful of such details, only to fail at the final step."

"It might have been practical. Cast iron is easier to work with than bronze. And you need to consider whether this was made locally—a workshop specializing in bronze might be more difficult to find in the boroughs."

Larkin steepled his fingers together, turned on his heel, and began to pace in front of his desk. "This mask was found in the crate with the skeleton. If it's indeed a cast of the victim's face, then John Doe is contemporary."

"That's right."

"Replicating the mask into metal is an extra step. Potentially a step with witnesses."

"Plaster would have disintegrated the first time the crate got wet," Doyle pointed out.

Larkin nodded as he reached the limits of the bullpen, turned, and walked past the desk again. "It's purely speculation, but if the extra step was seen as worth taking in the perpetrator's mind, perhaps they intended for the mask to weather time." He paused and looked at Doyle. "Masks are typically buried with the deceased?" There was that note of repressed curiosity again.

Doyle shook his head. "In Western culture, these masks can be traced back to the fourteenth century in France and England. They were used as part of the funerary rituals of kings, but no, the masks were never intended to be buried with the deceased—not then and not through the 1800s.”

Larkin picked up his pace again. “Interesting.”

“I assume the remains are at the OCME?”

“Yes.”

“How good are you at sweet-talking?”

Larkin stopped, turned.

Doyle chuckled as he flipped his notepad shut. “I think you practice that face in the mirror.” He rolled his sleeves down, buttoned the cuffs, and pulled his suit coat on. “Put in a request with the ME for a cast of the skull. They don’t like doing it, so you’ll need to be exceptionally charming—”

“You mean, manipulative.”

“Just stroke an ego for thirty seconds.”

“There is no reason to provide an ego stroke if I’m making a request that falls within the confines of their job description.”

Doyle slung the portfolio bag over one shoulder and said, “Larkin—may I call you Larkin?”

“That’s my name.”

“You’re looking exceptionally fine.”

“Excuse me?”

“I don’t often see men wearing pocket squares these days.”

Larkin narrowed his eyes and glanced down at his breast pocket.

“Even fewer who know how to match them.”

“It’s not difficult.”

Doyle took a few steps until he was standing before Larkin. Then he said, in that smoky purr of a voice that was admittedly attractive, and perhaps, Larkin thought, it was so because that was Doyle’s real voice and not an act, “It brings out the gray in your eyes. Like the moon.”

Larkin stared at Doyle.

"There, an ego stroke. And compliment for good measure. How do you feel?"

"Uncomfortable."

"If you want to ID your John-in-the-box, I need a cast," Doyle concluded. "I can do a facial reconstruction, and then you've got a leg-up on NamUs."

"But—"

"Unless you wanted the OCME to pull DNA and, *fingers crossed*, maybe get a hit from the database in four months?"

"No," Larkin drew out. "It's only… time simply runs at a difference pace in this squad."

Doyle exhaled, adjusted the strap on his shoulder. "A memento mori is also a keepsake of those lost. I can give John Doe back his identity so someone can remember him."

I'll remember him, Larkin thought automatically. Because when every day he felt as if he were a man in a strange land, unable to stop speaking of, unable to stop thinking of the dead and otherwise forgotten, because he couldn't—*just couldn't*—turn it off, and no one around him sympathized with that, understood that—as if Larkin spoke in tongues… Doyle had unknowingly touched on his love language.

Remembrance.

And that mattered.

For however brief a study this was between them, it mattered.

So Larkin nodded curtly and said, "All right."

CHAPTER THREE

"It's not an unreasonable request," Larkin said. He stood at his desk, phone to his ear, while a woman at the Office of Chief Medical Examiner, with a voice like a steam whistle, provided him with a dissertation on why it was *absolutely* unreasonable to be asking for a skull casting of his John Doe. "I can see your only intention is to roadblock me in this matter. Who's the ME—Dr. Baxter. I'd like to speak to Dr. Baxter, then."

"You're doing great," Doyle stage-whispered, watching Larkin from where he stood in front of the desk.

Larkin shot Doyle a look as he said into the receiver, "Ma'am, perhaps you don't fully understand the process of facial reconstruction, which is fine, but if that is the case, I need to speak to someone with a higher pay grade than yourself."

Doyle gave a thumbs-up. "Excellent first try."

"Will you please stop," Larkin hissed.

"I'm being supportive."

"You're like a kindergarten teacher in the wings of the school auditorium, miming the absolutely ridiculous gestures and lyrics to a song about a baby whale, while her students watch stage right like deer in the headlights—no, ma'am, I'm not addressing you." Larkin squeezed his eyes shut and pinched the bridge of his nose.

When the steam whistle finally stopped blustering, she put Larkin on hold and he let out a sigh of relief.

Doyle's whiskey-smooth voice fractured the welcome silence when he said, "'Baby Beluga' really did a number on you as a child."

Larkin muttered, "I regret agreeing to your assistance."

"No, you don't."

"I regret even shaking your hand."

"My earlier examples for you to follow must have been too subtle."

"You think I should tell Dr. Baxter they have eyes like the moon."

Doyle had the audacity to give the ceiling a contemplative expression. "Well, I don't recommend saying they've got an ass like the moon, or you're going to have HR on the line."

Heat rose up Larkin's throat, pooled in his cheeks, and by the way Doyle's smile grew, he knew the blush was visible against his pale complexion. "I ha—llo. Hello, Dr. Baxter. Everett Larkin, Cold Case Squad."

"Good save," Doyle said with a nod.

Larkin briefly entertained the fantasy that his stare could melt Doyle's face right down to the bone before he provided the medical examiner with the facts of his request: there was a skull, an artist on standby, and really, if the doctor didn't have to strip skin and muscle, was a cast even an extra step in his examination? "Yes, when you explain the mold-making process, I suppose it is two additional steps," Larkin said. He tapped his cell's screen and checked the calendar reminder a second time. He was going to be late for his meeting with

Mable McClennan. Hastily, Larkin blurted out over the ME, "Your eyes are like the moon. Actually, we haven't yet met, so this flattery might be inaccurate to your appearance. Please replace moon with the celestial body of your choosing and then reconsider my request."

Doyle slowly clasped a hand over his mouth.

A flush burned Larkin's face again. His stomach churned like it were full of sour coffee as he said, "No, sir, I'm not making a pass. Thank you." He set the receiver on the cradle.

Doyle dragged his hand down so his fingertips rested on his lower lip. "What'd the good doctor say?"

Larkin pocketed his cell, smoothed his suit coat, and straightened the already perfectly aligned accordion files. "He said his eyes are like quasars, and that he'd let me know as soon as the cast is ready for pickup."

"Wow."

"I need to go." Larkin started for the stairs.

Doyle was right on his heels. "That was incredible."

"No, it was extremely unprofessional. You've gotten me all turned around. The next time I need a favor from the OCME, they'll laugh in my face."

"Sounds more like you're one favor short of a hot date."

"Why are you following me," Larkin asked as he reached the midpoint landing between the first and second floors.

"The meeting at Parks and Recreation."

Larkin pushed his suit coat back past his shoulder holster and set his hands on his hips. "I didn't invite you."

Doyle came down the last step to stand beside Larkin. His body was so relaxed, so comfortable, like he'd just had one of those hour-long hot stone massages, and every stress the human body could carry, from head to shoulders to the arches of the feet, had been alleviated. Jutting a thumb over his shoulder in the direction of upstairs, Doyle asked, "Do you know what the mask is missing?"

"I'm not getting participation points every time you ask me a question," Larkin answered. "Tell me, so I don't need to guess."

"It's not guessing," Doyle corrected. "It's deduction, Mr. Holmes."

A sound escaped Larkin—if he intended for it to be a chuckle, it came out as a snort. "Hair is missing."

"So if your crabapple was planted in the '70s—"

"You can give John Doe muttonchops."

Doyle laughed. "I was thinking more like a porno 'stache, but if you've got a thing for men in ascots, I can pick one up from the Gentleman's Closet over in Hell's Kitchen…."

"Everett?"

Larkin pivoted on his heels, looked down the final set of stairs leading to reception, and locked eyes with— "Noah." He hurried down the steps, derbies once again squeaking against the wet linoleum. "Why're you here."

Tall, thin, blond, with cheekbones that could make a holy man sin, Noah's dark and stormy expression was out of place on a face that could have modeled for Ralph Lauren, despite his Gap wardrobe. Larkin hadn't meant anything by the comment that morning—had only pointed out Noah's outfit (pastels, all pastels) looked like the spring collection of an affordable, mass-produced, commercial brand undergoing an identity crisis. And now, in what seemed to be next-level passive aggressiveness, Noah had opted to wear his baby blue Converse, which completed an ensemble already rife with too-bubbly pinks, greens, and grays.

Noah angled his body so Larkin's touch missed his shoulder. He dug into his jeans pocket before producing a silver wedding band pinched between his thumb and index finger. "Forget something?"

Larkin raised his left hand and blinked in realization. "Oh."

"*Oh*," Noah echoed. "It was in your pocket."

Larkin looked at him.

"I was going to take that suit to the dry cleaner for you." Noah flicked the ring, hard.

Larkin scrambled and caught the band against his chest. "I misplaced it," he explained, working it over his knuckle.

"Here's an idea: stop taking it off."

"Can we please not do this right now." When Noah's gaze flicked from Larkin to over his shoulder, Larkin turned to see that Doyle had reached the ground floor. The other detective raised a hand in silent greeting. "This is Detective Ira Doyle," Larkin introduced. "Doyle, this is my husband, Noah Rider."

Doyle took a few long-legged strides forward and reached a hand out. "Pleasure to meet you."

Noah's expression was sharp, calculating. He shook Doyle's hand with an air of indifference. "Are you new?"

"Sorry?"

"I've been to enough holiday parties to be acquainted with the entire squad."

"No, no. I'm a sketch artist. Just here to offer my limited expertise on a case."

Noah crossed his arms, staring at Larkin. "For a minute I thought Everett might have forgotten to tell me something as important as being assigned a new partner at work."

With that final and very public dig, Larkin touched Noah's bicep and nudged him toward the front door, out of earshot of Doyle. "This is not a good day for me."

Noah's arms were still crossed, and coupled with the… Larkin didn't know how to politely describe his husband's day-off—*hip*?—attire… he looked a touch like a petulant teenager. "I shouldn't have to work an argument about *our* marriage into *your* schedule," he hissed.

"Noah, I *can't*." Larkin's throat was tight, and it was another moment before he could roughly get out, "I have had too many associations this morning."

Noah's jaw audibly cracked before he said in a clipped tone, "*There's* an excuse I haven't heard before."

"Honey, I need you to give me a break. I'm struggling today."

Color had rushed into Noah's face, those beautiful cheekbones now a feverish red. "Yeah. Sure. It's my fault, of course."

"Jesus Christ." Larkin put a hand over his eyes and massaged his temples. "I don't even remember taking off the ring. I certainly didn't mean anything by it. I'm sorry. I'm forgetful, Noah, not stupid."

"Selectively forgetful—"

Larkin raised his eyes and shot Noah a look he usually reserved for when playing bad cop.

And it worked, because Noah looked away and muttered to his shoes, "You have an appointment with Dr. Myers tonight."

"I know."

"Six o'clock."

"Right."

"I emailed her the notes for the last three weeks."

"Thank you."

Noah hesitated but then added, like he couldn't fucking help but wedge the last inch of the blade into Larkin's heart, "Maybe you should set a reminder on your phone."

"I don't need a reminder."

"You forgot—"

"Dr. Myers is habitual routine. Every third Monday at

6:00 p.m. I don't forget."

Noah's shoulders had barely worked their way down to resting before they were at his ears again. "Of course. It's just those inconsequential details you forget, like us being married."

Larkin gave up. He expelled a quiet breath, wanted to scream because he could feel how his chest shook with the effort, then scrambled for the carefully modulated tone that was his security blanket. "I'll see you this evening."

Noah raised both hands in a gesture that could have been "I'm going to strangle you" or "talk to the hand," and honestly, Larkin would have welcomed either outcome right then. But Noah managed to bite back whatever nasty comment was on the tip of his tongue, turned, and stalked out of the precinct.

Larkin watched the door shut. The details of the quiet but intense argument were already housed in his long-term memory. The words, the expressions, the sensation of having his soul scraped from his body with a melon baller, leaving only the raw skin behind—it was all one more goddamn association. Always there, ready to hurt, Larkin only needed to retrieve the memory like plucking a card. He closed his eyes, took another breath.

'Til death do us part.

Larkin squared his shoulders and turned around to face Doyle. "If you insist on joining me, we need to go." He pushed open the door and stepped outside.

The late-morning sky was still gray, but the black clouds, heavy with thunder and heartbreak, were now past the Hudson. The air held a cool dampness that chilled Larkin's sweat-slick skin. He moved down the steps and crossed the street between passing vehicles. He tapped the key fob in his hand, the alarm on his Audi chirping in time with the pound of shoes on asphalt. Larkin slid behind the wheel as Doyle hurried to squeeze by the front bumper and opened the passenger door. Larkin started the engine.

Doyle shoved his portfolio bag in the back before wedging himself into the front seat. Noah was tall, but Doyle still had to adjust the seat so his knees weren't knocking the glove compartment.

Larkin maneuvered out of his parking spot and pulled to the corner. He glanced uptown and made out Noah's back as he strode toward the subway among the morning foot traffic. Larkin kept driving west on Sixty-Seventh. The silence in the car was deafening.

"How long have you been married?"

Larkin adjusted his grip on the steering wheel. "Four years."

"What's he do?"

"Teaches first grade."

"Wholesome," Doyle stated.

Larkin said nothing.

"Sorry."

Larkin briefly looked at Doyle. "For what."

"I had no idea. I wouldn't have—if I knew."

Rolling one shoulder, Larkin said, "I didn't realize you were actually trying."

Doyle leaned an elbow on the door and dragged his fingers through his hair a few times before saying, "You're going to give me a complex."

"You did your best, I'm sure."

"Thanks."

"It was very cute," Larkin continued. "The way you used your height to impose yourself and compared my eyes to the moon."

"They're *gray*," Doyle protested. "And bright. Like the—forget it."

"I'm surprised you're single."

Doyle met his look. "It's a shame you aren't."

Larkin smiled—only a little. "So long as you don't comment on my ass, I'll keep HR out of this."

Doyle's smoky laugh chased away the claustrophobic silence.

The Arsenal was visible just beyond the budding trees lining Fifth Avenue, which bordered the east side of Central Park. Built a decade before the Civil War to act as munition storage for the state, the out-of-time medieval fortress, complete with a cast-iron eagle that oversaw from its roost above the double doors, had since become the headquarters for the Department of Parks & Recreation. Larkin hit the brakes at the corner of Sixty-Fourth as two women came up on his blind spot riding Citi Bikes. He tapped the horn as they wove in and out of the two lanes of traffic before reaching the bus lane and peddling downtown carefree.

"They should be wearing helmets," Larkin murmured as he crept behind a plumbing van attempting to merge into traffic.

"Want to get out and write them a ticket?" Doyle asked.

"I don't mean *should* as in *required*. A rider fourteen years or older is not legally obligated to wear a helmet unless their job is accomplished via bicycle. I mean should as in it's safer."

"We can always hope Darwinism teaches them a lesson."

"Doubtful. The benefits of a modern society have greatly reduced the process of natural selection." Larkin stole the parking spot the van vacated in its process of cutting off a taxi, which led to a screaming match through the vehicle windows in two unrelated languages—Spanish and Urdu, respectively.

"That was dark."

Larkin pulled the key from the ignition, opened his door, and glanced at Doyle. "Trials and tribulations. Then you die." He climbed out of the Audi. Larkin tapped the lock after Doyle exited the car, walked past a too-full trash bin on the corner that folks kept piling wrappers and empty soda cans on, like a game of urban Jenga, then crossed the street.

Doyle's long strides easily caught up to Larkin. They took the steps down into the park and toward the looming fortress, white flag of the Parks Department flapping overhead. "You can't have the day without the night."

"Is that a saying."

"Hmm? No. Scientific fact. Nighttime is caused by Earth's rotation on its axis."

Larkin glanced at Doyle from the corner of his eye before pulling open the door to the Arsenal. "I passed Earth science, thank you."

"I'm using allusion," Doyle corrected.

Turning to stand in the open doorway, Larkin stared at Doyle for a passing beat, then said, "I represent nighttime."

"Right."

"And nighttime is yet another meaning for death."

"Not what I intended, but given our respective careers, sure."

"That's a terrible allusion."

"Why?"

Larkin glanced at the welcome desk before saying, a touch quieter, "Because, first, it's imagery, not allusion. Second, if you have too much daytime—*life*—it is, in fact, just as bad."

"Isn't that what I said?"

"Yes. But you worded it in such a way as to suggest some kind of romantic malarkey."

Doyle smiled. "Malarkey. Got it."

"Jesus Christ," Larkin muttered in an almost absent, automatic manner. He walked to the front desk and said, "Everett Larkin. I have an eleven o'clock appointment with Mable McClennan."

A disinterested young man with adult acne, aggressively chewing bubble gum that smelled like artificial cotton candy, didn't look up from his cell phone. "Sorry—no appointments. She's in meetings all day."

Larkin reached into his suit coat, removed his shield, and tapped it against the counter until the receptionist looked up. "Detective Everett Larkin."

He snapped his gum loudly, studied the credentials, then directed his gaze to Doyle as the latter sidled up to the counter, shoulder brushing Larkin's as he displayed his own badge. The receptionist snapped his gum again, then said, "I watched a porno that started out just like this—Butt Police Volume Four. The guy in it, he broke his conditions of bail, so two cops show up, right? And they're gonna bring him to jail, of course, but he's like, *What can I do to change your minds?* He's so hot, too. Total gym bunny. So he goes down on both cops—I swear there's, like, sixteen… *eighteen* inches of meat between the two—then they get out their nightsticks—oh my God." He stood and leaned over the desk to look. "Do you guys have nightsticks?"

"If you don't call Mable McClennan in the next five seconds and tell her that Detective Larkin is here for their eleven o'clock appointment, I'm arresting you for obstruction of justice."

Letting out a huff, the receptionist plopped down in his chair. "*Rude,*" he mumbled, picking up the phone and dialing an extension.

"You know," Doyle said, his tone conversational as he tucked his badge away, "it makes you wonder."

"What does."

"The events of the previous three Butt Police and why they warranted a fourth storyline."

"—I mean, they have badges, so—" The receptionist popped a bubble and glanced at the two. He whispered into the receiver, "Kind of a jerk, to be honest—"

"That must be you," Doyle said to Larkin.

"—*super* cute, though," the receptionist concluded, drawing out the *super* to emphasize his point.

"That'd be me," Doyle continued.

Larkin glanced toward a staircase to the left before he said to Doyle, "You were right."

"About what, being cute?"

"No. I'll take the dead. You can have the living." Larkin moved past and started for the steps.

"*Sir*," the receptionist protested, but it came off as a sort of melodramatic whine. "Hey, detective!"

"What floor is she," Larkin asked over his shoulder.

"Third, but—"

Larkin disappeared around the corner to hike the steep set of stairs indicative of the building's age. By the time he was crossing the second-floor hallway and starting up the next flight, Doyle had caught up with him.

"Larkin," he called. "Hang on. I think we need to set some out-in-the-field ground rules."

Larkin turned on the step and was eye-level with Doyle. "I would like to take this moment to remind you I didn't ask you to join me. If you don't like how I work, that's your own fault."

"Listen," Doyle said, ignoring the jab. "Rule one: don't leave me to handle a DP aficionado who's making googly eyes at your ass and trying to give me his number in a singsong voice like he's auditioning for Meryl Streep's character in *Mamma Mia.*"

"There's a lot for me to unpack in that statement."

"It's an important rule, all right?"

"And extremely specific." Larkin hiked to the next landing, and then asked, "How do you know he's into—"

"He told me."

Larkin grunted, then nearly jumped as an office door slammed open, the doorknob cracking loudly against drywall.

A stout, middle-aged black woman, with eyes that cut like knives, stood in the threshold. She tapped a cigarette free from a Marlboro pack in her hand, stuck it unlit between her lips, then asked in that gravelly voice Larkin remembered from the phone call in his car, "Which of you is Larkin?"

Larkin raised his hand. "That'd be me, ma'am."

"You're late."

Larkin quickly pulled back his sleeve to check his watch: 11:02.

"Hm-hm." Mable addressed Doyle next. "Cookie, you'd best be a package deal, because unless you plan on asking me follow-up questions about recently deceased flora while I'm on the john, I've only got the time for one of you."

Doyle jutted a thumb at Larkin. "We're together."

Mable looked dubious, muttered, "I'll bet," then made a come-hither gesture with the cigarette before stepping into the office again.

Larkin followed first. The room was more the size of a glorified closet. A corkboard hung on the wall to the left of a desk that was planted in the middle of the room. Every square inch of the board was covered in memos, flyers, newspaper clippings, printed-out emails—some appeared to date back years. Clearly, it was not kept current. The desk held a dinky seventeen-inch monitor, sticky notes surrounding the screen, and an In-N-Out tray was overflowing with more crumpled printouts, receipts, a spiralbound notebook, half-eaten granola bar, and two mugs—one empty, the other half-full with what smelled like days-old coffee. Behind the chair that Mable sat at were two black filing cabinets with a potted and dying spider plant on top. (Were you allowed to have a black thumb and work for the Parks Department?) The remaining wall space was covered in aerial maps of Madison Square Park at what looked like different time periods and pointing out different artifacts. The window on the right was partially open and an ashtray full of butts sat on the sill.

Larkin's ability to cope day-to-day came from a strict sense of routine. Even with long hours and the curveballs thrown at career detectives, whether that was a line of questioning taking a sudden one-eighty or getting called into the precinct at two in the morning, Larkin had always been able to keep a sense of order among that chaos. And part was due to how he managed the stimulation around him—or lack thereof, if he were extremely lucky. Absolutely anything unessential was moved out of his space, and what was left was clean, organized, and arranged in such a way as to not be a distraction or association to a past event.

Mable's office looked as if they were testing military-grade bombs on the premises. There was so much to look at, to catalogue, to memorize, that Larkin very briefly considered walking out and conducting his line of questioning over the phone. But phone calls were never preferable. He needed to see the other person's posture, expression, mannerisms. Sometimes the nonverbal cues were enough to prompt Larkin to keep digging—deeper and deeper, until he uncovered evidence that would later stand in court.

Another win for Grim.

"Take a seat," Mable said, motioning to the single chair in front of her desk.

Larkin found himself looking toward Doyle, who in turn made the same gesture to the chair. He took a breath, picked up a manila folder from the seat, and set it on the leaning pile of crap atop Mable's desk before sitting.

"Aren't you chivalrous," Mable said to Doyle before glancing at her computer screen and jabbing her cigarette at it. "This shit never ends. I've got donators demanding answers like I'm the cops, subway rags begging for juicy details like I'm the killer, and this department is helping me about as well as to be expected from a bloated nonprofit."

"Why did you say 'killer,'" Larkin asked.

Reining in the start of her tirade, Mable said, "Whoever's in that box didn't bury themselves, right?"

"And how was it you came to be informed of the situation," Larkin continued.

"You kidding me? I hadn't been in the office five minutes before the *New York Beast*, some bullshit blog specializing in city politics and drama, was on the phone saying they'd seen detectives and crime scene personnel on that app, Local4Locals? They wanted the scoop. Got my number from a simple internet search." Mable pushed away from the desk, the wheels of her chair squeaking as she inched toward the window. "What'd you say you did? Cold Crimes?"

"Cold Cases."

Mable picked up a BIC lighter from beside the ashtray, lit the cigarette, and leaned close to blow smoke out the window. "Uh-huh. And what's that mean?"

"It means when the detective originally assigned to the homicide has retired, been transferred, or has otherwise concluded they are unable to solve the case, due to either an influx of new cases or lack of evidence and leads, it's handed over to me."

"And you figure it out."

"Sometimes."

Mable sucked on the Marlboro. "The cases are old?"

"They can be."

"Like Robert-Stack-in-a-trench-coat old? You might be too young for that reference."

Larkin wrinkled his nose. He kept his gaze pinned to Mable and did his best to block out the visual noise of the office around him. "My oldest case dates back to 1919."

Mable started coughing on her cigarette.

"The cost of healthcare directly related to smoking in the state of New York is ten billion dollars annually," Larkin stated. "And among the LGBT population, which the CDC estimates makes up approximately three percent of the U.S. population, smoking prevalence is twenty percent, as compared to fifteen percent among heterosexual people."

"Larkin—" Doyle began.

"There's some interesting reading on the influence of tobacco marketing," Larkin continued, still staring at Mable. "Advertising at gay pride festivals, donations to community organizations, etcetera, but the CDC has also suggested factors related to being LGBT—stress, social stigma, daily prejudice—directly impact the decision to smoke."

Mable coughed once more, for good measure, then said, "What does this have to do—?"

"It doesn't," Larkin answered. "I just thought you'd appreciate knowing you're being scammed out of money and good health." He could hear Doyle rubbing his face, whiskers scraping against the palm of his hand.

Mable stamped out the cigarette in the ashtray, then pushed back and rolled across the floor to her desk once again. "That jab about being LGBT."

"A statement of fact."

"Do I look dykey to you?"

"You don't look any way to me. One of the community's growing problems, in my opinion, is the tendency to judge our own's worthiness to be included, based on nothing more than physical appearance, an already widespread issue when set out among the heterosexual population." Larkin finally raised his finger and pointed at the disaster of a desktop, although he didn't look away from Mable. "Your wedding photo is highly visible."

Mable's brows furrowed. She looked at the 5x8 frame on the desk—herself in a white suit, arms wrapped around the waist of a black woman with dreads to the middle of her back who wore a hip-hugging white dress, both looking about a decade younger. Her defenses came down and Mable started laughing. "Monica's been begging me to ditch the Marlboros. Wait 'til I tell her a pretty boy gay cop rode my ass about 'em too." She shoved aside some junk and adjusted the frame. "We got married back in 2011, the day the Marriage Equality Act took effect in New York." Mable looked at Larkin. Glanced at his ring. "How long you been married, detective?"

Larkin crossed his legs, folded his hands into his lap, and said in a clipped tone, "Four years."

"It's a work-in-progress that never ends, hmm?"

That's enough bonding, Larkin thought. "The crabapple," he prompted.

"Right, right." Mable turned her attention to the computer. "That was the one near Shake Shack?"

"Yes."

Mable clicked the mouse a few times. "What was it you needed to know?"

"When was it planted."

She blew out a breath, shook her head, then swiveled in the chair and rocked her way toward the filing cabinets. "It's a pretty old tree, as far as urban parks go. I don't think that info is on the computer." Mable yanked open a bottom drawer and began to sift through hanging folders.

The phone on her desktop rang.

"It certainly wasn't Old Stumpy in age," Mable was mumbling. "Remember him? I still get weepy."

The phone kept ringing.

Mable shoved the drawer closed and yanked open a second. "It's so silly—crying over a tree stump."

The stink of the ashtray, the incessant ringing, the office that looked about to cave in on itself—the pandemonium of competing stimuli reached critical far quicker than Larkin anticipated. He lurched to his feet, spun around the chair, opened the office door, and stepped into the hallway. He grabbed the stairwell banister in both hands, closed his eyes, and took a few shallow breaths.

Doyle's smoke-smooth voice said something to Mable that Larkin didn't allow himself to decipher, and then the door quietly clicked shut and he joined Larkin. "Are you all right?"

Larkin nodded.

"It was a rhetorical question."

"My answer was also rhetorical."

"Okay." Doyle let a handful of seconds pass before he asked, "Can I get you—?"

"No," Larkin snapped. "I need a moment of quiet. That's all." He looked at Doyle. The other detective's brows knitted together, but he said nothing further and returned to the office, announcing in an easygoing, everyone's-best-friend tone that Larkin was taking a phone call.

Larkin closed his eyes again. He took a breath, counted, released it. His palms were sweaty against the banister, fingers aching from the white-knuckle grip. March 30 was not a good day. *Perhaps even a bad day*, Larkin considered. There were already too many associations—too many negative memories to now eat away at him every year, every spring, every March 30. The crack of thunder, the salty tear tracks, the insults and fights, the stink of Marlboros…. Larkin's breathing escalated, pinpricks of cold heat spread across his chest like he was about to start dry heaving. He groped in his pocket, retrieved his phone, gripped it so tight that the plastic case protested. He pulled Dr. Myers up in his contacts—

Doyle's laugh broke the escalation and gave pause to the grave Larkin was digging. Even muffled through the office door, Doyle had a top-shelf-whiskey sort of voice, with a heat in his words that pooled in Larkin's belly as if he had actually been drinking. His breathing slowed. He put the phone away. It wasn't a fix by any stretch of the imagination. More like a poorly patched pothole. One wrong move and he'd still fuck his suspension. But if Larkin were careful—very careful—he could drive this road—*March 30*—with the pleasantry of Doyle's voice being a much-needed positive memory.

The door opened again. Larkin straightened and turned.

Doyle was staring at him. "She found the file."

With the briefest nod of acknowledgment, Larkin slipped past Doyle and returned to the lone chair that, somehow, managed to look as if it were consumed by the landslide of shit even more than it had been—Larkin checked his watch—two minutes ago. He perched on the edge of the seat, laser-focused on Mable, who was turning discolored pages that had absolutely been spit out of a dot matrix printer. It said something as to departmental funding at the time.

"That crabapple was planted April 2, 1998," Mable said in her gravelly voice. "Looks like it was part of the massive renovation to save the park."

Doyle dug his notepad out and scribbled the date down.

"It was a goddamn mess back then," Mable continued, "but you're probably too young—"

"I remember Madison in the late '80s," Doyle broke in before Larkin had had a chance to open his mouth and say anything to the contrary. "Had a crackhead chase me with a knife."

Larkin turned and looked up at Doyle with a raised eyebrow.

Mable snorted, coughed, and said, "I knew grown-ass men who wouldn't walk through that park."

Doyle flashed that lazy smile. "Stupid, unsupervised kids think they're invincible."

Larkin turned to Mable once again. "Would there be any reason to dig the hole in advance."

She made a face. "It was before my time, but no, I can't imagine they'd do that without risking a safety hazard. That being said, millions were being pumped into the park. There was a lot going on."

Madison Square Park had once been the apple of Midtown's eye. Built before the Civil War (Larkin would have to look up the exact date), it'd fallen into a state of extreme neglect and disrepair, like so much had when New York teetered on the edge of financial collapse in the 1970s. The six blocks had become an epicenter of drug dealing, of prostitution, of murder—all the elements that made up what the NYPD had called the city once upon a time: Fear City. So it was possible, probable even, that John Doe was an unfortunate casualty of the violence during that decade. After all, homicides had skyrocketed by 1970—1,117—and kept rising for twenty years. When the crabapple had gone into the ground, homicides were at their lowest since 1965, with only 633 murders, due to the much-needed and aggressive crackdown on crime throughout the '90s.

But even with the reality of these statistics, the likelihood John Doe had been killed over a rock or fifty cents or just for the sadistic pleasure of hurting another human being—it didn't sit right in Larkin's gut.

Because of the death mask.

How exactly that piece of evidence fit into the puzzle, Larkin couldn't be certain yet. But the murder of John Doe had been methodically planned and orchestrated. Whoever had taken the man's life, stuffed his body into a crate, and seen him buried nearly four feet in the ground in the middle of the biggest and busiest city in the country, Larkin was certain they never intended for John Doe to be found.

So what did that say about the perpetrator?

Larkin had laid to rest plenty of cases that involved premeditated murder. The victim had been chosen because they were weak, they were blonde, they were wearing a baseball cap—whatever had scratched the itch of the killer. But what was the same in all those instances was that their relationship had been that of *strangers*. And while a certain attempt had been made by the perpetrator to cover their tracks by disposing of the victim in locations unrelated to the scene of the crime—in a dumpster behind a Midtown Whole Foods, left in the overgrown vegetation overlooking the Rockaways out in Queens, floating in the waters along the East River Greenway—the victim was still found and the breadcrumb trail of clues led all the way to an eventual arrest.

John Doe was different.

There was no indication he had ever died until today. Whoever knew him, remembered him, missed him—what had they been thinking for, at minimum, the last twenty-two years? That John had run away? Had been kidnapped? Taken a walk for a pack of smokes? If not for the morning's disastrous storm, how many more years would those who John had left behind keep wondering where he was, what he was doing, what sky he woke to every morning?

John Doe was never meant to be found.

And it wasn't the forensic evidence the murderer couldn't chance leading back to them, but John *himself*.

They hadn't been strangers.

"I need employment records," Larkin said. "The

renovation crew working at Madison Square Park during the '90s."

CHAPTER FOUR

"But you're not *dressed* like cops," the petite blonde whined.

Larkin's request for employment records had seemingly broken the fragile spell of patience he'd cast on Mable via their personal connection at the start of the interview. Her desk phone rang a second time, and she claimed he had exactly the information requested, she needed to get back to putting out fires, and anyway, did she goddamn look like HR? So Larkin and Doyle were directed to an office on the second floor, where they now stood in front of the desk of a young woman who undoubtably got carded every time she ordered a nine-dollar glass of wine at a restaurant.

A nameplate suggested the blonde's name was Kelly. Kelly wore her hair in a messy bun piled atop her head like an afterthought. She had big brown eyes, a button nose, wore a frumpy striped sweater that Larkin was about seventy percent certain was supposed to be frumpy in a *cool* way, along with a pair of mom jeans, which hadn't been cool when he was a child and *still* weren't cool, despite fashion's attempt to bring them back.

Before Larkin could reply to Kelly's absurd comment,

Doyle took the lead with the ease of a man who was paid to shoot the shit for a living. "We're detectives, ma'am."

"So no uniforms?"

"Ties and slacks, I'm afraid."

Kelly brightened, waved her hands, then said, "Oh! Like Detectives Stabler and Benson!"

Larkin narrowed his eyes. "*Law & Order* is a fictional—"

"Exactly like Stabler and Benson," Doyle agreed. He nudged Larkin. "You're pretty like Benson."

Larkin couldn't help it. He flushed.

Kelly's stare bounced between them like a cartoon character.

Doyle, the bastard, was grinning. He said to Kelly, "We need employment confirmation."

At Doyle's request, she narrowed her eyes and pursed her lips like she was seriously contemplating his words, but mostly, she just looked like she had gas. "Don't you need a warrant?" She added in a loud whisper, "I've always wanted to say that."

Larkin pinched the bridge of his nose. He needed to spend an hour—no, two hours—in a sensory deprivation tank, and it wasn't even noon. Not that he pulled in the sort of income that warranted being a member of a Manhattan spa that offered hour-long floats in Epsom salts. Not when he was married to a public-school teacher who was saddled with student loan debt for at least another decade.

A bottle of ZzzQuil was cheaper.

Doyle was saying, "We're looking to confirm dates. You don't need a warrant for that."

"Okay!" Kelly said brightly, eagerly, with stars in her eyes.

Larkin spoke on the exhale of a quiet sigh. "I want to know about the renovation crew at Madison Square Park in

1998. Although, if we can have 1997 to 1999, that would be more ideal."

Kelly snorted, then covered her mouth. "Sorry. No, I mean—" She struggled not to laugh. "My God. 1998? I wasn't even born."

"Yes, the neo-grunge on top and suburban mom acid wash on bottom was my first clue," Larkin answered.

Kelly furrowed her brows and glanced down at herself.

"Don't mind my partner," Doyle said, putting his hand on the back of Larkin's neck and giving a firm squeeze.

"Don't touch—"

"He's only had half a donut today," he continued, squeezing again. "Blood sugar is a little low. I promise I'll feed him after we're done here."

Kelly giggled as Doyle smoothed the conversation over, sounding very much the age waitstaffs likely mistook her for. She babbled something about how this was just like TV, clicked the computer mouse, and studied the screen in front of her.

With the reception-like desk tall enough to block the movement, Larkin jabbed his elbow hard into Doyle's side. Doyle grunted and released his hold. "Don't touch me," Larkin whispered.

"*Noted.*"

Shaking her head and looking up at them, Kelly said, "Yeah, sorry, but we don't keep records organized like that. I really can't find anyone without knowing their name. And if they've quit or were terminated… I mean, we only need to keep personnel files for, like, a year or so or whatever."

"What about OSHA records?" Doyle tried.

Larkin gave him curious side-eye.

"What about them?" Kelly asked.

"Legally, those have to be kept a lot longer," Doyle said.

"Five to thirty years, in some cases."

"Oh… sure, yeah, we have some really old ones."

"From the '90s?"

Kelly concurred.

Doyle looked down at Larkin.

"Do you… need a warrant for that?" Kelly asked into the brief quiet.

"Yes," Larkin answered.

She offered Doyle a dramatic wince and mouthed, "Sorry."

The front door of the Arsenal fell shut at 11:44. Larkin and Doyle stood side by side on the top landing. Sunshine cut through swatches of heavy gray clouds like a puncture from a dull knife, and light seeped like blood from a bandaged wound. Wind blew like the shudders of a man trying to hold back tears and breathe at the same time. Blossoms whipped across the bottom steps in a furious little cyclone. Eventually the air would still, and the petals would sprinkle the ground like confetti, then be trampled. They'd become muddy, torn, and then, forgotten.

"It's turning out to be a pretty day," Doyle said quietly.

Larkin crouched and collected a white petal from the shoestrings of his derby. He straightened.

"You want to tell me what happened back there?"

"We need a warrant."

Doyle sighed.

"Why did you ask," Larkin questioned. "Specifically about OSHA."

"Employers are required by law to keep documentation regarding any violations involving toxic substances for thirty years. I figured that's bound to happen now and then—isopropylamine is a volatile compound found in most insecticides and this *is* a parks department. And since HR wouldn't have the personnel files of employees from the '90s if they've moved on, an OSHA report is better than nothing. So-and-so might remember old coworkers, might still be in regular communication, that sort of thing. At least it would be a starting point."

Larkin pivoted on his heel to stare at Doyle straight on, albeit he did have to tilt his head up.

Doyle must have sensed the stare, because he turned and mimicked Larkin's stance. "What?"

"That's very smart."

"Should I be insulted?"

"I don't see why you would be. It was a compliment."

Doyle was smiling again—not that larger-than-life grin that encompassed his entire face, his entire body, the air around him, but one of subtle bemusement. "I am a detective, Larkin."

"I know that."

"Okay."

Larkin studied Doyle a moment longer before saying, "A judge won't sign a warrant for those records. I have nothing but a gut impression."

Doyle slid his hands into his trouser pockets. A strangled breeze rustled his artfully mussed hair. "You suspect an employee from the '90s because they had the means?"

"It's more than that."

"Lay it on me."

Larkin narrowed his eyes slightly before asking in that same neutral tone, "Are you familiar with the case of Larissa Brown."

"No."

"Train conductor for the MTA. Mother of two young daughters—four and two years old. On May 4, 2015, after failing to drop her children off at her mother's, who babysat during the day while Larissa and her husband, Donald, were both at work, and after being unable to reach Larissa by phone, her mother called the police. Donald worked in construction and had left for his jobsite two hours earlier. In their apartment, there were no signs of foul play. No indication she'd packed for an impromptu trip, although the baby's diaper bag was missing. She and the little girls had, for all intents and purposes, simply vanished."

"Are they still missing?" Doyle asked.

"No. They're dead."

"Back up."

Larkin spun the white petal between his fingers and said quietly, "I caught Larissa's case just before being transferred to Cold Cases. I had other work piling up—robberies, assaults, the typical bullshit—but it didn't sit right with me, this woman walking away from her life. But that's how it was being treated. She was an adult. They were her children. Maybe she'd had a disagreement with Donald, and he wouldn't fess up to a fight, and she was cooling off somewhere. That's what everyone said. I couldn't sleep the first two nights. I was physically sick from dread."

Looking down, Larkin realized he'd smooshed the petal. He let the remnants fall to the ground. "She wasn't anyone important, you understand. She wasn't rich and famous. But she lived an honest life. She was raising two babies. And I knew that—" He paused, shook his head, and said, "I knew that someone had acted as judge, jury, and executioner. I worked unapproved overtime. Got dragged out on the floor for it. I did it again. Noah threw a shit fit. 'She doesn't want to be found. You're more upset than her husband. A stranger's well-being shouldn't be more important than our anniversary.'"

"Huh."

Larkin spun the silver wedding band on his finger. "It was our dating anniversary, not that it makes a difference…. Noah's tirade led me to reconsider Donald as a person of interest. He acted the part well, but what he said with his face he failed to follow through in action. Donald wasn't pounding down my door, wasn't calling day and night, wasn't scared out of his mind. He was hiding the person he knew—*Larissa*. We all do it, to an extent. Hide someone. Whether out of shame or safety, we hide who we know in certain situations."

"He was hiding Larissa and the children."

"Yes. They had vanished without any signs of a struggle and seemingly hadn't gone with someone, so it must have been her choice. And if she chose to disappear, then it's not a homicide. It's not even a crime."

Doyle nodded. "I get it. No struggle because she left with her husband. She trusted him, of course. He took her somewhere… out of the city? State?"

"Pine Barrens out in Jersey. Her and her daughters' remains were found inside an oil drum July 2 of the same year. I had to tell the mother that Larissa had never walked away from her life. Her life was taken. Donald wanted to get a divorce and didn't want to get saddled with child support payments."

"God Almighty."

"When the connection is deeply personal—those are the victims most cleverly hidden. And until today, I don't think anyone knew John Doe was deceased." Larkin looked away.

A car heading downtown on Fifth Avenue drove past the Arsenal, windows down, "Stereo Hearts" by Gym Class Heroes pounding. Travis McCoy was asking to be kept inside your head like a favorite tune. Maybe, Larkin thought, that's why he was so… *different*. His memory. His inability to let go, to forget, to move on. It wasn't HSAM. It was an earworm.

He cracked a smile at his own joke. *If only.*

Doyle retrieved a pair of round tortoiseshell-framed sunglasses and slid them on. He started down the steps, calling over his shoulder, "Let's get going."

"I appreciate your professional expertise regarding the mask," Larkin said after him. "And I look forward to the reconstruction of the skull, but there is no practical reason for you to keep shadowing me at this time."

Doyle stopped, turned. Another gasp of spring air rustled his hair. "Do you know what I do most days?"

"You draw victims."

"No. I draw perpetrators. Rapists, mostly. Assailants and burglars too."

"At least your victims are still alive."

"Most are, thank God. But yours should be too."

And maybe Larkin understood what Doyle was trying to say right then. That his job as a forensic sketch artist was something akin to a middleman. He assisted in the pursuit of justice, but he wasn't responsible for it. That was glory, vindication, respite for the lead detective. And that this sort of unseen role he played came with the promise of eventual burnout.

Larkin imagined it was like communicating—Noah called it that—communicating their problems all evening long, but still, Larkin went to bed with his heart as heavy as lead and had troubled dreams all night long when not dosing himself on sleeping aids. Because for all of the talking, talking, *talking* they did about every perceived issue in the life they'd built together, it was really all about Larkin's shortcomings, right? He'd explained it all to Noah a hundred times, a thousand times, a million even, but his husband wasn't listening anymore.

So what did it matter?

All that work fell on deaf ears. There was never a chance to bask in hard-fought acclaim.

Larkin knew what that burnout felt like.

Doyle wasn't so terrible a detective to work with either. Minus his flirtatious habits, he was a natural conversationalist and quite smart. In fact, smarter than he seemed willing to let on, if the juxtaposition between what he said and how he presented himself was anything to judge by, which Larkin had. And Larkin was taking notice of his inaccurate deductions regarding the latter. Not that the lazy, rumpled appearance was a ploy or game to something bigger, something devious, but that it wasn't who Doyle was. Not entirely.

Anyway. If Doyle's schedule permitted further hands-on investigation, Larkin supposed he wouldn't… mind the assistance.

CHAPTER FIVE

At 12:07 p.m., as Larkin drove back to Precinct 19, Doyle's phone rang. He answered with that same liquidness in his voice—easy, accessible, reassuring. Yes, that was the word Larkin had been struggling to pin down. Doyle had a reassuring voice. Like he might have read aloud the lunch specials at a hole-in-the-wall joint with a C-grade notice in the window and the weighted blanket sensation of his words would have convinced Larkin they were about to have the best meal of his entire life, no need to worry about those health code violations. So it was rather surprising, when at a red light, Larkin glanced at Doyle and saw an intense frown at odds with that comforting tone.

Doyle's free hand rubbed up and down his thigh in a self-soothing gesture, the tweed fabric rustling under the touch. "How old?" He hadn't liked the murmured answer, Doyle's expression growing more pronounced. "Both of them? If I can have the particulars of the case beforehand… thanks. I'll be there in about twenty minutes." He said goodbye, tapped End, and pocketed the phone.

The light turned green and Larkin took his foot off the brake. He was silent—no reason to state the obvious, after all. When he turned onto Sixty-Seventh Street, all Larkin said was, "I'll be in touch when the OCME has the cast ready." He double-parked a few cars down from the blue Honda.

"That'll be great." Doyle paused before adding, "Sorry this changes our plans."

Larkin shrugged.

Doyle put his hand on the door handle, then said, "You know, whatever happened earlier, you should tell me."

This time, Larkin met Doyle's expression.

"If you're going to have some kind of, I don't know, fit…."

And like that, the frayed thread holding together Larkin's patience and composure for this godawful shit Monday snapped. "*Fit?*" he repeated, his voice rising sharply, suddenly.

"If it happens again during our interview—"

"*My* interview. This is my case. We are not partners. Do you understand?" Larkin asked, voice pitching harshly a second time.

Doyle said nothing.

Twisting in his seat to face Doyle, seat belt taut against his chest, Larkin said, "You have two victims—children, I suspect—waiting at 1PP. The lead detective didn't arrange an appointment with you prior to their arrival, which means these victims must have just come forward and they're afraid by delaying the session, the children might forget vital details as to their assailants. No cop wants a case involving children, but based on the rise in your vocal pitch, tension in your facial muscles, and subconscious attempt to calm yourself, this session will be particularly brutal. So it must involve Special Victims. See?" Larkin asked. "There was no fit. I am perfectly capable of handling a myriad of situations while making competent deductions and rational decisions."

"I never said—"

"Please get out."

"Larkin—"

"I'm asking that you respect my boundaries and get out."

Doyle pulled the handle, popped the door open, and climbed out. He collected his portfolio bag, shut the door, and walked toward the Honda without a glance back.

Larkin put his hazards on and sat there—shaking. "Fuck. Fuck. *Fuck*!" He punched the passenger seat several times before leaning back, breathing hard. Fumbling one-handed, Larkin opened the center console and removed a prescription bottle with his name on it. His hands continued to shake as he fought to get the cap off and then poured the contents into his palm.

It'd be easy. It'd be so easy. No more Grim. No more faggot. No more thunderstorms or sugar-and-smoke kisses or the city's unwanted dead. No more whiskey voice talking about a fit, like he had a single fucking clue what a monumental achievement it was to get out of bed some days. No more feeling as if being alive were akin to a hospital flatline.

People don't want to know what makes them uncomfortable.

Larkin clenched his fist around the pills, a few spilling between the seat and console, another into the footwell. He managed his phone free with his other hand and dialed Noah.

His husband's wary voice answered on the third ring. "Hi."

"Hey," Larkin breathed.

"Are you okay?"

"Yeah," Larkin lied. "I had a minute. Wanted to hear your voice."

"Liar," Noah said, but there was a smile somewhere in there.

Larkin let out a quiet, shaky laugh. "It's just been one of those days, honey. I'm sorry about this morning."

"It's all right. I know some of those cases get to you more than others."

Larkin squeezed his eyes shut. More pills spilled from his clutch. He laughed again, more brittle, and shook his head. "Right."

"Do you want to go out tonight after you see Dr. Myers?"

He cleared his throat and managed to say, "I'm usually tired after my appointments."

"We haven't had a date night in, like, a month, Everett."

Larkin opened his hand and the Xanax fell across his lap and between his legs. Tears rolled down his cheeks as he said obediently, "Yes, honey."

"But I guess I can order delivery… have it here by the time you get home."

"That sounds good."

"We can finish *Broad City*."

Larkin shook his head again.

"That new Indian place on Eighty-Ninth finally opened. Did you want try it?"

"Okay."

"Seven thirty, then?"

"Yes."

"Have a good afternoon." Noah disconnected.

Larkin dropped his phone in his lap. He wiped his cheeks for a second time that day, picked up one of the Xanax, and dry swallowed it. A moment later, he swallowed a second.

People don't want to know.

A search on his phone of the New York Public Library mobile site, with the keywords "death" and "mask," had unearthed a book on the third page of results called *Funerary Rituals: Faces From The Other Side, A Brief Account of Effigies and Death Masks*. The title was available for checkout at the Main Branch on Fifth Avenue, so Larkin submitted his personal patron details, and when the Xanax made it so he could no longer feel his heart jackhammering in his throat, he drove into Midtown to pick up the research book.

Upon returning to the precinct, Larkin sat down at his clean and orderly desk, took a moment to mentally block out conversations, phones ringing, and doors slamming, which was admittedly easier when riding a Xanax high, and then began to read.

The death mask, as we understand its importance today—tangible proof of rare and true greatness achievable by humanity, and that by surrounding ourselves with their likeness, we are reminded to strive for answers to the unknowns just as they once did—was not seen as valuable in and of itself, but as a means to an end: that being the effigies of royalty.

"Who the fuck moved the Hello Phone?" Byron Ulmer shouted from across the bullpen at 1:45 p.m. "I got a CI more skittish than a newborn colt calling in five fucking minutes!"

Throughout the Renaissance period, France's and England's utilization of death masks was that of a tool. Court painters applied the details of the recently deceased to a wax or wooden likeness of the king, but as he was known in life, thusly confirming our previous account of being nothing but an instrument. The serenity of death was avoided at all costs in the full-bodied effigies—

"Grim."

—but the death mask would eventually become treasured for what it was: realism artwork obsessive of the individual.

The death mask would become the symbol of all that embodied the man. His face undying.

"Grim!"

Larkin put his finger on the sentence and raised his gaze to see Ulmer, the lox-stealing detective who looked more like a linebacker in a suit, moving up beside Porter's empty chair and glaring down at him. He had a dark complexion, shaved head, goatee, and none of the patience seen in the squad's veteran detectives. Ulmer was newly transferred and had been hard-pressed to become the face of Cold Cases—that was, until he'd come to realize that Larkin stood in his way of that career goal.

"Do you have the Hello Phone?" Ulmer demanded.

"Does it look like I have the Hello Phone," Larkin answered in a subdued tone.

"What it looks like," Ulmer began, puffing out his chest, "is that you went to a Scholastic fucking Book Fair and forgot to pick yourself up a Lisa Frank pencil on the way out."

Larkin placed a bookmark on the page, calmly shut the library book, sifted through the cup of pens on his desk, then removed a pink pencil with hologram leopard prints stamped all over it. He tapped it absently against the desktop while staring up at Ulmer. "That's because I already have one."

"What the fuck. Those are for little girls."

"I don't believe there's a particular age or gender demographic when it comes to a pencil."

"It's *Lisa Frank*," Ulmer stressed, like maybe if he said it a few more times, he'd make his point understood.

"Yes. My husband is a schoolteacher and children like bright colors."

Porter was returning to his desk with a mug of coffee in the midst of the back-and-forth. He took a seat, the chair groaning under his weight, before saying, "We can hear your pissing all the way to the breakroom, Ulmer."

"I need the fucking Hello Phone," Ulmer snapped, glancing sideways at Porter. "And Grim is trying to lecture me on the fucking societal consequences of a grown man using a kitty-cat-themed pencil or whatever the fuck he's on about."

"They're leopard prints," Larkin corrected, raising the pencil up for Ulmer to see. "And I said there was *no* associated age or demographic for pencil utilization. At most, we're obligated to transition to blue or black ink pens due to the permanency and legality of adult careers, but otherwise, society hasn't frowned upon me using my gay pencil—I believe that's what you've been itching to say."

Porter had the rim of his mug to his lips before he started laughing. A few drops of coffee splashed his pant leg.

Larkin offered the pencil to Ulmer. "Unless this display of toxic masculinity is actually you trying to ask if you may borrow my Lisa Frank pencil. The answer is, yes, you may."

Ulmer grabbed it, broke the pencil in two, then threw the pieces, hitting Larkin in the chest. "What do you think of that fucking display of masculinity?"

Larkin said, without any perturbation, "I think it's very cute you needed both hands to snap a Number 2 pencil."

Ulmer's face darkened. He gritted his teeth and said, "Don't fucking call me cute."

Porter put his mug down noisily. "All right, Ulmer, chill out or you're going to get smacked with a discrimination lawsuit."

"I don't care that he's a fag," Ulmer said, hackles rising.

"The use of that term implies the contrary," Larkin answered easily, still floating on the haze of a relaxed high. "You're very uncomfortable around me and typically resort to violent outbursts, like right now. This sort of behavior is often accompanied by comments akin to 'you better not be looking at my ass, bro,' as if you expect all gay men to not only be attracted to you, but be eager to bend you over a desk. The overcompensation of heterosexuality has been viewed in the past as a repression of latent homosexual desires. Those are big words, I know, so I'll put it more simply: you want me to stare at your ass and that makes you angry."

Porter's eyebrows crept to his nonexistent hairline.

Ulmer might as well have had steam shooting from his ears as he moved around the desk to stand before Larkin.

Larkin casually pushed back from his desk and stared up at Ulmer from his chair.

Ulmer grabbed a fistful of Larkin's button-down shirt and yanked him from the seat in one impressive display of strength. "If you ever try to make a pass at me—"

"Let go," Larkin interrupted.

"—I'll smash your face into a brick wall so many times, the only way you'll be able to suck a dick again is if it's through a straw."

Larkin's mouth twitched in a smile. "You're not my type, Ulmer. Let go before I hurt you."

"What the fuck is going on out here?" Lieutenant Connor's voice boomed from the open doorway of his office.

"Ulmer is looking for the Hello Phone," Larkin answered, staring at Ulmer, still clutched in the brute's grip.

"It's in the Fuck It," Connor retorted. "Ulmer—get your hands off Grim."

Ulmer released Larkin with a not-so-gentle shove before turning to Connor and saying, "He started it."

"And I'm fucking finishing it," Connor barked. "Go do some goddamn work."

Ulmer shot Larkin a final, fierce stare—*and if looks could kill*—before he stalked off to the converted junk room.

Lieutenant Connor, a fair but short-tempered Irishman

with a tendency to micromanage, had come from a family who served the NYPD dating back to 1892, a fact that he was very proud of and happy to talk about to anyone who asked. He'd likely been a formidable flatfoot in his prime, as Connor's height and build rivaled doorframes, with features softened only by a smattering of freckles across his face. Nowadays, his job was to keep the understaffed and overworked Cold Case Squad in one piece, which meant he'd exchanged pepper spray for paperwork.

"Grim." Connor jerked his head and returned to his office.

Larkin smoothed his shirt, adjusted his tie, then walked across the bullpen. He stepped inside, shut the door, and took a seat in front of Connor's desk.

"Was that something I should be made aware of?"

"No, sir."

Connor eased back in his chair. After a pregnant pause, he said, "Last chance."

Larkin just stared at Connor. Because nothing good ever came from being a tattletale.

A smile slowly spread across Connor's face. "Tell me what's happening with that Madison case—the one O'Halloran phoned about this morning."

So Larkin did. He told Connor about the rudimentary knowledge gleaned from the crime scene. About Ira Doyle's analysis of the death mask and promise of a skull reconstruction. About the interview with Mable McClennan at Parks & Recreation. About the potential for information in the dated OSHA reports.

Connor grunted. "You need more for a judge."

"I know."

"So what's your next step?"

"Pending, until I get a call from the ME."

"I assume you've got other work that needs attention?"

The question was a setup, but Larkin nonetheless answered truthfully, "Thirty-seven open cases."

"And which of those thirty-seven were you working on, prior to putting Ulmer in an early grave?"

"I was doing research on death masks."

Connor straightened. "Is it relevant to the case?"

"I don't know yet."

"Then save that artsy-fartsy crap for—what'd you say his name was? Doyle."

"Doyle isn't working this case in an official capacity. I'm not even certain who his supervisor is. I can't pony off the necessary homework simply because he already has an elementary understanding of the subject matter."

Connor picked up the receiver of his desk phone. "I know his supervisor."

"If you're going to have some kind of, I don't know, fit...."

"I'd prefer you not do that, sir."

"You've never had a problem asking for help in the past," Connor answered, holding the hook with an index finger while he removed a directory printout from a desk drawer with his other hand.

"That's because I don't need help reading a book."

"Your time is better used elsewhere. The artist can read up on any relevant information and provide the CliffsNotes edition." Connor tapped a few numbers on the phone before leaning back to get comfortable for the conversation. "What's the latest on that Garcia case?" he asked Larkin.

"The mother has refused all attempts I've made at communic—"

"Darryl? Hey, it's Mikey Connor in Cold Cases," Connor interrupted, speaking into the receiver. "How's shit down at 1PP?" He glanced at Larkin and motioned to the door.

Larkin stood, walked to the door, and opened it.

"Yeah, hey, hang on one second…. Larkin!"

Larkin turned.

"June 2."

He let out a small breath. "What year?"

"2005," Connor said.

"That was a Thursday," Larkin answered. Then he shut the door.

CHAPTER SIX

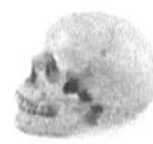

Marco Garcia had been eighteen years old when he was pushed onto the tracks in front of an incoming Q train. The case had been cold for nearly two decades, left unsolved once the assigned detective got tunnel vision, convinced that Marco had been rubbed out over a drug deal gone wrong. After the detective had retired—Florida, Larkin recalled— the case found its way to his desk, and Larkin had quickly deduced that drugs had never been part of the narrative.

Marco had no drugs on him.

Marco sold no drugs.

Marco did no drugs.

No drugs.

The mother, after being fed this line of bullshit for over twenty years, no longer wanted anything to do with the police. So when Larkin had reopened the case and reached out to her, she had refused to return his calls. He'd driven to her home last week—he heard the television, heard the clatter of pots on a stovetop, heard *life*, but she wouldn't answer his knocks—so Larkin called through the door that he understood his presence wasn't welcome, but he needed her to know that her son's case was now his, he knew there were no drugs involved, and he'd bring Marco some justice, no matter how long it took. He slipped his card under the door and left.

Sometimes people like Marco's mother eventually called back.

And sometimes they'd rather not open a blistering wound again. Those were the cases that Larkin chased away with pharmaceuticals. Because when people like Marco's mother, a shell of who they once were, looked him in the eye and asked, "What's it matter? It won't bring my baby back," Larkin struggled not to agree. Struggled not to say, "At best, it'll break your heart again. At best, the trial will haunt you. At best, the justice will taste like ash in your mouth. And for what. He'll still be dead."

It won't rewind life to a more innocent time.

It won't fix what's wrong with your brain.

It won't bring him back.

—the sun-bleached dock, rivulets of cold water running down every vertebrae, their entwined fingers hot with the fires of first love—

But it was Larkin's job.

He reread the Garcia file, even though the details had already imprinted themselves on his bones, placed some calls, left some messages, and was reworking the timeline of Marco's final days when an email popped in his inbox. Larkin raised his eyes at the quiet *ding* and saw L. Baxter, MD, in the sender column and John Doe's case number in the subject. He closed the Garcia file and clicked the email. Attached was the autopsy report and one sentence: *Come by the office before 5:00 for your cast. -Baxter*

Larkin checked his watch, returned Garcia's records to their accordion file, adjusted the neat stack on his desk, then stood and gathered his suit coat from the back of the chair in one fluid motion. He pulled his arms through the sleeves, collected his library book, and walked to the staircase, but then Connor shouted, *"Grim!"*—the open door of his office providing a perfect view of who came and went in the bullpen.

Larkin looked over his shoulder.

"Where you going?" he called.

"OCME."

"For John Doe?"

"Yes."

Connor nodded after a beat, then added, "Doyle's all yours, by the way."

"Great," Larkin heard himself say, but his tone was so tempered, he wasn't certain if he intended for it to come across positively or sarcastically. His gut wasn't so sure either.

Porter shuffled his feet across the floor as he lazily spun in his chair to look at Larkin. "That kid's gonna be shadowing you now?"

"I'm fairly certain Detective Doyle is older than me," Larkin corrected before he started down the steps.

"Age is a state of mind."

"How very zen of you, Porter," Larkin called back.

"He can draw you some funny cartoons while you do the actual detective work!"

"Goodbye."

The forty blocks downtown to the Office of Chief Medical Examiner would have been an easy straight shot at any time but the start of rush hour on a Monday. It took exactly thirty-two minutes, with Larkin flashing his badge to the front desk at 4:34. He inquired after Dr. Baxter's whereabouts—the basement, Larkin had presumed—but was instead directed to take the elevator to the second floor. Except when Larkin reached the office door with the nameplate L. Baxter, Medical Examiner, it was locked and no light showed at the floor.

"Dr. Baxter isn't here."

Larkin turned to an office that mirrored the good doctor's on the right side of the hallway. The door was open and a middle-aged woman with thick glasses and closely cropped brown hair was staring at him from where she sat at a desk. The workspace was cluttered with files and a government-assigned laptop, but there were no tchotchkes or family photographs that'd indicate the office was specifically hers. Larkin glanced over her shoulder, taking an automatic inventory of the space. Two other desks had been shoved into the cramped quarters, both currently unoccupied but with the same buildup of impersonal items. A squat bookcase on the far wall of the windowless room had several packages stacked on the shelves, as well as binders, loose sheafs of paper, and a tabletop microscope, like the sort Larkin used in biology class in high school when they had dissected a goat's eye and his partner, Susan Anderson, had projectile vomited and was sent home for the day. Larkin sniffed. The circulated air smelled a bit stale, a bit like someone's hours-old lunch of instant ramen noodles, and a bit like harsh cleaning chemicals.

Larkin decided the office was likely used by the rotating staff of mortuary technicians and that this woman, with the steam whistle voice, was the same he'd spoken to on the phone that morning. He removed his badge and showed her, saying, "Everett Larkin. I called about—"

"The skull casting," she said in a clipped tone.

"That's right. Dr. Baxter emailed to say I could come pick it up before five o'clock." He briefly considered, now that his comfortable Xanax high was a few hours old and on the decline, that Dr. Baxter might have been screening him. Larkin would have to apologize again for the improper comment he'd made that morning. Explain that he'd been given some poor life advice from Ira Doyle and that he'd never in the future attempt to imitate someone whose flirting skills were on a bar Larkin couldn't even jump to reach.

You owe Doyle an apology too.

The thought had been lurking just under the surface the entire drive to OCME.

Because Lieutenant Connor had felt it necessary to pull favors and get Doyle officially involved, and working together with a storm cloud overhead wouldn't help anyone. Because Doyle had seen something was very wrong with Larkin but kept a cool and professional attitude that allowed Larkin privacy, without tipping Mable off. Because it hadn't been Doyle's fault that March 30 mirrored August 2, 2002, in all the ways that required Xanax in order to cope.

People don't want to know.

But Doyle did. Well, he'd asked, at least. He'd regret ever showing an ounce of concern if Larkin told him—really told him—but for that singular second, Doyle *had* asked and he'd been… seemingly sincere about it.

Larkin blinked and returned his attention to the technician, who'd clearly been talking the entire time.

"—And so he had to attend the scene for the body transport," she was explaining.

Larkin glanced over his shoulder at Baxter's office before saying, "Then can you provide me with the cast."

Steam Whistle flashed a microexpression of contempt at the request.

Larkin said nothing more, just met her stare dead-on.

And like most who challenged him, she broke almost immediately under Larkin's unrelenting gaze. With a huff, Steam Whistle got to her feet and went to the shelf lined with packages. She returned with a sealed box and extended it at arm's length, as if Larkin were the bogeyman and he'd snatch her up if she got too close.

"Thank you," he said brusquely.

Larkin left the way he'd come, stepping through the front doors of OCME and into a mostly concrete courtyard. The *clink, clink, clink* of a flag snapping against the pole in the brisk breeze sounded overhead. Two administrator-looking sorts stood a dozen feet away with cigarettes. They held an animated conversation, smoke curling and stirring into abstract shapes around their moving hands. A playground sat west of the building, and even Larkin, a man known in professional circles as *Grim* or *Spooky*, thought its vicinity to the morgue pushed the envelope of morbid humor a touch too far.

Larkin stepped around concrete barriers, which jutted up from the ground like monstrous teeth, and onto the sidewalk while pulling his phone from his pocket. He opened the list of recent outgoing calls, hesitated on the number he'd dialed at 9:07, then edited the details with Doyle's name, title, and the inclusion of "office" so it was added in his address book. He placed the call and put the phone to his ear as he walked toward First Avenue on Twenty-Sixth, passing half a dozen white-and-blue medical examiner vehicles parked along the southside of the street. The call rang and rang and rang.

"Detective Ira Doyle, Forensic Artists. Please leave a message."

Larkin made a *tsk* sound under his breath before the beep. "This is Everett Larkin." Larkin held the phone between his ear and shoulder in order to check his watch. "It's 4:46. I just collected the cast of John Doe's skull from OCME and I'm on my way to 1PP to drop it off. Traffic is backed up on Second, so I'm taking the FDR."

He should have ended the call then.

But he didn't.

A child in the park, pumping their legs hard and fast on a swing set, screamed in delight as they reached maximum air.

—"We're too old for swings."

"Says who, Everett?"—

Larkin shivered and said into the recorded silence, "I hope you'll be available for an additional moment once I get there so that I might… apologize for my tone with you earlier. It was unprofessional of me. That's it. Okay. Goodbye."

Then he hung up.

One Police Plaza, an ugly-as-fuck love song to Brutalism architecture, had replaced the former headquarters of the NYPD—a gorgeous Renaissance Revival structure from the turn of the century—in the '70s, a decade where everything once beautiful was left to die. The monochromatic, minimalist structure of thirteen stories sat wedged between Park Row and Pearl Street on the lower end of the island—a turd that the entire neighborhood complained about as if it were an Olympic sport.

The reception area, which Larkin estimated his entire bullpen could have fit into, breakroom included, was bustling with the administrative sort whose careers resembled something closer to the mundane nine-to-five. And seeing that it was—he checked his watch—5:20, they were itching to complete their final task before clocking out for the day. Uniformed cops moved at the pace of those in the midst of the swing shift with several hours to go, and detectives acted like they never got home before midnight anyway, so what was the point in rushing? The ground floor echoed with ringing phones, dinging elevators, doors slamming, toilets flushing, a dozen competing conversations.

Larkin hated it.

Standing near the elevators and doing his best to ignore the shuffle of people coming and going at a consistent rate, Larkin studied the directory bulletin on the wall. He narrowed his eyes, read it a second time, then went to the front desk.

"Your directory doesn't state which floor the Forensic Artists Unit is located on."

A uniformed man set a desk phone down and flashed Larkin an irritated look. "What's that?"

"Forensic Artists Unit."

"Fifth floor."

"It should be on the directory."

"Yeah, well, there's only three of them."

"So."

The officer furrowed his bushy brows. "So there probably wasn't enough vowels to list a three-man unit, buddy."

"Those letters are packaged with three or four times the number of vowels to consonants, so it is extremely unlikely they ran out of 'i's. I'd like to leave feedback about the directory. Do you have comment cards."

"Are you serious?"

"If 1PP did, in fact, run short of plastic letters, a replacement package would cost twenty dollars. The NYPD has an annual budget of five billion," Larkin explained. "This way, myself and others won't need to interact with you again for simple directions."

"Hey—"

And in what was most definitely a power move akin to whipping out his dick and measuring it, Larkin said, "In the future, please refrain from calling me or any other plainclothes officer *buddy*. I'm a first-grade detective." He returned to the elevator banks as one of the car doors opened, slipped inside, and pressed the fifth floor.

Upstairs, Larkin followed winding halls lit with the same fluorescent overheads as his own precinct. The punch-out-style windows appeared to be relegated to inner offices for the most part. The air smelled like toner, like carpet cleaner, like the ever-present hours-old coffee that was the base note of most colognes and perfumes for police officers. A closed door on the west end of the floor had the nameplate Ira Doyle, Forensic Artists Unit, and Larkin stopped outside it. He could hear murmured voices inside, but wasn't able to decipher individual words. Then he picked up the hesitant laugh of a child, Doyle's patent smoky response, and the laughter grew more confident—if only briefly—reminiscent of the innocence lost.

He was still with the child victims. Had been all afternoon, in fact.

Larkin turned, backtracked to another office, and knocked on the partially open door. He poked his head in as a middle-aged man glanced up from a computer screen. He was skinny—not Larkin-skinny, who was toned because every effort was made to hit the gym several times a week, if for nothing else but the peace and quiet that accompanied cardio workouts—but skinny in the sense that this man hadn't much cared for his physique beyond being able to pass departmental endurance requirements. He had a Tom Selleck Chevron mustache, which, when paired with a tie covered in colorful macarons, gave him nerdy homeroom teacher vibes and not that of a forensic artist.

"Can I help you?" he asked in a deep, pleasant voice that absolutely did not fit the aesthetic of someone who would write you up for being late to class.

Larkin pushed the door open the rest of the way. "My apologies for the intrusion. My name's Everett Larkin, Cold Case Squad."

A knowing smile broke out across the artist's face. "You must be lead detective on that case Doyle was called to this morning."

"That's correct."

"Craig Bailey," he said, standing and leaning over his

desk to offer a hand. "Senior Artist."

Larkin stepped forward, shook, then raised his box in both hands. "I was dropping off a skull cast for Doyle. He was going to be assisting with a facial reconstruction of my John Doe."

"Yeah, I heard all about that. I got the rundown on his new assignment from our lieutenant this afternoon," Bailey answered as he took a seat again. "Starts tomorrow, though. He's doing composite sketches with SVU right now, and I'm not going to interrupt—"

"I'm not asking you to."

Bailey pursed his lips a bit, and his bushy mustache moved like a caterpillar. "I'll see he gets the package, then."

Larkin moved deeper into the office and handed over the box. "Thank you."

"Sure thing." Bailey drummed his fingertips against the lid.

Larkin stepped out of the office. The day had been hell. But underneath the addictive calm of pharmaceuticals, he rewound and replayed Doyle's passing comment about the day and the night—the light and the dark. He replayed Doyle's reassuring laugh. Its easiness and authentic notes. Its pleasure. *Jubilate up to the heavens.* Nietzsche—aphorism number twelve—the concept that pleasure and displeasure were so entwined that to have the extreme of one meant the same amount of the other. But if Doyle were the jubilance, did that make Larkin the *depression unto death* in this partnership they were about to embark upon?

Had Doyle read Nietzsche and simply dumbed down the profoundness of that philosophical concept in order to reinforce the lackadaisical front he projected?

Larkin wondered: was Doyle's laugh due to nothing more than the theory of relief? That it was merely a physiological mechanism in which to handle anger or pain or sadness or to cope with the existential crisis that is human mortality? Or did Doyle laugh because he was *truly* happy? Because if he chose to accept as much displeasure as possible, then by default he had already paid the price for which to experience boundless joy.

Larkin turned and asked Bailey, "Why was Doyle assigned his current session."

Bailey glanced up and said, as if Larkin should have known this all along, "He always takes the cases involving children. Those are the worst ones, you know? But he always takes them."

CHAPTER SEVEN

The office followed all the rules of basic psychology. Soothing wall color in a sage green. No harsh fluorescents, only warm tungsten floor lamps to keep the room luminated as the March skyline edged toward a sunset of golds and pinks. The desk and coffee table were a natural wood with a visible grain. Comfortable furniture at the midrange of price. Two pleasant, if somewhat bland, spring landscapes adorned the walls.

Larkin knew all the tricks.

Dr. Elizabeth Myers dressed like an appropriate accent to the room. Glasses that suggested intelligence, but with a large enough frame that her expression did not imply superiority. Steel-gray hair wrapped in some complicated affair. Pleated pants in a teal that complemented the walls, a billowy top that looked like something purchased in Williamsburg, and a chunky piece of jewelry around her neck that was styled to look rustic or smart, but not expensive, even though it most certainly was extremely pricey.

Her intern was a lanky fellow with a shock of red hair and a body that still hadn't been entirely grown into, in the way that twentysomething men were susceptible. But he was pleasant enough, which was all Larkin really cared about by 6:07 that evening. "Richard Walsh. It's a pleasure to meet you, Mr. Larkin."

Larkin stood to shake the student's hand. "Dr. Myers says you're working on your dissertation."

"Yes, sir."

"What is your area of interest."

"Cognitive neuroscience of human memory."

Larkin looked at Myers as she seated herself behind the desk. He returned to the couch. "HSAM."

"Specifically? Yes, sir," Walsh agreed as he took the chair left of the couch. "And I appreciate your willingness to be interviewed. I'm sure you've been asked these questions dozens of times already."

"I'm sure," Larkin agreed, his tone bordering on bland.

Color rose in Walsh's pale complexion. No doubt a mixture of the nervous excitement he was doing his damnedest to tamp down and the simple fact that Larkin's manner of speech tended to rub people in uniquely negative ways. He fidgeted with the pen in his hand, leaving pockmarks of ink on his legal pad of paper. "Can you describe how you assemble—or rather, the sensation of your autobiographical memories? I've spoken with another individual with confirmed HSAM, and they described it like viewing a board game."

Larkin glanced at Myers a second time, but the older woman gave nothing away. "A Rolodex," he answered, turning to Walsh. "Depending on the association I'm presented with, the Rolodex spins accordingly to find the memory. Then I can zoom in on specific incidents."

Walsh scribbled on his pad, but Larkin was too far away to decipher the chicken scratch. "So if I began with a calendar date, say… September 14—"

"What year. It has to be 2002 or later."

Walsh blinked a few times. "Is that when the HSAM began?"

"Yes. What year."

"2018."

"Friday," Larkin answered. "Overcast and humid. I was working the Archer case."

Removing a phone from his trouser pocket, Walsh asked, "Do you mind if I confirm that information?"

Larkin said nothing.

Walsh tapped his screen a few times, his eyes widened slightly, and then he cleared his throat and nodded. "Day of the week and weather are accurate. What if you're presented a more personal association? Like an individual's name?"

"It needs to be someone I'm already acquainted with."

"Of course." Walsh shifted a manilla folder he'd been holding underneath the pad and removed a few printed-out sheets of paper. "Dr. Myers explained to me the ongoing study the two of you are conducting—your husband assists with that?"

"Dr. Myers emails Noah a list of questions that he fills out over the course of three weeks and sends back without my knowledge of what's been asked. What I had for dinner Tuesday night. What he wore Saturday afternoon. On and on. They're never the same questions. Then she compares his answers with what I recall."

"The three-week minimum," Myers finally spoke up, addressing Walsh, "was decided upon as a baseline when clinical tests showed that an individual's ability to recall mundane autobiographical details without HSAM was severely impacted by this time."

Walsh scanned the document, then asked at random, "What shoes did Noah wear two Saturdays ago?"

Larkin shut his eyes.

It'd been the first day in almost a month that he'd been able to sleep in. He'd taken ZzzQuil to make the most of it. But Noah had stomped around the bedroom getting dressed—loud enough that their downstairs neighbor should have complained. Noah was going to the Greenmarket in Union Square. Noah was still upset from the night before when Larkin said no to a morning outing. He was running on fumes, needed to sleep, the market didn't close until six in the evening so where was the rush? Of course he wanted to spend the day with his husband, but he was so exhausted that his skin hurt and he needed to *sleep*. Larkin could see Noah sitting on the side of the bed, tying his shoes, then storming out of the bedroom. The front door crashed shut thirty seconds later.

Larkin opened his eyes. "Red Nikes."

Walsh looked excited again. "That's incredible."

"Not really," Larkin said dully.

"There's only about sixty confirmed cases, *worldwide*, of Highly Superior Autobiographical Memory. And of those sixty, the studies you've been a part of, Mr. Larkin, show that you're in the top percentile. I hesitate to use the word, but your ability to recall details is extraordinary. You don't think that's a gift?"

"My short-term memory is terrible," Larkin answered. "I miss appointments without reminders because I'm just… unable to recall a plan on its own that exists outside a strict routine. I misplaced my wedding ring today. Forgot about it entirely. Gun to my head, I wouldn't have been able to tell you where I'd put it because I was so immersed in a past event that I was running on autopilot in the here and now. It's not a gift when my husband confronts me about the missing ring. It's not a gift that I can't control intrusive memories because a date, a time, a voice, a crack of thunder is an association and now the past has to play itself out in full like a film projector with no controls. It's not a gift that I've developed obsessive-compulsive traits as a method of coping. It's not a gift that I can barely hold a regular conversation, because I'm too busy automatically cataloging every mundane and minute detail, and that if I focus—really focus on the other person—there's a constant fear that the conversation will take a negative turn and I'll have invested energy into something I now can't forget, a pain that doesn't diminish with time." Larkin wiped his cheeks and took a wet breath. "*None* of that is a gift."

Larkin quietly shut the front door to 3C, threw the deadbolt, and hung his ring of keys on a hook they'd installed after one too many times of Larkin misplacing the set. The apartment was a one-bedroom in a hundred-and-twenty-year-old walk-up on the Upper East Side. Furnishings were modern and simplistic, ornamentation kept to a minimum, lighting low and warm, curtains pulled shut across the windows overlooking Eightieth Street. The television was on in the front room, the murmur of a commercial barely audible. Noah was in the kitchen off to the left, rustling through a bag, setting plates on the counter—the takeout had beaten Larkin by a minute at best.

Walking across the room, Larkin dropped his library book on the couch and kept moving into the adjoining bedroom. He went through the motions: hang up suit coat, fold pocket square, store weapon and shoulder holster in the safe, watch, cuff links, and phone on the nightstand. He'd tugged his tie free as the old floor creaked, announcing Noah's presence in the doorway.

"Hey."

Larkin turned. "Hi."

Seemingly fine now, after Larkin had been the one to apologize earlier, Noah came forward, leaned down, and kissed him. "How was your appointment?"

Larkin caught Noah by the back of the neck, drew him

into a second kiss, then said, "It could have been better." He let go and unbuttoned his shirt.

"What happened?"

Larkin considered, pulled a T-shirt over his head, then said, "Just an interview with a new intern."

Noah laughed lightly. "Did this one call you superhuman? Like the last guy?"

"Almost." He dragged pajama pants on, and when Noah draped his arms over Larkin's shoulders, he instinctively pulled his husband closer by the hips.

"They treat you like an oddity."

"I am an oddity."

Noah raised a hand, tilted Larkin's head, and kissed his right temple. "Where your noggin got knocked loose."

"Don't joke about that."

"I'm not joking."

—Boom. Squish. Crack—

A quake shook Larkin from the inside out—rattled bones, warped muscles, flipped organs. He stepped back from Noah, scrubbed his face with both hands, and said, "Let's sit down and eat."

"Everett—"

"I'd like to sit down."

The petulant jut of Noah's jaw returned, but he bit back whatever venom he had ready to spit, turned, and walked out of the bedroom, saying something about the chicken vindaloo, vegetable curry, and naan in the kitchen.

Larkin shook his head. *Like walking on eggshells.* He collected his phone and stepped into the front room when he noticed a text message notification that'd come in over an hour ago. He swiped and opened the rarely used app (he was one of the few Millennials to prefer phone calls), tapped the message, and a gif loaded of a woman—was Larkin supposed to know who she was?—giving finger guns with a subtitle that read: *Don't worry about it, babe.*

Underneath the gif was a text: *It's Doyle, by the way.*

Larkin furrowed his brow before the voicemail he'd left earlier automatically replayed in his head: *—so that I might… apologize for my tone with you….*

"What're you smiling about?"

Larkin looked up. Noah stood at the couch with a plate in either hand. "A message from work." He quickly added Doyle's cell number to his phone, moved his book to the end table, placed his phone on top, then took the meal from Noah's hand.

"I take it to be good news?" Noah asked, sitting beside Larkin.

Larkin's mouth twitched. "Yeah."

They ate dinner without talking, with only occasional comedic one-liners from *Broad City* or commercials for auto insurance or the latest antidepression medication on the market penetrating Larkin's thoughts. Not that his thoughts were terribly cohesive or properly organized at that point. He'd been rode hard and put away wet today, and that wasn't taking into account the crash from the Xanax or the mental exhaustion that always lingered like a storm cloud after appointments with Dr. Myers. Mostly, Larkin felt fried. He'd have preferred to take the opportunity to turn in early, but that'd become another argument about how he didn't pay enough attention to Noah. So Larkin remained on the couch, trying to read a bit more on the history of death masks, but he was turning pages and studying pictures without absorbing any of the information, merely as a way of looking busy so he'd be left alone.

Noah had curled up beside Larkin after dinner, and that'd been pleasant. Larkin didn't enjoy physical contact from most people—it was just another sensory stimulation to fuck with him when his mental defenses were low. But Noah was different. Noah was okay. After all, they'd been together nearly seven years and married for four. Of course he liked it when Noah touched him. Except that lately—*all the time*—Noah wouldn't leave it at that: a comforting snuggle. He'd want more, like he'd traded libidos with an eighteen-year-old boy who knew only two truths in life: eating and fucking. And the longer Larkin flatlined between heartbeats, the more difficult it became to keep up with Noah's physical demands.

During a commercial break, Noah raised his head from Larkin's chest and kissed his neck, the blond stubble on his husband's chin like beach sand, gritty in a satisfying sort of way. A brief shock of physical interest popped inside Larkin, but as Noah kissed again, sucked Larkin's skin, the sensation dissipated and he was left flaccid and disinterested.

Noah yanked the book from Larkin's hand, tossed it to the floor, and straddled his lap. He kissed Larkin's mouth like a man starving, murmured against his lips, "I need you to fuck me," then reached between Larkin's legs. Noah stopped, leaned back.

"Not tonight," Larkin said quietly.

"What the fuck?"

"Noah—"

"Not even a semi?"

Larkin put his hands on Noah's hips and drew them up his flanks in a sort of placating manner, but Noah swore again and climbed off. "Fuck," Larkin muttered on an exhale.

Noah stood in front of the television, the flickering screen illuminating his form in a way that Larkin could only describe as hellish. Noah put his hands on his hips and asked, "Do I repulse you?"

"For God's sake, Noah."

"I have a right to know."

"You're being ridiculous."

"You want to know what ridiculous is?" Noah countered. "Ridiculous is your husband spurning your every advance for, oh, I don't know, the entire *year* thus far."

"I'm exhausted—" Larkin began.

"This isn't exhaustion."

"The fuck it's not," Larkin argued. He got to his feet. "I spend every day chasing down people who've gotten away with cold-blooded murder. I spend every day with grieving families, angry families—I've had doors slammed in my face, I've been threatened, spit on, all because I'm trying to find out who killed their mother, their brother, their child. I spend every day carrying that emotional baggage on my shoulders, and today was a bad day, I *told* you that. You *know* what thunderstorms do to me, Noah! You know it brings back Patrick—"

"I'm not having this argument again," Noah spat. "I'm not going to sit here and let you guilt trip *me* over *your* career choice and then have you bring him up as an easy out."

"Easy out?" Larkin echoed. "You know what, Noah— I've been on Xanax for the last six months. I've been falling apart right in front of you. When was the last fucking time you asked if I was okay and actually meant it?"

Noah looked as if he'd been slapped—his eyes wide, jaw open. The silence crumbled inward as he asked, "Why the hell are you taking Xanax?"

Larkin snorted and shook his head. His chest was heaving, cheeks hot like a child had turned a magnifying glass into the sun and was trying to burn a hole right through him. Larkin wiped his eyes and said, "If the future of our marriage hinges on you getting a satisfying deep-dicking, go buy yourself a dildo." He grabbed his phone, walked into the bedroom, and slammed the door.

ZzzQuil had been losing its potency over the years.

5:22 a.m. and Larkin was already wide-awake. He was alone in bed. A sanitation truck rumbled on the corner of Eightieth and First as it compacted garbage. The wind—strong enough to sway and rub the limbs of the gingko tree together outside the bedroom window—created a pleasant, if somewhat eerie, lullaby. Larkin's phone buzzed, and the noise was like a missile launch in the stillness.

He rolled onto his side, picked it up from the nightstand, and winced when the screen lit up.

Text message from Ira Doyle.

Another gif. This one Larkin recognized. Marilyn Monroe from *How to Marry a Millionaire*, wearing chic '50s glasses, holding a coffeepot, and looking startled. Text bubbles populated while Doyle typed, and a moment later came the message: *Good morning, sunshine. Swing by 1PP when you're up and at 'em.*

Larkin glanced toward the closed bedroom door. Noah had slept on the couch and it didn't sound as if he were awake yet. Usually he got up just as early as Larkin did, but with this week being spring break for the public school, he'd take the opportunity to sleep late. And Larkin would never admit it aloud and chance either a divorce or a beheading, but he loved Noah's vacations because it meant he could get ready for work by himself. In silence. Larkin was a morning person by necessity, not nature. Noah, on the other hand, was like a Disney princess when he woke up—the forest animals were there to greet him in song, and he was chitchatting until they went separate ways for their respective jobs. Part of that, Larkin was certain, was because Noah spent his day with kids who could hold about a thirty-second meandering conversation about their poodle named Puddles and also, Mr. Rider, do you think grass cries when I step on it?

Noah wanted to have a conversation with an adult. Preferably the one he'd married.

But Larkin was a miserable fuck, *at best*, before a shower and cup of coffee, and grunting his way through morning banter with Snow White was… tedious. And it looked like his new—temporary—partner was one of these "happy before the sun's up" sort too, which was Larkin's luck.

But he carefully slid out of bed and got ready for March 31.

Because habit and routine were infinitely easier to maintain without distraction, Larkin could shower and dress—a gray checkered suit, pale blue button-down, navy tie, pink pocket square, two-toned gold wingtips—and be out the door in exactly thirty minutes. With the sky that hazy grayish blue, a whisper of the incoming sunrise they called nautical twilight, he could reach Penn Station in fifteen minutes, when Krispy Kreme's coffee was piping hot and the donuts were fresh and soft and perfect. The drive along the FDR to 1PP, just Larkin and the thrum of the Audi's tires eating up the miles and the golden sunshine rising over the East River—he felt different from last night.

Better.

And as if he'd won the lottery of mornings, the fifth floor was still quiet at 6:37 and Larkin crossed paths with no one on his walk to Doyle's office. The door was closed, but not shut, and a sliver of light shone through the crack. Larkin could pick up a barely audible but constant drone from within. He knocked lightly and pushed the door open with his free hand.

The left side of the office held a large white drafting table with a closed 11x24 sketch pad on top and a currently unoccupied chair. A squat shelf lined the wall behind the chair, stuffed with what appeared to be reference books, binders of old six-packs, and a laptop and portable scanner, as well as an astounding amount of art supplies and tools.

A corkboard was covered in drawings. Nothing official like wanted posters, but the sort of art small children did in school, the nonsensical scribbles that held a place of honor on the fridge in so many homes. Doyle sat at a worktable on the opposite end of the room, his back to the door. He was hunched over a bust, his big hands molding the red clay into the shape of some facial muscle Larkin didn't know the name of, head bobbing absently in tune to music leaking from his earbuds. His sleeves were rolled back to the elbow, and it appeared he was also wearing an apron—to protect his suit, Larkin assumed.

Larkin got close enough to tap Doyle's shoulder.

Doyle startled and spun on the stool. He tugged the earbuds off by the cord and said, "*Jesus*."

"Larkin."

Doyle laughed under his breath. He tapped his phone's screen, turning the music off. "You didn't text back, did you? I wasn't expecting you so early."

"I don't text."

"Uh-huh."

Larkin felt warmth pool in his cheeks, and he wasn't certain why. "Noah turns on the 'read' feature. So he knows I've seen the message."

"'Read' is a power move."

Larkin shrugged.

Doyle raised one of those thick, expressive brows. He gathered the apron, wiped his hands of red pigment, then collected his phone and swiped through the setting options. "Are you taking those coffees for a walk?"

Larkin held a cardboard takeout tray in his hand. Two coffees and two individual bags secured between the cups. He shimmied one free and held it out as Doyle set his phone aside and looked up again. "Cream and sugar."

Doyle accepted the coffee before hesitating. "Come on. You didn't deduce that by a stain on my shoe or something, did you?"

Larkin glanced down at Doyle's shoes. "I like your wingtips."

"Thank you."

"Sixty-five percent of coffee-drinking Americans prefer to add sweeteners. Cream and two sugars is a fairly safe assumption to make." Larkin set the tray on the corner of the table, picked up one of the bags, and held it out. "I don't, however, know what sort of donuts you like. Some people have very strong opinions about sprinkles or filling or traditional cake."

Doyle accepted the offer and removed a simple glazed donut. "Good choice." He popped the top off his coffee and dunked the donut. After taking a bite, he said, "You look very nice."

"You're flirting," Larkin remarked absently as he busied himself with a cake-batter-filled donut.

Doyle smiled, and when he stood, Larkin was reminded again of exactly how tall and perfectly proportioned he was. Doyle untied his apron, pulled it over his head, and set it aside. "I got dolled up for you. What do you think?"

Larkin studied Doyle's navy three-piece suit in a cut that hugged... *everything*. A white shirt kept it understated and an orange tie—bold but not crazy—added a pop of much-needed color. Doyle had said he looked good in blue. Larkin couldn't find the lie.

"You're frowning."

Larkin set his donut down. He sucked the frosting off his thumb, took a step forward, and undid the bottom button of Doyle's vest. "This should always be left unbuttoned."

"Is that so?"

"There are four predominate theories behind the custom."

"I'll take your word for it."

Larkin met Doyle's gaze and asked, "Why did you get dressed up."

But Doyle didn't answer, merely smiled again and returned to his seat. He sipped the coffee, finished the donut, then pulled forward the bust he'd been working on by its base. "I'm not quite done yet," he explained. "I started last night—"

"I didn't mean to imply that I expected—"

Doyle waved the comment off. "I don't get to work with clay very often. It's a nice way to decompress. The ME left a copy of the autopsy report in the package. You read it, I'm sure."

For a second time, Larkin felt his cheeks heat. "I… didn't, no. I had an appointment last night."

"No problem." And that was all Doyle said before launching into an abridged narrative. "Male, twenty to twenty-five years of age, five ten in height, average in build. I'm using Caucasian tissue markers, by the way. That was an intelligent guess, based on the orbital sockets and nasal cavity. I didn't want to base this reconstruction on the death mask."

"Make the details fit," Larkin murmured.

"Exactly. Anyway, the ME noted that the bones lacked any sort of wear and tear common to manual labor or extreme sports, but he did have numerous fractures in the phalanges of both hands, as well as his left radius. A deviated septum too." Doyle touched his index finger to the half-molded shape of a broken nose he was constructing. The tip of one tissue marker stuck out from among the clay. "An old break, but a pretty bad one. It'd be an obvious facial feature. You can't help but notice that particular detail aligns with the mask."

Larkin pulled out his cell, opened the email app, and

found the autopsy report from last night. He quickly scrolled through the attachment while asking, "Anything on the bones that would indicate cause of death?"

"Cervical fracture."

Larkin looked up. "He died from a broken neck?"

Doyle nodded. "Extreme force from behind with a blunt object. Your pitch has risen twice, by the way."

"Unfortunately that happens when I'm interested."

"I'm honored."

Larkin ignored that comment and studied his phone again. "The nonfatal fractures were only a few years old, so we can likely rule out childhood abuse. They *could* be run-of-the-mill, although…."

"Intimate Partner Violence predominately affects females," Doyle began. "And I can't say how much the CDC has studied this among LGBT people, but I've worked with enough victims of violence to know the visual differences between random and domestic assault. There's been papers written about an abuser's tendency to avoid areas like the spine or neck until late stages, which can and has resulted in death."

"You think John Doe was LGBT."

"Not necessarily. Over ninety percent of men who report being victims of IPV say they've only had female partners. But that does leave a small percentage who have male partners, and in comparison, nearly ninety percent of men who report rape had a male perpetrator. I'm just saying, with male victims, it can be a bit trickier to narrow down assailant likelihood."

Doyle was doing it again: exhibiting that lazy physical posture—he'd fall off the stool if he wasn't careful—while his pyrite eyes sparkled like every stone had been overturned and what was found underneath was a deep pool of intelligence, that sunshine skittering across its surface.

"I'm going to read the ME's report in full before I hypothesize further."

Doyle pointed to the empty seat at the drafting table. "Make yourself at home."

Larkin collected his breakfast and sat on the other side of the office. He sipped coffee and read a sentence or two at a time on his phone, but found himself, more often than not, watching Doyle resume work on the bust. He'd put those earbuds on again, and while he didn't sing along outright, Doyle's deep voice created an almost subaudible hum that seemed to vibrate the very air around them.

It was a bit like reading *Hamlet* through Alice's looking glass.

An upside down and inverted evaluation of the Gravedigger by the Prince of Denmark.

Has this fellow no feeling of his business, that he sings at grave-making?

Except Doyle wasn't digging a grave, was he? He had found Yorick and was bringing him back to life, if only for a moment, so as to kiss those lips a final time.

Larkin swiveled in the chair, putting his back to Doyle so that he might read without interruption. And the report, it turned out, had little to offer that Doyle hadn't already covered in their discussion. John Doe was in his twenties at the time of death, suffered from multiple instances of violence in his past—the ME noted that while he had no soft tissue damage to go off of, the number of breaks would have been enough for a mindful nurse or physician to suspect something was happening at home—and that John Doe had indeed died by extreme blunt-force trauma to the back of his neck.

Blunt-force trauma.

Larkin frowned as he considered. The weapon could have been anything, really. And while that thought wasn't even remotely helpful, the fact that it was an up-close-and-personal assault lent credence to his developing theory that John Doe wasn't a stranger or randomly chosen victim to the killer. It was too personal, especially with the suggestion of domestic abuse on his bones. Of course, the violence inflicted on John Doe could have been accidental—*highly* unlikely—or by an abuser prior to whomever might have killed John—unlikely but not out of the realm of probabilities. People are creatures of habit. Without building a new pattern of behavior, victims were often sucked into the same cycle of suffering over and over.

Now the question Larkin had to ask, as caffeine worked through his system: was John Doe the only one? In any other situation, Larkin wouldn't have been scratching at that question as if he were trying to remove adhesive residue from a poorly placed sticker. It was the death mask that turned this on its head. The unnecessary step. The clue that brought this beyond a probable fatal domestic. And if John Doe *wasn't* the only one, was he the first or the last? His personal, likely intimate, connection to the killer would have either been what pushed him to kill, or who the perpetrator was building up the courage *to kill*.

A text notification popped at the top of the screen.

Noah Rider.

Larkin didn't want to deal with him. Not now. Not this early. Not when he was still seething from the night before— the genuine shock on Noah's face when he learned Larkin was taking Xanax and he had the audacity to question why. Wasn't the why obvious?

Because Larkin was a neurotic mess.

Because he cried every time it rained.

Because his life was hell.

Larkin tapped the bubble and opened his texts, because even still, Noah was his husband and 'til death do us part and maybe he was going to apologize.

I need you to communicate with me.

Larkin snorted and closed the app, leaving the message as read and without a response. Hadn't he done that last night? Communicated? Or did he imagine that fight where Noah got pissy over their lack of intimacy as of late, and Larkin said, in no uncertain terms, he was exhausted—physically, mentally, emotionally—and on medication that had clearly been wreaking havoc on his sex drive? He thought that had been quite clear. And as usual, Noah hadn't listened, was more aghast that Larkin kept the medication to himself than the fact that Larkin had reached a point of needing pharmaceutical aid. And maybe Larkin should have said something six months ago. Probably. But Noah hadn't been listening *then*. That'd been, in part, the reason Larkin had asked Dr. Myers for the prescription.

Larkin tucked his phone away and studied the corkboard of crayon drawings. One picture was clearly a rainbow, although it didn't follow the ROY G. BIV arrangement of colors, and that sort of artistic irresponsibility would only lead to a future exhibiting at the MoMA. Another drawing might have been a dog or a four-legged child with no neck or a unicorn, sans horn. Larkin was still trying to figure it out—

"It's a fairy princess pony."

Larkin turned around. "What is a fairy princess pony."

Doyle stood at the drafting table, wiping his hands on the apron. His eyes cut to the drawing over Larkin's shoulder and he shrugged, smiled a smile that, for once, didn't reach his eyes, and said, "Come take a look at the bust."

Child victim, Larkin thought as he rose, but he said nothing. He looked at his watch—after eight—then followed Doyle back to the worktable.

John Doe had risen from the dead. At least, that's what it felt like to Larkin, staring at the skull reconstruction. The muscles and tendons in his neck looked taut and alive, his cheeks were full and lacking that suggestion of slack seen in the death mask. John Doe had ears too, another feature that'd been missing from the mask, as well as eyebrows that'd been created by scoring the clay with some sort of tool along the brow ridge. Most importantly, Larkin noted, was that Doyle understood how to work genetic statistics into his art and had given John Doe brown eyes. The probability that he was correct was over fifty-five percent and would work in their favor when it came to databases like NamUs.

Doyle opened the door to a closet that was likely intended for coats, hats, umbrellas—you know, normal things. Instead, it was stuffed, floor to ceiling, back to front, with boxes. Thank God it'd all been hidden, because it would have undoubtedly been enough visual clutter to set Larkin off. Doyle grabbed a banker's box by the handles and pushed the door shut with his foot. Setting the box on the worktable, Doyle flipped the lid and sorted through… wigs.

"You're still thinking mid- to late '90s?"

"It's the most logical theory," Larkin said, watching curiously.

Doyle removed a brown wig—nothing particularly high in quality, but Larkin could only imagine the hoops he'd jumped through to get departmental approval on such a purchase to start with. "Two abominations came out of that decade: frosted tips and middle parts." Doyle moved around Larkin and took a moment to wiggle the wig into place on the bust. He combed the synthetic hair with his fingers. "But I don't think John Doe was in a boy band. We'll go with the Leo DiCaprio look."

Larkin grunted.

"Not a Leo fan?"

"I was a gay preteen in the '90s. What do you think."

Doyle's smile lit up the room. "*Titanic.*"

"*Romeo + Juliet.*"

"Somehow, that doesn't surprise me."

"Baz Luhrmann is far more innovative than James Cameron," Larkin replied. "Luhrmann's utilization of exaggerated and evocative visuals—"

"I meant the romantic tragedy."

"*Romeo and Juliet* is strictly a tragedy. The romance is merely the vehicle that drives the hero, and most of the cast, quite frankly, to the required death at the play's conclusion. Besides, they were two idiotic teenagers—children, really— and Romeo mistook a boner for love at first sight."

"Is this the sweet talk that landed you your blond bombshell?"

Larkin pushed his suit coat back and settled his hands on his hips. "I think it was my badge, actually."

"Authority is hot."

Larkin raised his eyes.

Doyle adjusted the wig a moment more, then picked up a rag that looked vaguely like terry cloth and began to press it lightly against the bust's face in various places.

"What're you doing," Larkin asked.

"Skin isn't smooth," Doyle explained. "We have pores, fine hairs—deerskin on clay leaves a more realistic surface. It cuts down on the artificial aspect and adds an element of life." He set the skin down. "Facial hair was pretty low-key in the '90s, short of Kurt Cobain or Bob Vila, so I'm leaving him clean. He was in his early twenties and still had a bit of a baby face." Doyle glanced down at Larkin. "If he did have something, it probably wasn't much. Certainly not enough to make a difference in being recognized."

"You're very good at this." Larkin frowned, rewound, tried again. "That is, utilizing facts and statistics to construct something reasonable out of inherent chaos." He motioned to the bust while adding, "And art. You're a good artist. Very good."

"God, I might be a little in love with you."

"I'd rather you weren't."

"It's too late," Doyle said with the ease and casualness of a man long-practiced at this sort of interplay. He undid the tie of his apron and removed it. "You're incredible at dirty talk—"

"Eye color probabilities isn't bedroom—" Larkin tried to correct.

"And you offer such passionate accolades," Doyle continued without missing a beat.

Larkin blinked. "I was merely stating an obvious—"

But Doyle was shaking his head. "I've been thinking about this for a long time, and I think we're ready to take the next step in our relationship." He picked up a black band from the tabletop that might have belonged to one of the wigs, got down on a knee, and held the hair tie out like a ring. "Will you marry me?"

The door to Doyle's office opened without warning, and Senior Artist Bailey poked his head inside. "Doyle, don't forget you're working with that Cold Case fellow—what're you doing?"

Doyle didn't seem fazed in the least as he said, "Proposing."

Bailey looked at Larkin, rolled his eyes, and said as he saw himself out, "I keep telling Hannah I'm hanging on until the big six-oh—but this place is a zoo." The door shut.

"Congratulations," Larkin said. "You'll likely be promoted due to the stroke your supervisor is going to suffer."

"Is that a yes or no?"

"I'm already married and polygamy is illegal in the United States."

"You would strictly be my work husband."

"Absolutely not."

"I'm really hanging out on a limb here."

"Please get up."

Doyle raised the band higher. "Don't break a guy's heart."

Larkin snatched the hair tie, pondered what to do with it for half a second, then tugged it onto his left wrist. "There. Happy?"

"Thrilled," Doyle answered, getting to his feet. He flashed that all-caps smile one more time before reaching across the table for his notepad and Larkin's molested pen that he'd not returned. "Do you have digital copies of the mask?"

Larkin opened his emails again. Detective Millett with CSU had sent him plenty of crime scene photos yesterday afternoon. He scrolled for a time until he found what they needed, tapped, and enlarged the photo. To be polite, he studied the already memorized details of eternal sleep for a second, then directed his attention to the bust. "John Doe is the face of the death mask."

"Yeah." Only one word, but there was gravity and fire in Doyle's voice.

—a directional shift of the wind, the heat and the smoke kissing his face, a lingering taste of burned marshmallows and Jameson on his lips, with nobody in the entire world to see them but the banished queen overhead—

It wasn't an association.

Not exactly. A similarity. A comparison. Something more.

Something *better*.

CHAPTER EIGHT

"Well?"

It'd been the first thing Doyle had said since setting Larkin up at his work laptop and leaving him to go nuts with NamUs.

Doyle had, in the meantime, done a few more touchups on John Doe's bust—the sort of modifications that a man like Larkin wouldn't notice, but that clearly dug under the skin of an artist. Then Doyle had snapped several photographs of his work to use in the event they found jack in the missing persons reports and had to submit a new case to the unidentified portion of the NamUs dashboard and hope someone else found *them*. He had been cleaning his worktable when he finally spoke.

And Larkin couldn't help but note that the silence until then had had two admirable qualities: it had been natural and welcomed. Doyle didn't force small talk and didn't chatter to fill the space the way so many people often did. He hummed sometimes, but Larkin was certain that wasn't due to nerves, and was nothing but a personal habit. Briefly—*very briefly*—Larkin wondered if Doyle woke early, woke happy, but valued the quiet that accompanied those moments before the sun rose.

Larkin didn't look up from the screen. He'd been methodically combing through the listing of missing persons in the state of New York, but beyond that, was hesitant to filter his search based on assumed details. Because he couldn't be certain, beyond a reasonable doubt, that John Doe had disappeared in the mid-1990s, nor could he be certain the young man had resided in one of the five boroughs. He might have been from Ossining, Poughkeepsie—hell, Albany.

Or he might have even been from out of state. Nearly one million daily commuters came into the city from Jersey and Connecticut, and although Larkin felt this probability was far less likely, he couldn't rule it out. If his search of New York state came up empty-handed, he'd have to get on the phone with NamUs and build a unique profile for John Doe's search across the entirety of their missing persons before he could safely conclude the young man had never been listed.

Larkin hoped that wasn't the case.

Not only because it limited his avenue of detecting, but also because it was too heartbreaking to consider.

"There are just over 1,000 open cases in New York," Larkin said. "Some go back as far as the '60s."

Doyle opened the closet door, probably putting away the banker's box of wigs, then shut it. "That's terrible."

Larkin grunted in acknowledgment.

A moment later, Doyle was dragging his drafting chair up beside Larkin, who was seated on the stool. He sat, got comfortable in a way that seemed like there was too much of him and not enough air between them, and stuck the tip of his thumb between his teeth as he studied the computer screen. It wasn't a self-mutilating gesture. Not even a nervous tick. It appeared to simply be ingrained, repetitive behavior born out of a need to control fidgeting.

Doyle glanced at Larkin, caught him staring, and took his

thumb from his mouth. "What?"

"You were the class troublemaker," Larkin stated. "As a child. Before you directed that energy into drawing."

Doyle's eyebrows—thick and expressive and probably as gorgeous as an eyebrow was capable of being—rose. "Did you run a background check on me after chewing my ass out yesterday? Ms. Steinfeld would be about eighty now, but I'm sure she remembers me from third grade when I flicked a cap eraser so hard, it launched across the classroom and got stuck in her wig."

Larkin fought to control the tug of a smile at the corner of his mouth. "You display restless energy that's coped with by harmless fidgeting, is all. You chew on things."

"I chew on things?" Doyle repeated.

"My pen. Your thumb. I suspect you snack a lot too. But not mints or gum."

"Why not?"

"I haven't smelled spearmint or peppermint on your breath."

Doyle's quizzical expression shifted to something like playful amusement. He'd given a go at shaving that morning, although it wasn't as close as it really should have been, but the stubble on the bold and powerful cut of Doyle's jaw looked… nice. "Maybe I've run out."

"There's a Duane Reade on every corner in this city." Larkin returned his attention to the computer. He was on page sixteen of forty-seven. From the corner of his eye, he saw Doyle raise his thumb, stop, and lower his hand. "I didn't mean to make you self-conscious," he said in his usual modulated tone. "I don't always filter my deduction process."

"Not since I met you."

"It's bothersome."

"No, that's not it."

Larkin looked at Doyle a second time.

"Lemon drops," Doyle said. "I like hard candies because—"

"They last longer."

"Exactly. I special order them, and my delivery hasn't come in yet. You probably know why I do that, don't you?"

Tactfully, Larkin said, "Price-to-flavor ratio of drugstore-brand candy isn't in your favor." But after a handful of seconds, like he truly couldn't help himself: "You're dedicated to a specific brand either not found in New York or not found in stores at all. So perhaps an old-fashioned recipe, which would typically be something ordered from a specialty vendor. Childhood candies aren't necessarily good—they're nostalgic. You buy a very particular lemon drop candy because there's a positive association for you when eating it."

"And maybe I also like lemon candy."

"Also maybe, yes." Larkin swallowed and redirected his attention to the screen. Quieter, he added, "I—I have some minor obsessive-compulsive tendencies. By saying it aloud, I can control the obsessive thoughts a bit more. At least, it makes my brain feel more organized."

Larkin stared at his hands—long, slender fingers poised over the keyboard. His wedding band shone. A cascade, a tidal wave, an avalanche built in his mind, in his chest. Each memory of when Larkin used his desirable detective skills in an undesirable situation. Each time Noah got mad, got embarrassed, got defensive. Each time Larkin bit his tongue around his husband—shutting down, choking out one- or two-word answers to avoid a fight, and then he'd spend the rest of the night trying to calm the thoughts that never turned off and lick emotional wounds that'd be in his long-term memory forever.

"That was inappropriate of me," Larkin said to the computer.

Doyle reached across the keyboard, pinched the hair tie between his thumb and index finger, gave it a tug, and let it snap against Larkin's wrist.

"Ouch." Larkin pulled his hand away.

Doyle was smiling again, but it was smaller, gentler, calmer. He sat close—smelling the same as yesterday: neroli and sandalwood and cardamon. "My grandmother always kept a dish of Clancy's Candy Counter lemon drops in the house." He let that confirmation hang between them for a minute, then made a slight gesture at the computer with a nod of his head.

The maelstrom that'd been building in Larkin began to subside. It wasn't gone, not entirely, but the way Doyle had dropped Larkin's anxiety to a manageable, almost ignorable level by simply letting him spew his nonsense without taking offense was a pleasant variation to how Larkin had been living his life as of late.

Neither spoke again. They studied the screen. Larkin scrolled through five more pages.

And then there he was—John Doe.

Larkin's finger skittered to a halt on the touchpad the same instant Doyle said, "That's him."

"Andrew Gorman," Larkin stated, trying out the name.

Even with his photograph being a small thumbnail in a sea of tragedy, his resemblance to the reconstruction sitting with them at the worktable was… uncanny. Andrew had been a young man running that final stretch into adulthood. His slightly rounded cheeks were what many would consider a baby face, which Doyle had accurately produced, although that could simply be due to his understanding tissue marker mathematics and how individual muscles played over human bone. For Larkin, the surprise was in Andrew's clean-shaven face and *Teen Beat* heartthrob hairstyle.

"You were correct about his hair."

"Good guess."

Larkin looked at Doyle. "That wasn't a guess."

"There's some psychology that goes into reconstructions or aging processes."

"But you didn't have a profile of the victim."

"That'd have certainly made it easier," Doyle said by way of answer. He nudged Larkin's hand away from the touchpad and clicked the link.

Doyle had big hands with big knuckles, and the veins in his arms were pleasantly defined and close to the surface. That attraction came from a subconscious place, Larkin knew. The biological imperative to find the ideal partner—a strong and healthy physique being an incentive for most. Not that Larkin was in the market. But it was nice to window-shop now and then.

"Andrew Gorman, date of last contact was March 28, 1998." Doyle let out a breath. "What day did McClennan say the crabapple went in the ground?"

"April 2, 1998."

"You were right."

"Not entirely. There's a five-day discrepancy."

Doyle leaned back in his seat, staring at Larkin. "And those five days are going to tell the story of Andrew going missing and how his remains came to be found over twenty years later. You don't like compliments, do you?"

"No. And neither do you."

"Oh, I've got an ego," Doyle corrected. "You've just got a curious way of stroking it that I'm still adjusting to."

"Noted."

Doyle raised his hand and made like he was—was going to reach for Larkin's arm. As if to confirm understanding through physical touch. But he stopped midway, caught himself when Larkin raised an eyebrow, and dropped his hand to his thigh. Doyle returned to the screen and said, "Missing age was twenty-two years old. That lines up. Five foot ten, Caucasian—good, good. God, look at his nose. I'd bet he never saw a medical professional for that. Poor kid."

"Scroll down to last known location."

Doyle did, and read, "New York, New York. No exact address… oh, the circumstances of his disappearance: Andrew was last seen by his roommate leaving their apartment at 8:00 p.m. to take the subway—"

"Where."

"Doesn't specify… Andrew took his wallet and has not been seen or heard from since. That's all it says."

Larkin made a sound. "Someone is concerned for Andrew and then supplies as little information as possible to NamUs. Was the case filed by an individual or law enforcement?"

"Boys in blue," Doyle said after another click. "Point of contact is Detective Byron Ulmer."

"Sonofabitch," Larkin said under his breath.

"Not a chance in hell!" Ulmer bellowed as he jumped out of his seat in front of Lieutenant Connor's desk.

"Sit down, Ulmer."

"When Whitmer retired," Ulmer protested, gesticulating with both hands, "the Gorman case became mine. *Mine*, not Grim's."

Larkin sat in the second chair, a forced study in Calm, Cool, and Collected. His legs were crossed and hands folded in his lap as he presented a request for Andrew Gorman's file to become his own. This conversation wasn't new to Larkin. He'd made the appeal plenty of times since being transferred to Cold Cases, and his astounding track record usually got him what he wanted. The problem this time—he wasn't asking for Homicide to give up a case they no longer had the time or energy for. He was asking a detective in his own squad to give up the reins. Not only did the request suggest intellectual superiority, but to say that cops were territorial was the understatement of the century.

Larkin's gaze cut to Ulmer as he said, "You transferred from Missing Persons *with* the Gorman case. You've had it in your stacks for eight—"

"Seven—"

"Eight years," Larkin said, tone clipped. "Your submission to NamUs was two sentences."

Ulmer blustered. "I adopted that fucking case from Whitmer. Two sentences is all he goddamn wrote down."

Larkin said to Connor, "Detective Doyle and myself were the ones to identify Gorman."

"And that information should be added to *my* case file," Ulmer interjected.

Larkin felt the rubber band of his patience snap. He got to his feet, turned on Ulmer, and without any concern to the other man's bigger build and height, he retorted, "In the last twenty-four hours, I've constructed a plausible timeline based only on skeletal remains, got the cast for Doyle to give this forgotten man his identity back, and then found your joke of a report on NamUs by digging through hundreds of missing people. What have you done, besides scratch your balls on the city's dime."

"*You little—*"

"Both of you shut the fuck up," Connor said. "Ulmer, when's the last time you filed a DD5 on Gorman?"

Ulmer's jaw clenched before he ground out, "I'd have to check my records, sir."

After a moment's consideration, Connor said, "Give it to Grim. I don't want to hear one fucking word." And to Larkin, he added, "We've gotten a few calls from the press since yesterday. A body in the park is scandalous shit for these artisanal waters and twelve-dollar gourmet-coffee-drinking motherfucking Midtown office drones looking for some excitement in their lives, and the subway rags want to cash in. Talk to them and I'll have you writing parking tickets for the rest of your career."

"Yes, sir."

"Both of you get out," Connor concluded with a wave of his hand.

Ulmer came short of yanking the door from its hinges on his way out. He stormed off to the left, deeper into the bullpen to where his desk was, presumably to get the Gorman file.

Larkin stepped out of the office and looked toward his desk by the stairs. Doyle leaned his backside against the furniture, his long legs stretched out, big hands resting along the siding, looking comfortable—like he belonged. Larkin didn't like unnecessary ornamentation, which left his workspace as sparce as a military barrack, but this current embellishment was....

Keep that locked up.

Doyle offered a thumbs-up that somehow translated into a question.

Larkin nodded.

And Doyle's face lit up like sunshine on pristine snow. Blinding, but so beautiful, you didn't want to look away until an afterimage was burned into the back of your skull.

"Andrew Gorman."

Larkin turned toward Ulmer's voice in time to catch the accordion folder thrown at him. That extra second to snatch the file and secure it against his chest had allowed Ulmer to penetrate Larkin's personal space and back him against the wall, out of view from Connor's open door. "Get away from me," Larkin said.

"If you ever try that shit again," Ulmer began, his voice an almost animalistic growl but low enough to not be overheard, "running to Connor, whining about how I run my investigations, demanding control of *my* caseload—"

"Get away from me right now," Larkin said again.

"Or what?"

"Or I'll break your nose and you can spend the next month explaining how you walked into a doorframe, no big deal."

Ulmer slammed the meaty side of his fist against the wall beside Larkin's head, hard enough that the reverb was like the *boom* of thunder.

—the squish *of mud underfoot and the devil about to steal the yellow of his summer flowers, the orange of his campfire, the red of his love—*

—disgusting words he knew existed in an unjust world, but still, it shouldn't happen to him, it wouldn't happen to him, it couldn't happen to him, and then the crack *of the baseball bat—*

Boom. Squish. Crack.

Larkin reacted on instinct to protect himself, to protect his face, *his head*, and raised the file with the intention of whacking Ulmer across the face. But then Doyle was there, yanking the accordion file from his grasp. He put a hand on Larkin's chest, pushed in between the two, and used the folder like a shield to force Ulmer back.

"Hey, man," Doyle said to Ulmer, his voice steady, the smoke tangible—a buoy to anchor Larkin in the now. "I think you need to cool off for a few minutes."

"Who the fuck are you?" Ulmer spat.

"Ira Doyle. I'm working the Gorman case with Larkin."

"Oh yeah? Are you just like him? A fucking know-it-all faggot?"

Doyle's fingertips tightened fractionally against Larkin's chest, that touch like five simultaneous shots: little fiery bullets burning his ribcage to ash. But calmly—Doyle was still so frustratingly calm, Larkin distantly acknowledged—he said, "That's enough. And I'm going to ask that you take a few steps back."

"I stand corrected," Ulmer replied, a cruel laugh chasing his words. "A condescending faggot is what you are."

"Ulmer?" Porter was walking out of the breakroom with thin-as-a-rail-no-matter-how-many-donuts-she-ate-Miyamoto. He studied Ulmer, Doyle, and Larkin, still pinned to the wall. "Everything okay?"

"Everything's fine," Doyle answered. He looked at Ulmer a final time. "Right?"

Ulmer raised his hand, pointing at Larkin, but he didn't—couldn't—get any words out before he moved through the bullpen like a gale and down the stairs, the front door of the precinct crashing in his wake.

Doyle removed his hand from Larkin's chest, turned, and asked quietly, "Are you—?"

He didn't finish.

Larkin knew why. Could see himself through Doyle's eyes. Pale face red and blotchy, ash-blond hair shaken free from its conservative side part, the panic in his washed-out gray eyes. Larkin gulped air like a landed fish, but none of it seemed to reach his lungs.

That had been just like—*almost like*—August 2, 2002.

"Come with me." That request from Doyle penetrated the panic and stuck a pin in Larkin's mental Rolodex, preventing it from spinning out of control. He gently took Larkin by the sleeve of his suit coat and gave a little tug. And when Larkin willingly moved with the momentum, Doyle plopped the accordion folder on his desk and guided him down the steps to the ground floor and into the men's restroom.

Larkin pulled free from Doyle's hold, moved to one of the two sinks, turned the faucet, and splashed his face with cold water. Again. And again. Until he inhaled and choked and coughed. Larkin turned off the faucet, gripped either side of the porcelain, and watched droplets fall from the tip of his nose.

Plunk.

"So Ulmer is a first-class asshole," Doyle said, voice echoing off the tile walls.

Plunk. Plunk. Plunk.

"It's rhetorical, but are you all right?"

Larkin moved to the paper towel dispenser, grabbed a wad, and pressed the recycled paper to his face. He leaned back against the far wall, lowered his hands, and wadded the papers into a ball. "People don't want to know," he whispered, not looking up.

"Know what?"

"What makes them uncomfortable," Larkin specified. "Sometimes they don't know what to say, don't want to make a bad situation worse. Other times, they only pretend to not know because the empathy required is too big a burden. They pull back. They become distant. They ask how you are the same way they ask if it looks like rain or if you watched that Mets game on TV. People don't really want to know."

The bathroom door opened.

Larkin raised his head.

Doyle turned. "Sorry, but can you use the other bathroom?"

A man in a suit, sweating despite the cool day, jutted a thumb to his right, saying, "It's the ladies' room."

"A toilet is a toilet," Doyle corrected. "Just knock first."

Suit rolled his eyes as he left.

Doyle went to the door, threw the deadbolt, then walked

across the bathroom. He leaned against the wall beside Larkin—close enough that their shoulders were a breath apart. "People don't want to know." He was quiet, so absolute in his agreeance. Doyle cast Larkin a sideways glance. "But I do."

Larkin put a hand over his mouth as one very big and very heartbroken sob tore through him, wracking his entire body like a leaf battling a hurricane. Huge hot tears spilled down his cheeks and he considered: Had anyone ever said that to him?

Not his parents.

Not Dr. Myers.

Not Noah.

None of them.

They wanted Larkin to keep quiet because *It's been a year of this, Everett, you're upsetting your father and he needs to focus on making partner.*

They wanted Larkin to talk about the resulting change in his memory because *Everett, research like this might one day help us discover a cure for Alzheimer's.*

They wanted Larkin to stop being sad because *When you talk about him, Everett, I feel like you don't want me.*

Larkin was not okay. And people didn't want to know.

"I'm a world-class hugger, if you—" Doyle didn't have a chance to finish before Larkin turned into him and grabbed the other detective in a back-breaking embrace. Doyle let out a *whoosh* of air, choked out, "—want one," and then wrapped his arms around Larkin.

Doyle smelled nice. He was warm. He was strong, all lean muscle under the cut of his suit. Best of all, he really did give an exceptional hug.

Larkin couldn't remember when he'd allowed himself to be touched like this. Noah, of course, but when was the last time it'd felt like acceptance and not a means to an end? It wasn't a hug that conveyed apology or jealousy or lust. Doyle's hug was simply a hug, and Larkin was so fucking traumatized that—that sometimes—even his aversion to touch couldn't overpower that single-most desire all humans craved.

To be loved.

After a moment, Larkin peeled his arms free from around Doyle's neck and took a step back. He wiped his face dry with the paper towels still clutched in one hand, cleared his throat, and said, "I have a memory condition. HSAM." He looked at Doyle. "Highly Superior Autobiographical Memory."

"I've never heard of it."

"Most haven't. It's rare. Fewer than one hundred cases worldwide. I know what you're thinking: a cop with memory problems. I should be on disability, not employed with the city."

Doyle gave a small microshake of his head. "I wasn't thinking that."

Larkin wiped his nose on the paper wad, then threw it away. "Having HSAM as a detective is beneficial. Every interview, every location, every case file—I never forget any of it." Larkin felt restless, his hands so awkward at his sides. He put them on his hips. "The problem is that I really have very little by way of short-term memory. Everything that your brain promptly forgets once it's no longer a necessity—what you wore, what you ate, the weather, a phone number, a name— that all goes in the long-term for me. And it's overwhelming. So I do what I can to manage sensory input, and I employ habitual routines so that I don't misplace my keys or wallet or overlook some mundane errand or appointment.

"But sometimes my brain will pluck out a memory, unprompted by me wanting to consciously remember it. It's an association. Sounds, typically, are what do it for me, but dates too. And some of those memories… aren't good. They're just as vivid as they were five or ten or fifteen years ago. And so are the emotions of that moment." Larkin shook his head. "It sounds unbelievable, I know."

"You were born with HSAM?"

"No." Then Larkin said something only his parents, Dr. Myers, and Noah knew. "On August 2, 2002, I was struck in the head with a baseball bat."

CHAPTER NINE

It was 10:27 a.m. when Doyle segued from the walk to Larkin's Audi to stand in line at a coffee cart on the corner of Sixty-Seventh and Lexington. A woman with purple hair and stilettos was currently cleaning the guy out of his everything-bagel inventory. Larkin slowed to a stop, his eyes on the paperwork of the Gorman file that Doyle had graciously gone upstairs to collect while Larkin made himself presentable before rejoining society.

"What do you want?" Doyle asked, tugging his wallet free.

"Already ate. Detective Whitmer cut every perceived corner available when he took the initial report regarding Andrew's disappearance."

"You ate one donut four hours ago," Doyle corrected. "Unless you snacked in your car beforehand."

"I don't eat in the car."

"Okay, well, one jam-filled donut—"

"It was cake batter."

"God. Even healthier. What do you want?"

"Listen to this," Larkin answered, still studying the file.

"Andrew was reported missing by his roommate on March 30, 1998—that's three days before the tree went in the ground. The roommate, Jessica Lopez, said when Andrew didn't come home the next day before work, she wasn't too concerned. Said Andrew had gone to a friend's the night before and sometimes went directly to work from there. But on the thirtieth, she and Andrew were supposed to go to the movies together. He never showed. She called the friend in question, who said Andrew hadn't been there on the twenty-eighth."

"What movie?" Doyle asked.

Larkin smiled but didn't look up. It was a smart and simple detail to confirm, one that could catch a liar in a snare. "Whitmer didn't ask."

Doyle muttered something under his breath before moving to the cart window as the purple-haired woman walked away with her prized bag of bagels. "Got any egg-and-cheese left? Great, two, on bagels, please."

"I said I already ate."

"Are you a vegetarian?" Doyle asked.

"No."

"Allergic to anything?"

"Strawberries."

Doyle said, "You need to feed that big, beautiful brain some protein."

Larkin finally glanced up from the file. "He's going to put American cheese on it."

"Yup, probably."

"The amount of sodium in a single slice of that plastic-y, cheese byproduct—"

"And you ate cake batter for breakfast."

Larkin pursed his lips before saying, "Nothing with a shelf life of half a year is healthy."

Doyle paid for the late breakfast, accepted the foil-wrapped sandwiches, and joined Larkin. He held one out with a placating smile. "Out-in-the-field, rule two: if being hangry can be avoided—avoid it."

Larkin snapped the folder shut, tucked it under one arm, and took the offering. The foil was warm, and as he unwrapped the food, had to admit that it was difficult to be annoyed by Doyle's insistence when the aroma of melted cheese, hot egg, and the unique majesty that was a New York bagel hit him hard and fast. Larkin's stomach growled. He took a bite, and while standing on the street corner beside Doyle, who had left the conversation of HSAM behind in the bathroom, who hadn't pushed for an inch more of information, who had allowed Larkin to collect himself and pretend he was okay even though he wasn't, so he could focus on the job, well… Larkin didn't really care all that much about the cheese's shelf life anymore.

"What's typically your first move on a case like this?" Doyle asked between bites.

"Visit the crime scene, dump site, or last known location of the victim."

"Despite twenty years having passed?"

"Twenty-two. Yes." Larkin looked up and added a bit more gently, "I understand it seems a waste of time, but seeing a location, or as much of a location that still exists, bridges the gap between the past and present. It's humbling, in a sense, to be reminded of people who lived and died before us."

Doyle didn't argue. "The apartment he and the roommate shared, then?"

Larkin took another bite of his sandwich, nodded, and said after swallowing, "Edith Stanislaus was raped and strangled in the bedroom she and her younger sister rented on Twenty-Third Street. This was 1945. Police took plenty of evidence from the home—the most important being her stockings, which were used to choke her. They had interviewed four men they considered persons of interest. Despite this, they couldn't poke a big enough hole in any of the men's alibis, and of course, there was no DNA testing to be done at the time. The case went cold. I took it over when I was transferred into the squad. Of the three boxes of hard evidence stored with the Property Clerk, I was only able to recover one—not the stockings, but the bedsheet was second-best. Of course, I still had no one to test it against and no one was still alive from then except Edith's sister, Leona, who was nearly ninety.

"So I returned to the scene, as Leona still lived there—seventy years later and she still lived in that little studio. There had been a few cosmetic updates, but for the most part, it was a tomb to her sister. The same bed frame, Edith's suitcase and a few hat boxes were stored underneath, her moth-eaten clothes still hung in the closet. Leona had bought a couch. She slept on that. Didn't want to disturb what was once Edith's. I was standing inside a time capsule. So I did a search. I didn't know what for, but maybe—*maybe*—the detectives before me, now dead and gone, missed something."

Doyle's crow's feet were back as he cast a thoughtful expression. "Something was under the bed."

"Yes. How did you know?"

"You said her suitcase and boxes were still there. Makes me think no one had any reason to look. Or *clean*."

"I found a gold tooth among a dust bunny the size of a dog. Leona cried. Their stepbrother, Matthew, had a gold tooth he'd lost the same time Edith was killed. He'd told Leona he'd gotten into a fistfight at a bar. She never had reason to doubt his story. I won't bore you with the details, but Matthew was already dead, so I had him exhumed. A forensic odontologist confirmed it was his lateral incisor. The samples from the bedsheets were enough, barely, due to degradation, to run a test. Matthew had raped and murdered his stepsister and hadn't been a person of interest because the police never even considered a family member could have been responsible for brutalizing her in that manner."

"Leona had closure?"

"Yes. She passed one week after Matthew had been charged, posthumously. The point of this story," Larkin said in conclusion, "is that sometimes I get very lucky. Not usually. But sometimes there's a memento mori beyond a case number, and I'm not the only one mourning."

Andrew Gorman had shared an apartment with Jessica Lopez in Alphabet City—East Sixth, between Avenues C and D. It was a neighborhood that'd lived through a lot of drugs, a lot of murder, a lot of crime. The façades of walk-ups lining either side of East Sixth looked tired in a way that only brick and mortar could: awnings of ground-floor businesses were discolored from the sun; exterior stonework around apartment windows dirty from maybe mold, maybe soot, or maybe just a long and hard life; oxidized fire escapes; and one front door had recently been tagged with the declaration that *John smokes cock.*

Despite the wear and tear of the past, Alphabet City was alive and thriving. An elementary school on the block was clean and bright, the trees old but greenery well underway with the return of spring. A young couple was unloading a moving van double-parked with its hazards on, and folks of all ages walked up and down the sidewalks, going about their Tuesday morning.

Larkin parked in front of a church, denomination unknown, and turned off the engine. He watched a six-story walk-up on the north side of the street, and when a man in jeans and a sweatshirt stepped out of the front entrance, Larkin opened the driver side door and climbed out. He heard Doyle follow, and by the time Larkin had reached the other side of the street, Doyle was at his side, the strap of his black portfolio bag slung across his chest.

"Excuse me," Larkin called to the man, now busily tugging full trash bags from the building's bins and knotting them closed. Larkin removed his badge and flashed it. "My name is Everett Larkin, and I'm a detective with the Cold Case Squad. Do you have a moment to speak."

The man had a face and hands that'd been weathered and worked hard. He was big, but not gym big or overweight big—there was just a lot of him. He moved like he was middle-aged, despite looking older, and smelled like sweat and pot. The man glanced up from the trash and flashed a pair of dark, dead eyes. "Yeah?" He drew the word out oddly before offering a crooked smile.

"Do you live here." Larkin jutted a thumb at the door.

"I'm the super," he said by way of an answer.

"For how long."

Super hummed, staring straight at Larkin. He hadn't blinked. "A long time," he finally said.

Larkin tucked his badge away. "How well do you know your tenants."

Super finally, methodically, lowered his gaze to the bag before him. He finished knotting it, dragged it to the curb, then returned, saying, "I fix all sorts of things for them."

Doyle asked, "Have any of the tenants lived here since the mid-1990s?"

"Ms. Lopez."

"Is that Jessica Lopez," Larkin asked, for clarification.

"That's right," Super drew out again in that strange, almost singsong sort of speech.

"Which apartment is she."

Super directed his dead stare back at Larkin. "It's about the body in the park?"

"Why would you ask that," Larkin asked.

Super slowly reached into the pocket of his ratty jeans. He retrieved a newspaper clipping folded over about half a dozen times, spent several excruciatingly long seconds opening the article, then held it up for the two detectives. He read the memorized title aloud: "Cold Case Squad investigates found body in Midtown. Fear City is back!"

Larkin said nothing as Super methodically folded the clipping back up. He was well aware that both sides of the law had a tendency for attracting a cast of characters that touched on the entire gamut of humanity, but crime groupies made his skin crawl. There was no other way to put it. He felt gross.

Doyle came to the rescue. "Is Ms. Lopez home?"

"She's always home." Super tottered toward the walk-up, ushering them to follow. He unlocked the front door, then the vestibule door, and led the way up the first set of stairs. Super stopped outside of 2C and knocked like he meant "Shave and a Haircut" but missed a beat. "Ms. Lopez?" he drew out. "It's Ricky."

A dog—*a small dog*—started yipping and yapping as movement drew closer to the door. A chain lock was undone with a *shiiick*, a deadbolt twisted, the knob lock clicked. Jessica Lopez was middle-aged, dyed-blonde hair pulled up into one of those "I woke up like this" style buns, showing where her roots needed touch-ups. And maybe she *had* just woken up, because she wore pink zebra-striped pajama pants, a tank top, and an oversized, unbuttoned flannel shirt.

She looked at Ricky. She looked at Larkin and Doyle standing behind the super. Her eyes were sharp—someone born and raised in New York, someone who'd seen enough shit for a few lifetimes. "Ricky, why've you brought cops to my door?"

Larkin raised his identification and spoke before Ricky

had the chance to creep him out a second time. "Ms. Lopez, I'm Everett Larkin. I'm a detective with the Cold Case Squad. This is my partner, Ira Doyle."

That sharp edge in her eyes softened suddenly, like a knife dulled from years of use and abandoned to the back of a kitchen drawer. She said to Ricky, "Thanks. You can go—it's fine."

Ricky turned without a word, squeezed between the two detectives, his belly rubbing Larkin's front in a way that felt entirely indecent, and started down the stairs. He stopped once, looked back at the second-floor landing, then disappeared from view.

"Sorry," Jessica said over the barking of her dog trying to sneak out of the apartment. "Ricky's kind of off, but he's harmless. What's this about?" Something in her tone suggested to Larkin that she already knew.

He said, "I understand it's been a long time, and this might not be a subject you wish to revisit, but we'd like to speak with you about Andrew Gorman."

Jessica licked her lips. Whether or not she actually smoked—Larkin didn't believe she did—she looked like she needed a cigarette right then. "Yes. God. Finally. Come in." She opened the door wide, scooped up a black-and-white papillon, and ushered them inside.

Around a sharp corner, the single-file hall opened onto a surprisingly spacious kitchen, big enough for a table to fit three—four if it was pulled away from the wall. The counter, which looked like Jessica's dump-and-forget spot for junk mail, grocery store receipts, empty Starbucks cups, and a myriad of other typical household items that made Larkin's skin crawl was also a full six inches wider than his own kitchen counter, and underneath his sensory tick was a touch of jealousy. An open door to the right had sunlight spilling in through two big windows. Inside was an unmade bed, a television mounted to the wall, a diminutive couch, and messy stacks of books and tchotchkes on an unappealing shelf that listed to one side. The bedroom doubled as the living room, it seemed. The open door beside the kitchen table looked into an equally messy, albeit impressive, home office setup.

Jessica shut the front door, twisted the knob lock, turned the deadbolt, slid the chain lock.

The patter of tiny doggy feet echoed on the tile floor, and then the papillon came skidding around the corner, barking and spinning in circles.

"PomPom doesn't bite," Jessica called before her slippered feet shuffled after the dog and she entered the now-crowded kitchen. "You can pet him."

Doyle crouched and did just that, becoming PomPom's best friend in about three and a half seconds.

Jessica fussed with her hair, but it was still a mess when she finished. "Sorry, I'm not really dressed for company."

"That's all right, Ms. Lopez," Larkin answered.

"Jessica is fine," she corrected. "I work from home. I only wear a bra when I need to go to the store." She pointed to the table. "Larkin, was it? Sit down. Either of you hungry?"

"No, ma'am," Larkin said, taking a seat.

"Thirsty?"

"No," he repeated.

"*I'm* thirsty," she stated. "What time is it?"

Larkin pulled back his right sleeve to check his watch. "11:12."

"Close enough." She opened a cupboard and removed a bottle of whiskey. She poured two fingers into a water glass printed with flowers, paused, then added a third. Jessica screwed the cap back on and took the seat across from Larkin. "I haven't heard Andy's name in a long time." She took a sip and said, her voice a bit huskier with the burn of alcohol, "But

I've never stopped thinking about him. For the first year or two, I figured he just… *left*, you know? People who aren't city natives do that. Up and leave because they can't hack it here anymore. You two from around here?"

Doyle stood from his crouch and leaned comfortably against the counter. PomPom was still dancing in circles around his feet. "Born and raised in Hell's Kitchen."

"One of those Irish families still clinging to life, huh?"

"By our fingernails," he confirmed.

Jessica tried to smile, but it didn't reach her eyes. "I was born a few blocks from here. My *abuela* raised me."

"Mine too," Doyle said.

She perked up a little and looked at him a second time. "Yeah? I always thought most grandmas share certain traits. Did she always have that one framed picture of Jesus?"

"As any good Irish Catholic granny would."

Jessica tittered. "A bowl of hard candies?"

Doyle glanced at Larkin before he smiled. "Always."

Jessica's stiff posture relaxed. Just like that. It hadn't been the sip of alcohol, although Doyle's voice could have made anyone feel a little punch-drunk. "Andy was a sweet guy. My best friend. We met third year of college. Andy was… erm… you know."

"Andrew was gay," Larkin clarified.

Jessica dropped her gaze a bit and nodded. "So when he asked if I wanted to be his roommate, I said sure. I felt safe around Andy. God, I know, that sounds so terrible to suggest—that women can't trust men unless they're friends with Dorothy—but I think my *abuela* instilled a lot of her own fears in me."

"Certainly not unfounded fears during the '80s and '90s," Larkin said. "Reports of sexual assaults against women were four times higher than they are currently."

Jessica shuddered a little. When she looked at Larkin again, her brown eyes were glassy with unshed tears. "He's dead, isn't he?"

"I'm very sorry," Larkin answered, his modulated tone shifting *a little* to something warmer, gentler. "Andrew's remains were found yesterday."

She took a soggy breath and wiped her nose on the flannel shirt sleeve. "He's been dead the whole time, hasn't he? I mean, since I filed that stupid missing person report."

"We believe so."

"He was murdered?"

Larkin settled back in the seat. He left his hands flat on the tabletop. "Yes."

Jessica wiped her face again.

Doyle tore a sheet from a paper towel roll on the messy counter, then took a step forward and handed it to her.

"I knew it," she said, scrubbing her cheeks with the rough towel. "Deep down, I mean. Because your best friend wouldn't up and leave. Not without a note, a phone call, hell, even some cash for next month's rent, because believe you me, I was scrambling without him here." Jessica took another, longer, sip of whiskey. "I guess it hurts less to ignore what you know is the truth."

Larkin's palms were sweaty against the worn wood. He resisted curling his fingers into fists. "That is true," he agreed.

But Jessica didn't appear to have heard him, because she asked with a spike of frustration, "What was I supposed to do? That cop, the one who took my report, he didn't care. Kept saying Andy was a grown man capable of making his own decisions and he didn't have to get his beard's approval to do nothing. He said that. Called me Andy's beard. What an asshole." Jessica tore the paper towel into several smaller pieces. "Andy was proud of who he was. I worried, of course. Even twenty years ago, it was dangerous for him, but we weren't like that. That cop was homophobic. I called for months, asking for updates. Nothing. Then I started calling yearly." Her anger subsided, her voice hitched, and those big fat tears started rolling down her face. "Just so the cops knew I hadn't forgotten Andy. Everyone else did, but not me. *Not me.*"

These were the worst cold cases.

Andrew Gorman had been gone twenty-two years, and Jessica Lopez had been living with a hole in her heart the entire time. And even now, she wouldn't be any better off. The best she could hope for was that the truth could be used like gauze, to pack the wound, so she'd stop bleeding out.

Offering a personal connection was time and again Larkin's least favorite tool in the detective arsenal, because he felt so raw, so vulnerable afterward, but sometimes he didn't have a choice. Not in moments like this—when someone like Jessica, the closest he'd ever get to Andrew himself, deserved to know her pain was being acknowledged. He peeled one hand from the tabletop, rubbed it against his pant leg, then reached across the table to take Jessica's. She gripped his tight, her knuckles blanching.

"I won't forget Andrew," he said simply.

PomPom's whine broke the quiet. He scurried into Jessica's bedroom and returned with a squeaky ball, which he dropped at her feet. He left to fetch another toy, this time a stuffed bunny.

She cried for a bit longer. Doyle fetched her another paper towel. When she'd… not calmed so much as ran out of stamina, she asked, "What do you need from me?"

Larkin gently pried his hand free. "How long were you roommates."

Doyle removed his notepad from his suit coat pocket and uncapped Larkin's pen.

"I think a year? No, it'd been just over a year. I remember, because we signed the lease before spring semester of senior year, and had already renewed it before—what happened."

"In your initial report, you said you had cause for concern when Andrew failed to show for a movie."

"That's right."

"Why."

"We were gonna see *Grease*," she said simply. Jessica glanced at Doyle. "You can google that. *Grease* was being re-released in theatres, and Andy loved musicals. Is that a stereotype?"

"Not if it's factual to his person," Larkin replied brusquely.

"Oh. Well, Andy had been waiting all month. He was so excited. He wouldn't have missed that night if he were on fire."

"You said that on March 28, he had left in the evening to visit a friend."

"That's right."

"I need the friend's name."

"He wasn't a friend," Jessica corrected. "If you get my meaning."

"Andrew had a boyfriend?" Doyle asked.

"I don't know. I don't know if they were *that* serious yet. That's why I said friend. But, God—that was over twenty years ago. I honestly don't remember his name."

"Did you meet him?" The level of curiosity in Doyle's tone was notable.

Jessica nodded. "Once or twice, for, like, a hot minute."

Doyle flipped the little pad shut, met Larkin's studious gaze, then asked, "If I were to sit down with you and do a composite sketch, would you be able to describe him? I know it's been a long time, and if you say no, that's okay. But close your eyes for a moment, think about him, and tell me if you could describe Andrew's friend."

The doubt on her face was overt, but Jessica dutifully closed her eyes and was quiet for five seconds… ten…. Larkin counted thirty-seven long seconds before she blinked and said, "I think so."

Larkin had switched places with Doyle, standing at the counter while Doyle took a seat. He removed his suit coat, apologized to Jessica when she cringed at the sight of his shoulder holster, made a wholly believable comment that he liked it about as much as her, and then flipped open the portfolio bag he'd dragged along. Doyle set a sketch pad on the table and sharpened a few pencils by hand as he began conducting one of the most casual, friendly, and impressive interviews Larkin had seen by another officer since making detective.

"So where'd Andrew meet this other man? Did he ever talk to you about that?"

"We both went to FIT." Jessica laughed at that and plucked her pajama pants with one hand. "Obviously not the career path I stuck with. I do coding for websites now. Andy was the better designer anyway. After graduating, he'd gone to… geez… some show or gala or whatever, I don't even remember, and they met there. I recall Andy saying this guy had gone to FIT the same time we did, and I'd found it funny that we'd never crossed paths."

"Oh yeah? Did they have the same degree and everything?"

"No, I don't think so. Andy and I were in fashion design. This other guy designed accessories… pretty sure."

"What makes you so sure?" Doyle asked, flipping back the cover on the pad.

"It must have been a conversation we had." Jessica reached for the glass of whiskey and tipped it back and forth thoughtfully. "Jewelry, maybe."

Larkin's gaze shifted to Jessica. He interjected from across the room, "Designing or constructing jewelry?"

"You'd have to learn both," she explained.

Doyle looked at Larkin, seemingly waiting for more. When Larkin gave a headshake, Doyle assumed the lead once again. "I want you to think of the time you were around Andrew's friend the longest."

She began to nod, then said, "But he's not going to look the same today—"

"That's okay," Doyle insisted.

Jessica leaned back in her chair, reached a hand down, and absently patted PomPom, who was curled up with his small mountain of gifted toys. Larkin could see when the memory returned to her: it was like the pop of an incandescent lightbulb on Jessica's face. "Oh, wow. Okay. Andy and I were walking home from a bar in the Village. It was cold as hell, so I guess they'd met in winter, yeah? Andy called the guy from a pay phone to meet us. We must have waited for him around the Q? Maybe the 6. One of those trains. I know he had to come downtown. He walked a few blocks with us, then, I don't know, either Andy wanted to get more drinks in the East Village or his friend did—I can't remember—but I do know I told them to have fun and I'd walk home. Andy asked if I wanted company. It was dark. I was twenty-one. I was a little tipsy. I said no. Of course, about two or three blocks from home, some guy started following me. I totally freaked and made a beeline for my *abuela*'s. She was on that block. I stayed the night with her."

That's when Doyle went to work. A composite sketch has three stages, he'd told Jessica. The first focused on general proportions. Jessica said the man had been a fit white guy in his early twenties. *But who looked older*. She was very insistent on that point. The three were of the same graduating class, but this man Andy was smitten with could have been in his mid- or late twenties if she hadn't known better. Doyle fetched a few six-packs from within the portfolio bag, sifted through the pages, then placed several of the reference photos in front of Jessica. Faces of strangers, but all of white men. The point was not to find someone who looked like their unknown love interest of the past, but to pick and choose elements that were similar to him. Eyes, nose, ears, etc.

After Jessica had chosen a few references, Doyle had her drag her chair around to him and he put pencil to paper. He sketched the outline of a very generic and entirely forgettable face. Then he started asking questions. Nothing leading, but very general, so as to force Jessica to focus on her own memory. How were the eyes? Should they be closer, farther, or stay as is? Should the hairline be higher or lower? What do you think of the length of the nose?

Characteristics was the next stage. Doyle spent several quiet moments adding more in-depth linework and shaping the hair. He asked Jessica more questions: How is the shape of the head and hairstyle? Do the eyes and nose appear similar? Is this sketch within the realm of possibility? This stage ended up taking much longer—fifty-seven minutes, by Larkin's count. Jessica was uncertain at times, referring time and again to the photos she'd chosen, hemming and hawing over the eyes in particular, growing frustrated when fragmented memories failed her.

"I know this isn't easy," Doyle said, "but you really are doing a great job."

"I bet you say that to everyone."

"Most everyone needs to hear it," Doyle answered.

After they'd settled on the characteristics, Doyle explained that the final stage was rendering. This was where he'd add contrast, tone, lighting, and shadows. Conversation lulled. Doyle's pencil scratched the surface of the expensive-looking paper. PomPom snored. Jessica got up to pour herself more whiskey.

"He's very good," she murmured against the rim of the glass, her eyes cutting to Doyle.

Larkin glanced across the kitchen and studied the composite sketch. It'd gone from a pile of nonsensical lines to a living portrait in just under two hours. Larkin had seen police sketches that were akin to political cartoon caricatures, anatomical abnormalities such as a missing jawline, or drawings done by someone who simply could *not draw*. But Doyle? Doyle was the real deal, and if the skull reconstruction hadn't been enough proof, this sketch solidified his skill and merit.

"Yes, he is," Larkin answered. Jessica was smiling at him when he returned his attention to her. "May I ask you another question about Andrew."

"Okay."

"Tell me how he broke his nose."

She lowered the glass sharply, amber liquid sloshing. "How would you know that?"

"Autopsy reports and facial reconstruction."

"They might be wrong."

Larkin frowned at her suggestion. He retrieved his phone, pulled up the profile from NamUs, and showed Jessica. "You supplied this photo."

Jessica's shoulders drooped and she nodded meekly. "Yeah…. God, his nose looks so fucked-up in that picture."

"How'd it happen."

"Honestly, I'm not sure. We'd been roommates for a few months and it was right before graduation. Andy had seen a few guys senior year, so I guess I assumed one of them got rough with him. But when I'd asked the first time he came home all bloody, he'd only say, 'Jessie, baby, don't worry about it.'" She looked down, tilted the glass, and watched the whiskey catch the overhead light on its surface. "I guess I should have worried."

"You're certain this happened before meeting his jewelry-designer friend."

"Oh yeah," Jessica answered confidently. "Like I said, it was shortly after we moved in together. Andy didn't meet What's-His-Name for another half a year? I guess it was more like a month or so before he disappeared that they met…."

"Was Andrew involved in anything illegal."

"Like what, drugs?"

"That's a start."

"God, no. He drank, but he waited until his twenty-first birthday. I don't think he'd ever even smoked a cigarette. Andy was a good boy."

Larkin considered, then tried, "Did he know anyone who worked for Parks and Recreation."

Jessica's brow furrowed in sincere confusion. She slowly shook her head. "No. At least, I don't think so."

"Which room was Andy's." Larkin motioned over Jessica's shoulder.

"The office."

"Did you keep any of his belongings."

Jessica stared at the open doorway, as if looking for an answer somewhere in the dimness beyond. "Some photographs. I think I still have his copy of *The Idiot*. I tried to give some of his belongings back to his parents when I realized he… he probably wasn't going to come home, but they didn't want any of it. The rest—clothes and furniture—I donated."

"His parents—"

Jessica was shaking her head. "I'd have no idea how to get in contact with them today. You might have some luck, being a cop, but they didn't want anything to do with Andy, you understand?"

"I do. May I see the photos you've kept."

"Sure." Jessica set her glass on the counter and went to the bedroom.

Doyle didn't look up from his sketch as he asked, his voice low, "What're you fishing for?"

"I don't know." Larkin approached the table.

Doyle set his pencil down, raised his arms back as if he were sitting at a pec deck machine, and stretched them backward until something in his shoulder or maybe collarbone audibly popped.

Larkin glanced down.

Doyle said, "A kitchen table isn't the best place to sit and draw for two hours." He rubbed his right shoulder while inclining his head at the sketch pad. "What do you think?"

"I think it's a very well-done composite sketch of a man who can't be identified and will now need to be aged twenty-two years so that I can beg my lieutenant to have it uploaded to Local4Locals, asking that he phone the police to assist in the cold case of a man he knew briefly back in the 1990s."

"May I watch you beg?"

"No, you may not."

Doyle chuckled under his breath.

Larkin watched Doyle rub his shoulder a moment longer before saying, "Tilt your head down."

"What?"

"Chin to chest."

"Is this one of those trust exercises?" Doyle asked, doing as instructed.

Larkin put his thumb and two fingers on either side of Doyle's exposed neck and dug into the muscle while dragging in a downward motion. "Your shoulder might hurt, but the tension begins in the neck."

"*Sweet Jesus*," Doyle hissed.

"I assure you, it's Larkin."

"I take back that crack I made about your sense of humor."

Larkin smiled a little. He repeated the motion, saying quietly, so Jessica didn't overhear, "Something's off about the violence perpetrated against Andrew."

"How so?"

"Statistically, victims of domestic assault don't receive help combating the abuse for up to two years. Jessica said he'd been seeing a few different men. None of that sounds particularly serious or long-term."

"I think we both assumed this fellow," Doyle began, pointing at his sketch and then grunting when Larkin seemed to have found the knot causing discomfort, "would have been the one to inflict the mortal blow."

"Yes."

"He still could have. Victims also have a tendency of becoming entrapped time and again without proper education on how to protect themselves against predators."

"This is true." Larkin dropped his hand and took a step back.

Doyle looked up and said, "Thanks for that."

Larkin shrugged off the comment. "He studied jewelry design at FIT."

"Yeah. Why did that stick out to you?"

"He'd have learned metal casting and welding—necessary skills for creating Andrew's death mask."

CHAPTER TEN

It was 1:27 p.m. when Larkin and Doyle exited the walk-up.

Upon seeing the fully rendered sketch, Jessica was surprisingly confident in the entire face, not only the elements she'd selected. She had touched the corners of the pad, like caressing a memory, and said, *That's him.*

Jessica promised to clean her apartment, top to bottom, and if she found anything squirreled away that might help put a name to his face, she'd call Larkin on the card he provided. And before the interview's conclusion, she offered a few photos. Her and Andrew Gorman in sunglasses and ballcaps, standing outside of Nathan's, each holding a hot dog. Another of just Andrew standing in line outside of what Larkin suspected was a theater, given his adoration for musicals. The last was outside of the walk-up, both of them in winter clothes and Jessica being given a piggyback boost by Andrew. She displayed a key for the camera—their apartment key, most likely. Two men were maneuvering a mattress through the door in the background.

"Are those pictures going to be useful for anything?" Doyle asked as he put his portfolio bag in the backseat of the

Audi.

"Maybe," Larkin answered. He stood at the driver side door, puzzling over the pictures. He shuffled through them over and over—Nathan's, theater, move-in day. Nathan's, theater, move-in day. "There's a clue in most everything."

"Doing a little light reading?"

Larkin looked up. Doyle stared at him over the roof of the car, holding the library copy of *Funerary Rituals: Faces From The Other Side, A Brief Account of Effigies and Death Masks*. That's right. He'd picked up the book from the living room floor on his way out the door that morning and had forgotten about it completely once he'd put it in the backseat. Larkin tucked the photos into his inner suit coat pocket, then removed his phone. "I need to mark the return date in my calendar…."

"Did you read it yet?"

"Hm-hm." Larkin saved the reminder, turned off the phone screen, and pocketed it. "Yes. Well, a good portion of it." He watched Doyle page through the book. "The death mask would eventually become treasured for what it was: realism artwork obsessive of the individual. The death mask would become the symbol of all that embodied the man. His face undying."

Doyle briefly met Larkin's steady gaze. "You forgot you left it in the car?" he guessed.

Larkin shifted. "The act of borrowing a library book for work research is not routine to my life. So… yes, I forgot."

"Just clarifying," Doyle said, his whiskey-voice easygoing. He looked at the pages again and echoed, "'Obsessive of the individual' is a touch melodramatic, but it's honestly not a bad description of death masks."

"It resonated."

"Why's that?" Doyle bent, set the book back on the seat beside his bag, then shut the door.

"It reinforces the belief that there was a relationship between Andrew and the perpetrator, and that Andrew was tucked away because the truth of that connection would out his killer. Obsessive of the individual."

Doyle tapped his fingers against the roof for a moment. "Do you suspect Jessica was at all involved?"

"No." Larkin raised one fine eyebrow. "Do you?"

Doyle shook his head. "No. She sincerely loved Andrew. Maybe was even a little *in love* with him. But her sense of being… unmoored, I guess, that's real." He smiled and added, "Just making sure we're on the same page."

Without warning, a gunshot fractured the air, like a pianist slamming their fists down on the keys and the crash ricocheting back and forth against the walls of an empty auditorium. Larkin and Doyle both reached for their holstered weapons and drew a SIG P226 and Glock 17, respectively.

"That was on this block," Doyle said.

A second shot was fired, and somewhere overhead, glass broke. Children at the public school a few doors back began screaming.

"Recess," Doyle said.

"Go," Larkin snapped. "Tell the teachers to put the school in lockdown."

Doyle left the Audi in a full run, as if the hounds of Hell were snapping at his ankles.

Larkin turned toward Jessica's walk-up when the front door was thrown open and Ricky stepped outside, tucking something into the small of his back. The front of his sweatshirt was speckled with red. Larkin checked over his shoulder. Doyle stood at the gates of the school, badge raised, voice steady but loud and insistent as he ordered teachers to quickly escort the children inside. Swearing under his breath, Larkin turned to Ricky, raised his gun, and shouted, "NYPD, Ricky! Stop where you are!"

Ricky startled, looked across the street, and when he spotted Larkin, he broke into a run toward Avenue D.

"Ricky!" Larkin called again, immediately giving chase. He cut across the street, narrowly avoiding being hit by a car. Brakes screeched, a horn honked, the driver shouted out his open window, but Larkin didn't stop. He jumped a sizable puddle at the curb, remnants of yesterday's storm, and pounded down the sidewalk after Ricky. The super hadn't bothered to hide his weapon underneath his sweatshirt, instead leaving the handgun on full display at the waistband of his jeans. Larkin stretched his legs, pushed himself to sprint harder, faster, and barreled his shoulder square into Ricky's back.

Ricky's arms flailed for purchase and he crashed to the ground like the giant falling from his beanstalk.

Larkin's momentum kept him going past Ricky's prone body, and he managed to barely remain standing and skid to a stop before he crashed headfirst into a trash can on the corner. Breathing hard, Larkin swiveled around, keeping his weapon drawn as he demanded, "Hands on the back of your head, right—so help me if you reach half an inch more for that gun, I will blow your fucking nuts off, Ricky. Hands on your head, right now."

"You broke my nose," Ricky wailed in his slow speech mannerism.

"*Hands*, Ricky!" Larkin snapped.

"Larkin!" Doyle was holstering his weapon as he came toward them. "You okay?"

"Yes. Take his gun."

Doyle crouched, yanked the pistol from Ricky's jeans, and removed the magazine. "Two rounds missing," he confirmed before pocketing it, sliding the gun into his own waistband, and retrieving a pair of handcuffs.

"Whose blood is on your shirt," Larkin demanded.

Ricky moaned something into the ground.

"Whose blood is it," Larkin asked again, more forcefully.

"She'd always been the one who got away," Ricky sobbed.

Larkin lowered his firing stance and said to Doyle, "Read him his rights. Call it in." He started running toward the walk-up.

"Where are you going?" Doyle shouted after him.

"Jessica Lopez!" Larkin reached the front door—locked, of course—and began pressing the buzzer to every unit. "NYPD," he announced, when someone had finally answered in a skittish voice.

The door immediately buzzed open and Larkin plowed through the vestibule and up the stairs two at a time. He raised his SIG at the second-floor landing and moved carefully toward Jessica's open door—the door she had shown to keep methodically locked.

But she had known Ricky for God only knew how long, had no reason to not open the door when he knocked.

2D opened. A wizened old man and another man who was likely his adult son both glanced into the hall. "We called 911," the old man warned in a shriveled voice, like he had pegged Larkin as the attacker.

The son was holding a cell to his ear and said with courage he clearly wasn't feeling, "Y-you better get the fuck outta here. The cops are coming."

"I'm a detective," Larkin said. "Everett Larkin. Tell the dispatcher that right now. Tell them I'm alone and I'm going into Jessica Lopez's apartment."

The father tried to open the door a bit more and peer into 2C, but his son pulled him back by the shoulder.

"Tell dispatch my partner is outside with a suspect," Larkin ordered.

And he must have come across as honest, sincere, believable, because the son nodded vigorously and began relaying the information into the phone.

Larkin reached Jessica's doorway and called, "Ms. Lopez, it's Detective Larkin. Are you able to respond." He waited only one breath. "I'm coming inside."

He moved down the hall and entered the untidy kitchen. PomPom was cowering under the kitchen table. A slick trail of bright red blood covered the tile floor, heading into the next room. Larkin cleared the dark office before moving into the even more disorganized bedroom. Jessica lay facedown, a number of trinkets having fallen from the cheap shelf, her cell phone among them, like she'd been trying to reach for it. One of the windows had a hole through the glass and was cracked like a spiderweb.

Larkin holstered his pistol, eased Jessica onto her back, and yanked a sheet from her unmade bed. He wound it several times and then pressed it to the bloody gunshot in her abdomen.

The scene on East Sixth between Avenues C and D at 1:49 p.m. looked like a chaotic law enforcement block party. Black-and-whites with strobing lights were haphazardly parked along the sides of the road. One of two ambulances was pulling away with Jessica in critical condition, sirens screaming. Radios of uniformed officers crackled in the bus's wake. Any minute, one of the fifty CSU detectives employed by the city would pull up and begin processing Jessica's apartment.

Larkin sat on the bumper of the second ambulance. One of the paramedics was washing his hands of Jessica's blood. A cabernet to a rosé to no one ever knowing he'd packed the gut shot of a dying woman with retro Rainbow

Brite sheets. Larkin looked away from his hands. He studied Doyle, his exclusive-to-this-case partner, speaking with one of the responding detectives from Precinct 9. He was giving an official report as to their presence on the scene and the pursuit of Ricky when Larkin saw blood on his sweatshirt and had reason to believe an immediate connection to the gunfire. It was better that Doyle was taking the first pass. Larkin wasn't feeling particularly amicable, and his report would undoubtably reflect that.

"Detective?"

Larkin blinked a few times and looked to the paramedic standing over him.

"I asked if you wanted to remove your ring for a moment—get the inside of it."

"Oh." He tugged the silver band free. Dried blood discolored his finger.

The paramedic wiped it clean, then did the same to the wedding band.

Doyle strode across the sidewalk, jumped a puddle, and joined Larkin. He sat on the bumper and snapped the hair tie around Larkin's wrist.

The gesture translated so suddenly and so simply in Larkin's brain that he almost started laughing in some sort of hysterical relief. Then he almost started crying, because, no, he wasn't okay. Of course not. No one would be after what had just transpired. But that question—*Are you okay?*—rang so hollow for him because people *never* wanted to know.

But I do. And Doyle had found a way to communicate that.

Larkin nodded and said quietly, "Thanks."

Doyle smiled. He leaned forward to rest his elbows on his knees. "2D took PomPom."

"Good."

"It all seems pretty straightforward," Doyle explained. "No signs of forced entry, so Ricky must have knocked after we stepped out. In the kitchen, he shot Jessica in the stomach. She stumbled to the bedroom, for her phone, most likely. He shot her again in the shoulder. That was a through and through—broke the window."

"She'd always been the one who got away," Larkin stated. "That's what Ricky said."

"He's a few Fruit Loops short of a cereal bowl."

Larkin glanced sideways.

"Not professional, I know. In my defense, he shot a woman."

"Yes. Also yes." Larkin stood. "But he's known Jessica for how long. Why was it vital he scrub—"

"Rub."

"—her out now." As Doyle followed suit getting to his feet, Larkin was struck with the realization of what it was that Doyle's movements reminded him of. A big cat. The way they stretched, posed, hell, *strutted*. But Larkin set the thought aside and went to the cruiser that had Ricky cuffed in the backseat. He opened the door and asked, "Why was Ms. Lopez the one who got away."

Ricky's nose had been tended to by a paramedic, but despite no longer bleeding, it was bruised and swollen, and a bit of snot ran down his philtrum. "A long time ago, she got away," he whispered, not looking at Larkin.

"You attacked her before," Larkin tried to clarify.

But Ricky sneered, sniffed, and said, "She got away. But she was just like the others. Would have been just like the others."

The shiver that whispered across the back of Larkin's neck felt like a kiss left by a ghost. The sensation of someone having stepped over his grave, and Larkin was now painfully aware of what it must have felt like to be on the receiving end of his stare. He repeated, voice inflecting on the one word, "Others?"

CHAPTER ELEVEN

Detective Philip Bosman from Precinct 9 was not a particularly handsome man. He was at least in his midthirties, gangly, his cheeks pockmarked with acne scars, and had strawberry-blond hair, which, of all the foods used to describe hair color, was the one that irritated Larkin the most. Red hair wasn't red. It was orange. And strawberries were not orange. But more irritating than lacking a proper descriptor for Bosman's hair was Bosman trying to pick an argument with Larkin outside of Ricky's apartment door on the first floor of the walk-up. It was out of sight from the main entrance, located on the back side of the staircase.

"Ricky Goulding isn't part of your cold case—"

"Ricky Goulding attempted to brutally murder the one witness in the investigation surrounding the murder of Andrew Gorman less than five minutes after myself and Detective Doyle concluded the interview," Larkin countered. "The subject matter of that interview being something Ricky correctly deduced upon my introducing myself."

"How would he—"

"He reads the papers," Larkin interrupted. "He was forthcoming with a clipping from this morning's issue of

The City, which specifically mentioned the Cold Case Squad. He's lived and worked in this building for a considerable time, as he knew Ms. Lopez's tenant history. Ricky might have actually known Andrew Gorman when he was alive. The suggestion that there might be other victims, however tenuous that connection currently is in relation to Andrew, absolutely makes Ricky part of my investigation. Do not make me ask you again to open this door."

An uncomfortable few seconds settled over the three detectives, and then Doyle said, "Do you watch Animal Planet, Detective Bosman?"

"Sorry?"

"Big cats toy with their prey. Not as an act of sadistic pleasure, but out of self-preservation. And once the prey is too tired to keep fighting, the cat strikes."

Bosman slowly shook his head. "Why are you telling me this?"

"Because Detective Larkin is playing a verbal back-and-forth with you, and I don't think you realize he hasn't struck yet."

Larkin kept his expression a practiced neutral, but it was difficult. Pride skimmed very close to the surface, like little nips of electricity along his skin. And while he'd have preferred a comparison like *Larkin would send Rosencrantz and Guildenstern packing in a game of questions*, big cats were king, so it'd do.

"Fine, fine," Bosman snapped. "Stay here. I'll grab the keys and some gloves." He pushed past them and headed out the front door.

Larkin leaned one shoulder against the wall. He was staring straight ahead at the unit labeled 1A as he said, "It's interesting."

"What's that?"

"Outside, I was thinking about big cats."

Doyle said, "Synchronicity bodes well for the longevity of our relationship."

"We're not in a relationship."

"I beg to differ, work husband."

Larkin pinched the bridge of his nose with one hand and slid his other into his trouser pocket.

Doyle chuckled and asked, "Big cats?"

"Never mind."

"You brought it up."

"I'm *un*bringing it up."

"I'll tell everyone about how you seduced me."

Larkin dropped his hand and looked up. "I did no such thing."

"Really? You fed me, complimented me—"

Larkin blurted, if only to get Doyle to stop, "I thought that sometimes, you—you sort of move like a cat."

Doyle raised an eyebrow.

"It's because you're very tall," Larkin continued, struggling for an air of professionalism. "And lean. Like…."

"A cat."

"Yes."

"Is this a roundabout way of saying I'm hot?"

"Jesus Christ." Larkin's cell buzzed in his pocket, and he dug it out while Doyle laughed to himself.

Text from Noah Rider.

Stop ignoring me.

Larkin closed the app and tucked his phone away as the main entrance opened from behind, the hubbub of the scene outside following Bosman inside before the door fell shut. Bosman's tread on tile echoed, growing more pronounced as he rounded the corner. He wore a pair of latex gloves and held extras in one hand, which he offered them both, and a set of keys in the other—taken from Ricky, most likely. Bosman unlocked the apartment, felt along the wall, then flipped a switch. "So what're you looking for?" he asked, stepping aside and allowing Larkin and Doyle to enter.

"I'll know when I see it," Larkin said, then abruptly stopped walking.

The studio, large and spacious for an old Manhattan walk-up, was a pigsty. The floor didn't look as if it'd been swept in… *months*. Dirt, dust, hairballs, and crumbs littered every conceivable inch. An old couch pushed against one wall was sagging in the middle, and most of the fabric covering the armrests had been torn away to reveal the padding underneath. It looked as if Ricky had methodically plucked at the yellowed foam and then threw it every which way like confetti. Partially eaten frozen dinners, dozens of them, were stacked on the coffee table and floor. The bed was unmade, a tangle of blankets kicked to the foot and a sheet stained from lots of sweat and no washing. The kitchen counter was absolutely covered in dirty plates, cups, bowls, pans, and a small mountain of silver Coors Light cans. The studio had a heavy funk of body odor, microwaved lasagna and meatloaf, stale beer, and cheap pot. Piled all around this… *shit* were newspapers and magazines. Stacks of them. Towers, even. Newsprint going back years. Maybe decades.

Bosman swore from where he stood in the doorway. "It's amazing this building isn't completely infested with roaches."

Doyle turned to Larkin and asked quietly, "Is Ricky a hoarder?"

Larkin swallowed, took a deep breath, then regretted it as the stink of the apartment left an aftertaste in his mouth. "Certainly seems to be the case." He put on a pair of mental blinders, forced himself to not study the studio as a whole but in sections, and then one particular area of filth within that to analyze. Because if he raised his head, saw the walls closing in, and automatically began cataloguing every single object in the home of a disturbed man—not because of the junk, but the violence perpetrated—Larkin was going to snap.

He moved to a stack of yellowed newspapers beside an ancient and blocky RCA television that probably weighed half as much as him. Larkin picked up the paper on top, pages so old, the corners crumbled like dust. He checked the headlines of the next paper, then the next. "David Berkowitz."

"What about him?" Doyle asked before the sound of a cupboard opening followed.

"These newspapers. They're from the '70s. It's the entire timeline of the manhunt for Son of Sam. Ricky has the papers with the police composite sketch of Berkowitz too."

"Thanks for the nightmare fuel."

Larkin moved to a smaller pile, the papers looking a touch more recent, if the coloring and curling of the edges was anything to judge by. "Joel Rifkin."

Doyle opened the fridge, made a sound of disgust, then slammed the door shut. "Rifkin… the guy who murdered sex workers in the '80s and '90s?"

"Yes." After some more digging through headlines, Larkin sighed and said, "LISK."

"They haven't caught LISK yet," Doyle answered. Larkin was able to follow his movement through the studio by the shift in his voice and crunch underfoot.

"Is Ricky a goddamn serial killer?" Bosman asked from the doorway.

"No," Larkin said without looking up. "Ricky is a groupie. It's more common in women. Have you heard of Bonnie and Clyde Syndrome, Bosman."

"Like the robbers?"

"Yes, like the robbers," Larkin replied with a touch of irritation. "It's the act of being aroused by a partner who commits violent crimes. Bonnie died alongside Clyde in a shootout with the police because she wouldn't leave his side. It's slang for hybristophilia, which is a psychological condition caused by a number of factors still being studied today. The common thread is that of an individual who is infatuated with a killer. They follow the killer's story in the paper or attend court hearings, write fan letters, love letters, meet them in prison, some even marry the killer."

"You want me to ask Ricky if he thinks he and LISK are in a committed relationship?" Bosman asked dryly.

Larkin finally raised his head and stared at Bosman in the doorway until he averted his gaze elsewhere. "My concern is that, in rare instances, those who exhibit groupie tendencies will start a relationship with the perpetrator in order to learn intimate details of the committed acts. It's a way to vicariously experience the crime without having to spill the blood themselves." Then Larkin pushed the coffee table aside, got down on his knees, and looked under the couch.

"I've yet to see a single connection between all this," Bosman said, and he was probably gesturing at the room, "and your cold case."

Doyle blew out a breath that had a hint of attitude, but said in his smooth politeness, "Larkin is suggesting that Ricky might have attacked Jessica today based on some firsthand knowledge he could have gleaned from a relationship with Andrew's killer. Ricky might have been reenacting past murders—might have viewed Jessica as a match to previous victims. We're not suggesting that Ricky killed Andrew twenty years—"

"Twenty-two," Larkin corrected, his voice muffled. He'd squirmed halfway under the couch and was using his phone's flashlight to study the underside of the furniture.

"Larkin, what the hell are you doing?" Doyle asked.

"You think," Bosman interjected, "Ricky knows

Andrew's killer? Has a relationship with him?"

"Ricky sure has proven he's open to being besties with a serial killer," Doyle answered.

"But what're you going to do, trawl every unsolved murder involving women with a box dye job?"

"Thank God we've got a Cold Case detective, hmm?" Doyle had tapped the sole of Larkin's wingtip with the toe of his own in emphasis. "Larkin, I swear to God, I need a shower watching you wriggle around on this floor."

"Just a moment," Larkin answered.

"It sounds like a hell of a stretch," Bosman said. The wood groaned as he shifted his weight in the doorway.

"We have evidence that suggests Andrew knew his killer," Doyle said. "I think the truth lies a lot closer to home than suspected."

"I don't buy it."

Larkin reached his hands out from the couch, pushed himself clear, then took Doyle's outstretched hand and was yanked to his feet like he weighed nothing. Larkin brushed the front of his suit coat while saying, "Whether Andrew was intentionally selected or his death was collateral, Doyle is correct—this case has a great deal more happening under the surface, and this building, Andrew's relationship with Jessica, with *Ricky*, are all vital clues."

"Per the FBI," Bosman said, like a man who'd once skimmed an article and was since desperate to show off that knowledge, "these days, most serial killers don't have a relationship with their victims."

"That's correct," Larkin answered. Then he held up a few Polaroids that were bent and weathered, directing his attention to Doyle. "But Andrew Gorman's death mask says otherwise."

Doyle looked away from Larkin's face and down at the

photos—three separate masks, all rudimentary, one of plaster and two of what seemed to be papier-mâché. Each laid over the face of a woman prone on her back, heavy bruising on their necks, and each nude from the waist up.

CHAPTER TWELVE

"I need to know how old those Polaroids are."

"Hang on."

"Doyle."

"I said, hang on," Doyle said, glancing up from his phone. "Unless you want to read a fifty-page manufacturer's manual yourself, give me a minute."

When it'd come time to take Ricky in for questioning, there'd been a territorial dispute with Bosman. Ricky was now a person of interest in Larkin's case, but he'd shot Jessica in an unrelated—according to Bosman—incident on his turf. The argument had spiraled out of control when Bosman declared having heard about the fucker everyone called Grim, what an egotistical prick he was, and that as far as he was concerned, Larkin could take a walk into rush hour traffic.

Larkin hadn't been particularly insulted. He *did* have a headache throbbing behind his left eye, however, a combination of stress from the shooting and finding Jessica slowly bleeding to death, irritation with this newbie detective so ready to prove himself that he was about to whip his dick out and literally mark territory, and the overwhelming stimulation from Ricky's apartment. Every time Larkin blinked, he saw a negative of the studio space. And the dank, spoiled smell had permeated his clothing, every movement stirring that combination of rotting food and pot and morbid curiosity from Larkin's suit.

"One in every five employees in a committed relationship cheat on their partner with a colleague," Larkin had told Bosman after he'd finished pitching a fit.

"*What?*"

"Spray tans on light skin last an average of five days. Yours looks to be at the midpoint. Something you got done over the weekend, then, and you didn't remove your wedding band for the process. Only now it's gone and there's an embarrassing ring of white skin in its absence."

Bosman glanced at his hand before quickly shoving it into his pocket.

"You've got a touch of lipstick on your shirt collar too," Larkin continued. "Sure, you might have come to the scene after some afternoon delight with your wife, but unless you're still in the honeymoon phase of your relationship, this is doubtful. Plus, you'd have no reason to remove your ring around her. Ergo, an affair. And not with a beat cop—she wouldn't bother with lipstick. Another detective perhaps, but I think you enjoy the power trip of the '*d-e-t*' title too much to share the glory. So a young and impressionable administrator at the Ninth."

Doyle had said nothing during the back-and-forth, but he did sigh once or twice.

A furious blush had worked its way through Bosman's tan, and he'd finally suggested that Ricky be brought to his precinct, but that he'd allow Larkin and Doyle first dibs on an interview.

"You're mad," Larkin stated, staring at Doyle. They stood

in a hallway outside one of the interview rooms at Precinct 9, with Doyle leaning against the wall, scrolling on his phone.

"I'm not mad," he corrected in that ever-smoky voice. "I'm trying to read." He must have sensed Larkin's stare, because Doyle raised his gaze after a beat. "I wouldn't have used an affair as leverage."

"I couldn't possibly care any less who Bosman is actually sleeping with." Larkin slid his hands into his pockets and began to pace the hall. Upon his return to Doyle, he added, "It was the only clear deduction I had of his person at the time."

"Hm-hm."

Larkin passed a second time. "If you don't like the way I work—"

"We're partners now. That's no longer a valid fallback," Doyle cut in.

"I don't know what you want me to say, then," Larkin murmured on his third pass.

"I would like you to apologize to Bosman."

"No."

"And," Doyle continued calmly, as if Larkin hadn't just so brazenly disagreed, "I'd like, with regard to personal relationships, that you keep those intuitive deductions to yourself. I know you can't help it, and if you want to blurt it out when we're alone, that's fine. But don't weaponize someone's romance. In fact—" He paused and looked up from his phone again. "—that's out-in-the-field, rule three: love and sex can only be used for good."

Larkin cast Doyle a look upon his fourth or fifth pass. "Bosman needed to be brought down a peg. He's a detective in the same way an honor student needs CliffsNotes in class."

"Evie," Doyle said, and there was a gentle sternness in his voice, in the stress on Larkin's first name—well, sort of his first name.

Larkin stopped and stared at Doyle.

"Unless you want someone pointing out your own domestic troubles, apologize to him."

Larkin didn't respond as a cold sweat broke out under his arms. His jaw tightened. Throat muscles tensed. He felt struck by both the need to simultaneously fight and fly.

Doyle returned to scrolling on his phone.

Seven years. That was how long Larkin and Noah had known each other. And it had been good in the beginning. Like waking from a restless sleep and getting an overdose injection of serotonin and dopamine. The effect had been immediate and intense, and Larkin should have known to slow down, to be careful, because he was damaged goods and most people weren't in the market for those bruised apples at the bottom of the produce display. But the love had felt so good. And Noah had said he understood. He'd listened, sympathized with Larkin when no one else had.

Until he hadn't.

Larkin had warned Noah that he couldn't change. It wasn't a matter of enough therapy or a cocktail of medications— his brain had completely rewired itself after August 2, 2002, and who he was now… this was it. Larkin knew the way he spoke was frustrating, sometimes rude, and he did his best to maintain a moderated and subdued presence, albeit he still came off as intense when in public, but Noah had promised him he didn't have to hide his… *quirks* at home.

He'd *promised.*

But now Noah was always angry, always offended, always lashing out, and Larkin was shrinking, collapsing back into that exhaustive blackness he'd been in the decade following the incident, hinging his ability to drag himself out of bed on doses of anxiety pills and sleeping aids and—Noah hadn't known. Didn't realize. Didn't care.

Larkin thought of the Xanax downstairs in the Audi. He

could excuse himself for a minute. Hell, if he ran, he could retrieve a dose and be back in forty-five—forty seconds. Just one. He'd still be focused enough to interrogate Ricky.

Doyle tugged lightly on the hair tie around Larkin's wrist. He hadn't looked up from his phone as he motioned Larkin to join him against the wall.

Just one, Larkin thought again, but he took a few steps and reluctantly stood beside Doyle. He scrubbed his face hard with both hands, and when he let out a breath, it was shaky.

Doyle had been clutching an evidence bag between his arm and torso. He removed it, studied the back side of the three photographs they'd taken from the hiding spot under Ricky's couch, looked at his phone once more, then said, "If I'm understanding this correctly, one of the papier-mâché masks was taken on film manufactured in September of 1991. The second, as well as the plaster mask, were both manufactured in March of 1992."

"That doesn't mean the photograph was taken then."

"Only that the film was manufactured and for sale," Doyle confirmed.

Larkin took the evidence bag and studied the photographs with the professional detachment that made his job possible. "How long does Polaroid film last."

"Hmm… it's best to use most films within twelve months."

"Well before Andrew's murder, then," Larkin murmured. He drew the pad of his thumb back and forth across one of the papier-mâché photos.

"What're you thinking?"

Larkin said, "Children love penguins. Every year, Noah has a penguin week in class. They take a field trip to Central Park Zoo, watch some kid-friendly documentary, he reads them *And Tango Makes Three*, and they make papier-mâché penguins. The week before, I'm usually up all night helping him fill a trash bag with strips of newspaper. You have to prepare certain steps, of course—otherwise six- and seven-year-olds will never finish the project. But it's a fairly simple craft."

Doyle had pocketed his phone, crossed one arm over his middle, and seemingly unaware of it, was chewing on his thumbnail.

Larkin suppressed a smile at the return of Doyle's fidgeting. "Plaster of Paris is beyond first graders."

"It's a bit more nuanced," Doyle agreed. He met Larkin's eyes. "The killer was experimenting with their signature?"

"It reads to me as a clear progression in artistic knowledge."

Doyle hastily removed the notepad from his suit coat. He flipped to a blank page, turned it sideways, then drew a line across the length of the paper. "Papier-mâché in '91. Again in '92, followed by plaster of Paris. And then there's Andrew with cast iron in '98."

"Clear escalation in both the perpetrator's desire to commit murder, and the skill surrounding his ritual with the body."

Doyle scribbled notes underneath the basic timeline. "Our questions would be: why does Ricky have these photographs, which are clearly souvenirs. Because you don't think—"

"Ricky is the Bonnie to the unknown perpetrator's Clyde," Larkin said with finality.

"Who is Clyde, then?"

Larkin finally smiled. "Arguably our most important question."

"Are there more than three victims?"

"Yes," Larkin agreed.

"Why three women and then a man?"

"To understand that deviation, especially with Andrew's

body dump implying a necessity to hide a personal connection, we need to know who the women were," Larkin explained. "Did the perpetrator know them as well. Were they strangers all chosen based on nothing beyond a sexual compulsion unique to the killer. Where are their remains. How were they disposed of."

"I can't write this fast."

"Shorthand classes should be brought back." Larkin waited for Doyle to catch up. The moment of suspended quiet allowed him to realize that Doyle had flawlessly redirected Larkin's energy from its escalating fixation on everything wrong between him and Noah to the case—something that required a considerable degree of emotional distance in order to properly investigate. That redirect had caused his accelerated heartbeat to slow, his breathing to even out, and the insistent craving for Xanax to wane, if only a little.

Larkin studied Doyle, who was bent at the waist and using his thigh as an impromptu surface to write on. Maybe, admittedly, there was a thrill—purely physical—in calluses and cardamon and whiskey and pyrite. And maybe there was also a wonder—something more abstract—of pencils over pistols and sweetened spice and the contrasting taste of austere and rich, depending on which way the light hit the smoke, and gold that was anything but the fool he presented as.

Larkin had been wrong about Nietzsche's aphorism, that Doyle was the joy and he was the depression. Such an assumption was an insult to their characters—the suggestion that neither were complete without the other. A partnership shouldn't fill missing pieces, but instead enhance what was already present. Doyle's acceptance of extreme heartache in return for unbridled happiness was a representation of who Larkin, too, could be, if he wanted it.

And sure, he'd likely have more shadows than sunlight.

More night than day.

More despair than hope.

But there would be thrill and wonder and partnership too.

'Til death do us part.

And then, quite suddenly, Larkin's mind silenced and only one thought rose to the top: *I'm dying.*

Doyle said something.

Larkin blinked, shook his head.

Doyle's eyebrows rose.

"I didn't hear what you said," Larkin said, catching the tone in his own voice—the gentleness, the delicacy, like his breath would snap in two.

"Spoken like a true work husband."

Larkin snorted, and then he started laughing. He clutched his middle and slid into a crouch as he was overcome with a full-bodied explosive sort of laughter that threatened to crack his ribs.

"He's fine," Doyle was calling to someone farther down the hall who was clearly startled by the outburst.

Still laughing, Larkin raised his head. Doyle squatted down in front of him with a confused smile. He was as alive as summer flowers and as warm as a lone campfire and—

"It wasn't that funny."

"It was," Larkin insisted. He took a deep breath, and another chuckle escaped as he said, "I don't remember the last time I laughed like this. It feels good."

"You have a nice laugh."

As Larkin wiped his face, he caught a curious look flicker across Doyle's face. There was no universal microexpression for shame. That reaction existed within the family of sadness, but by its very nature was a look humans instinctually sought to avoid broadcasting at all costs. Because to reveal shame meant receiving a reaction of disgust from others.

And yet there it was.

For just a second, laid bare.

Then Doyle smiled that light-up-a-room-before-you-even-walk-in smile, stood, and pulled Larkin to his feet. "Let's talk to Ricky."

It was 4:22 p.m. when Larkin opened the door to the interview room. It was nondescript: white walls, battered table, office chairs that'd clearly been rotated around the precinct until winding up here for the last leg of their lives. A public-school clock was on the wall, metal cage covering the face so no desperate suspect thought to utilize the minute hand as an impromptu weapon. And other than Ricky, his arms crossed on the tabletop with his head down, that was it.

Larkin took a seat across from the super.

Doyle shut the door and sat against the wall, notepad and pen ready.

Larkin was silent. He'd counted to thirty-three before Ricky raised his head and met his gaze.

"You ain't a cop," Ricky said, his voice almost too loud after the silence.

Larkin removed his wallet and displayed his badge. "Detective Everett Larkin, Cold Cases. I told you that."

"You're too pretty."

Larkin tucked his badge away.

"Like those store dummies," Ricky clarified.

"Mannequins," Larkin corrected.

"Perfect but plastic."

Larkin leaned back, propped his ankle on his knee, and folded his hands in his lap. He waited. But Ricky never changed position. Never shifted subconsciously to mirror Larkin, to build a bridge between them. *Interesting*. Larkin raised the evidence bag from his lap, holding it just out of Ricky's reach. "Tell me about these women."

Ricky stared at the Polaroids. He shrugged and met Larkin's eyes. Dark, dead eyes, like old fish on a bed of ice, met reaper gray in a standoff. A childish grin creased the wrinkles of Ricky's face, and he whispered, "You can see their boobs."

"Why were they chosen."

Ricky finally straightened his posture, his hands still on the tabletop. There was dirt under his nails. "I like those store dummies with faces and big boobs. Zallie's Pleasure Box has one in the window. It's my favorite."

Larkin put the evidence bag back in his lap so Ricky couldn't gawk at the victims. "When were these women killed."

"Oh, a long time ago."

"When," Larkin asked again.

"It was a long time ago," Ricky insisted, but now agitated.

"How."

Ricky furrowed his brow. He studied his hands, picked at a hangnail. "They were… shot…?" He said it without looking up, but more like he asked, as if looking for clarification.

Larkin narrowed his eyes. "Where were their bodies left."

"Lots of places." Ricky started picking at another finger.

Larkin slammed his fist on the tabletop and Ricky jumped in his seat. "*Where*, Ricky."

"L-let me see those pictures."

"No."

Ricky flashed a look of panic. He licked his lips. "But I need to see the pictures to know!"

Larkin considered, met Doyle's look briefly, then raised the bag.

Ricky sat up from his seat and leaned over the table. He pointed a thick, grimy finger at the photographs and muttered, "Simone, Baby, Nadia. Yeah. Yeah, that's right. Simone, Baby—"

Larkin lowered the bag a second time when Ricky's preoccupation suggested sexual excitement. "Where were Simone, Baby, and Nadia's bodies left."

Ricky slowly returned to his seat. He smiled again. His face contorted into something devilish as he said in that weird, singsong voice, "Now I remember… Tompkins Square Park."

Larkin shot Doyle a second look. His partner met his gaze and nodded once in understanding. A few years after the riots in 1988, Tompkins Square Park had closed and undergone restoration in an attempt to curb the same levels of crime, drug use, and mass gatherings of the homeless as seen at Madison.

"Have you ever worked for the Parks and Recreation Department," Larkin asked.

Ricky shook his head in a wishy-washy way. "I'm the super."

"For how long."

Ricky shrugged. "I'm not very good at reading time."

Larkin reached across the small room to hand the evidence bag over to Doyle. He watched Ricky follow the photographs like a hawk and lick his lips again. "Tell me about Andrew Gorman. He lived in 2C."

"He lived with Ms. Lopez."

Super since at least 1997.

Doyle was writing as he cut into the conversation. "You're pretty good with names, Ricky."

"Uh-huh."

"But not dates?"

"Numbers confuse me," he said in a long, drawn-out breath.

Doyle looked up from the notepad. "I get that," he said with the perfect amount of understanding and sympathy. "Did you like Andrew?"

Ricky shook his head.

"Why not?"

"He was mean." Ricky shot Larkin a dirty look. "Like him. All plastic pretty. One time I found a dummy, but she had no head and a dog had shit down her neck."

"Don't be rude, Ricky," Doyle said in a placating tone.

"I want my pictures back."

Doyle shook his head. "Tell us about Andrew."

"He was mean."

"Mean?"

"No talking to Ms. Lopez, is what he said. He yelled at me that I'd be in trouble. So much trouble, Ricky! *So much trouble!* So when I had to fix her sink one time, I didn't even say nothing."

"Even after Andrew disappeared?" Doyle asked.

Ricky nodded vigorously. "He might be a ghost." He patted his jeans pocket, turned it inside out, and picked some lint from the lining.

"Is Andrew dead?"

"Of course."

Doyle looked at Larkin. Exactly one person outside law enforcement had been privy to that detail: Jessica Lopez.

"Where's Andrew's body?" Doyle asked next.

"*He* went to Madison," Ricky answered, glancing up.

"Someone killed Andrew Gorman," Larkin said, and Ricky was nodding his head once again. "Who."

The corner of Ricky's mouth rose in a contemptuous smile. "Me."

CHAPTER THIRTEEN

"It's duping delight," Larkin stated. He stood before Lieutenant Connor's desk at Precinct 19. It was 6:07 in the evening and Ricky Goulding had been hauled away, booked for the murder of Andrew Gorman and attempted murder of Jessica Lopez—assuming she didn't take a turn during the night.

Tungsten orange from the streetlamps filtered through the partially drawn blinds at Connor's back. The glint of light picked out the copper in his hair. The halo glow did nothing to compliment the flush on his face.

"Larkin," Doyle tried, his voice steady. He was seated in the second chair beside the one Larkin had shot out of. He reached a hand out, saying, "Sit down."

"What it is," Connor corrected, his voice overpowering Larkin's in a way that suggested he'd spoken from his diaphragm his entire career, "is a slam dunk. One cold case ends up closing four—"

"We don't even know who those women are. Their names were obviously—"

"Don't interrupt me, Grim," Connor snapped. "You

arrested Gorman's murderer in less than forty-eight hours and it won't even need to go to court. The DA's gonna throw you a ticker-tape parade."

"No," Larkin said, shaking his head. "No, no, *no*. Ricky didn't do this."

"He says he did," Connor countered. "Video surveillance of that interview has him answering you point-blank. We can pin those women on him—"

Larkin interrupted a second time. "Duping delight is a unique expression of contempt and excitement. It's a literal high the person gets when they think their lie has been believed. The energy they get from the experience can't be contained, so it leaks out in tiny flashes of emotion."

"I'm not letting that shitbag go because he gave you a goddamn crooked smile."

"He's not going anywhere," Larkin agreed. "He shot Jessica Lopez. But none of those women in the Polaroids were shot, and neither was Andrew."

"He had photographs of the victims," Connor argued. "Photographs *you* found."

"They're trophies," Larkin said. "But not in the way you think. Ricky has hybristophilia. He's obsessed with, perhaps even sexually aroused by, the individual who committed these crimes. And I think Ricky has successfully established a relationship with this person. Those photographs were given to him, like a gift. He was living in a dumpster, but he made sure those photographs were safe and secure in a place he could be sure to find them. They meant something to him."

"Meant something because he fucking took them, Grim."

Larkin was almost shouting. "He didn't know how those women were killed. He was guessing. *Fishing*."

Doyle stood, took a quick sidestep to block Connor, who was seated at his desk, and, looking down at Larkin, said calmly, "Please sit."

Larkin scrubbed his face while letting out a *whoosh* of air.

Doyle hovered his hand just below Larkin's elbow, directing him without actually touching him into the chair he'd abandoned. Once Doyle had returned to his own seat, he picked up Larkin's train of thought without delay. "The photographs of the three unknown victims don't show any evidence of a gunshot. There *is* a great deal of post-mortem bruising around the neck, however, which would have been the same for Andrew. Plus, Ricky's clearly a hoarder."

"Clearly," Connor echoed. His face was still tight with agitation.

"But specifically of newspapers and magazines," Doyle continued. "Hoarders view their items not as junk, but as a prized collection. And two of those masks were made of papier-mâché."

"What's your point?" Connor asked.

"I think it would have been… extremely difficult, if not impossible, for Ricky to destroy something he loved— newspapers—to make those. The thing about hybristophilia is that they get to live vicariously through the killer, right, Larkin?"

Larkin was well aware that Doyle knew the answer. Even if he hadn't known the psychology prior to their conversation while at Ricky's apartment, Doyle certainly hadn't forgotten Larkin's explanation over the course of a few hours. But it was clear, now that the tension in the room was dissipating, that Doyle was asking a question as a means of returning control to Larkin. He was, after all, the senior detective on the case and the one whose disgruntled lieutenant sat before them.

On a quiet exhale, Larkin said, "The intimacy of the relationship between Ricky and this unknown perpetrator allows him to experience the violence he craves but cannot see to fruition himself. As for the papier-mâché, I do believe these were early attempts at constructing a death mask. Ricky might not be aware that those attempts have since escalated to cast iron. He sees those paper ones and can't replicate them because he can't bear to part with anything in his collection. And anyway, he doesn't need to, because he has those gifted Polaroids to look at."

"Why shoot Jessica Lopez, then?" Connor asked. "If he can't handle the violence?"

"I should have said *brutality*," Larkin corrected. "*Depravity*. I do believe Ricky has the capacity to be violent—in fact, we saw that today. But it's violence from a distance. He shot her. He wasn't up close and personal with a blunt object, like what transpired with Andrew."

Connor leaned back, the chair creaking as he adjusted his weight. He rolled a fountain pen back and forth across the desktop, never breaking eye contact with Larkin. He was anything but happy when he asked, "You say those three women and Andrew Gorman are all connected to the same perp?"

"Without a doubt."

"Those names Ricky gave you, of the women," Connor continued. "They're all stage names—you're aware of that, right?"

"More likely street names," Larkin corrected.

"My point is," Connor growled, "I understand the mask connection—I see it—but why go after three, if not more, who knows, sex workers, then take out a gay college boy? Maybe Ricky did help in the killings, since one hardly matches the majority."

Larkin shook his head. "It's all one and the same man. I believe *who* Andrew was is the clue to identifying the perpetrator. He beat to death at least four people, perhaps more, as you've said. We don't yet know if there're more photographs hidden in Ricky's apartment. But the perpetrator is still out there. And if you let Ricky hang for this, you'll be feeding right into his desires while the real monster gets away with it." He leaned forward in his chair to say, "The psychology of place is key in this case. That apartment building, those parks. I just need a moment to… to figure it out."

Connor opened his mouth, but Doyle, opening the portfolio bag leaning against his own chair, said, "We have an additional avenue that still needs to be considered." He tugged the sketch pad free, flipped the pages, and showed Connor the composite sketch of Andrew Gorman's unknown love interest. "Ms. Lopez assisted me. This man was sexually, if not romantically, involved with Andrew at the time of his death, yet never came forward in the initial missing person report."

Connor's brows rose in renewed interest.

"And according to Ms. Lopez, this man's schooling would have made him familiar with welding."

"Andrew's death mask was cast-iron," Larkin added.

"I didn't forget," Connor said.

Doyle said, "This sketch is what he looked like in 1998, but I can age him. We can get both versions submitted to the Local4Locals app, see if he's still in the greater New York area and is willing to talk."

Connor eyed the sketch a long moment before he said, "Do that. Submit it to public relations tonight. I want his mug on that app before sunup tomorrow. Grim, I want you to excavate whatever bug's crawled up your ass."

"Yes, sir," Larkin said stiffly.

"You really couldn't get Ricky to roll?"

"No. But then again, threats of jailtime wouldn't work, would they. It'll be a matter of dismantling his claim by proving he's lacking knowledge only the real perpetrator would have."

"Then you better fucking do that," Connor concluded. "Put names—real names—to those women."

"Of course."

"Loop Ulmer back in on this. Have him work his connection with Missing Persons."

Larkin's gut plummeted like the first drop on a roller-coaster. "Sir—"

"Check Homicide's stacks for any cold cases. Find those women. Names, remains, forensics—everything we've got floating around. The DA's going to want every *i* dotted and *t* crossed on this one."

Larkin stood. Doyle gathered his bag and moved to the office door.

"Grim."

"Yes."

Connor raised his pen and pointed at Larkin with it. "Not a whisper. One news article is already one too many. I don't want this guy spooked. And if word gets out before we've got our ducks lined up that Homicide brushed off victims of a serial killer, there's going to be an interdepartmental war. Understand?"

"Yes, sir."

Connor pointed the pen at Doyle next. "You too, van Gogh. One word and there's gonna be a Help Wanted sign where your nameplate used to be."

"Understood," Doyle answered. He opened the door, allowed Larkin to pass through first, then shut it behind himself. He said to Larkin, "I better get going."

Larkin looked over his shoulder toward his desk and the one just to the left, currently unoccupied. He turned back to Doyle. "Detective Baker is on sick leave until the end of next week. Her desk is beside mine."

"Yeah?"

"I may need to consult you."

Doyle's eyes twinkled like sunshine glittering atop raw pyrite. "Probably not." He smiled, moved for Larkin's arm, then stopped short—for a man whose love language was physical touch, the necessity to second-guess his nature was seeming to prove exceedingly difficult. Doyle dropped his hand to his side. "But thank you." He walked across the bullpen and sat down at Baker's desk.

Larkin closed his eyes, rewound the day in his mind, returned to that morning—the men's restroom downstairs. The flood of emotion was immediate, a sucker punch that stole his breath.

—Boom. Squish. Crack.—

He wanted to cry. And it wasn't because of how Ulmer had spoken to him, how Ulmer had scared him. Ulmer was irrelevant, had only been the association, the catalyst, the reminder. The panic and fear and heartache was from August 2, 2002, and the near-twenty years that'd since transpired had done nothing to soften those reactions in Larkin. It was as fresh as if it had been yesterday. Today. Five minutes ago.

He fast forwarded.

Plunk, plunk, plunk of the water.

The twist of the deadbolt.

But I do.

The memory of Doyle's hug—heat and strength and acceptance—*there* was his positive association for today. March 31 would be remembered by the embrace he'd received from… *God*, practically a stranger, but he'd liked it.

Loved it, in fact, that Doyle had struggled with the desire to touch him again but was clearly respecting Larkin's personal boundaries. No. *Desire* wasn't the right word. He didn't like the sexual connotation it held. Because despite

Doyle's flirty personality, that hug hadn't been physically suggestive. It'd been genuine. Doyle had a wish… an inclination… an *impulse*. That was it. An impulse to touch Larkin again. Something so essential to his personal makeup that a man of lesser intelligence or understanding would have violated Larkin in order to fulfill that need.

But not Doyle.

Because those eyes weren't fool's gold.

They were the real deal. Twenty-four karat.

Larkin strode across the bullpen, stopped in front of Baker's desk, and put his hands on top.

Doyle looked up from his sketch pad.

"You're an extremely competent detective," Larkin said. "And my poor attempts at past compliments have been a disservice to you."

Doyle set down his pencil and sharpener.

Larkin reached across the desktop, pulled back like he wasn't quite certain, then went ahead and took Doyle's hand. He brought it up to the hair tie still around his own wrist, and smartly, Doyle understood and gave it a tug. Larkin let go of Doyle, who was smiling again and swallowing up all of the oxygen in the room. "Thank you," Larkin said. Then he turned and marched to Ulmer's desk in the opposite direction.

"Fuck off," Ulmer murmured, clearly having seen Larkin's approach from the corner of his eye despite not looking away from his computer screen.

"I require your assistance."

"The hell you do."

"I like it as much as you do."

Ulmer growled and kept typing.

"I have three murdered women from 1991 and 1992—Simone, Baby, and Nadia."

"Prostitutes."

"Sex workers," Larkin corrected. "I believe their deaths are precursors to Andrew Gorman's."

Ulmer stopped and looked up.

"But due in great part to both the decade in question as well as their careers, I worry that if they were reported as missing, the case might have stagnated within Missing Persons or never been connected to a case established at Homicide."

"Don't try to blame me for department shortcomings before either of our times."

"I wasn't."

Ulmer looked like he could grind his molars to dust.

"They were supposedly dumped in Thompson Square Park—very likely while the area was closed for restoration. I'm unable to provide an accurate age bracket beyond the three were between adulthood and middle years. One black, two white—"

Ulmer held a hand up to stop Larkin. "Just give me their fucking photos, since apparently digging up a dead hooker is too much for you."

"Sex worker," Larkin corrected a second time. "These women were beaten to death and left to be forgotten. Please show an iota of respect." Ulmer stood from his chair, towering over Larkin with only the desk between them, but Larkin continued without missing a beat. "As for photos, I have none. Correction, I do, but their faces have been covered by—" He stopped.

Ulmer's brows rose and he asked shortly, "Covered by what?"

"Masks. Check with OCME too. I need absolutely any report written up or evidence gathered." Larkin began to walk away.

"Grim."

He looked over his shoulder.

Ulmer was grooming his goatee with one hand in a self-soothing gesture. After a beat, he pointed and said, "I'm doing this because it's my job."

"It sure is."

"As far as I'm concerned, you can drink Clorox."

Larkin's mouth twitched. "That's certainly more creative than simply telling me to fuck myself." He returned to his desk, took a seat, and looked at Doyle. Earbuds in, right leg bouncing—he probably didn't notice—busily tracing the composite sketch from earlier to make a second rendition. Considering Doyle's proven scientific understanding of bone and muscle structures, Larkin had no doubt the aging process would be just as accurate and impressive as the work he'd done so far.

Larkin left Doyle to it.

He picked up his phone, checked his department extensions, then dialed.

"Bosman" came the answer on the first ring. Good to know the newbie wasn't clocking out at five.

"Detective Bosman, this is Everett Larkin."

Silence.

In fact, Bosman was so quiet, Larkin could pick up the sounds of his bullpen through the line.

"Evie…. Apologize to him."

Larkin cleared his throat and said briskly, "I would like to apologize for our last conversation. It was inappropriate of me to point out your personal… business."

"Yeah, it was."

"I, of course, don't have the complete story, nor do I care. You have your reasons."

"Are you still apologizing, or have we moved on to some sort of vague insult?"

"I'm still apologizing."

"You're not very good at it."

"I don't usually have reason to apologize for my deductions."

Bosman laughed at that. Not a cruel or angry laugh, but one of honest amusement. "You're a weird fucking guy."

"I've been told that once or twice."

"I bet. What did you need?"

With his free hand, Larkin grabbed the evidence bags containing the Polaroids and Andrew's death mask. "Is CSU still at Ricky's apartment."

"Oh yeah. You saw it—crawled around in it, actually. They'll be there all damn night."

Larkin reached into his suit coat, retrieved the photos Jessica had supplied him with before the shooting, then stood. He cradled the phone between his ear and shoulder while shrugging the coat off and draping it over the back of his chair. "Have they found masks or more Polaroids."

"Not to my knowledge."

"Keep on them."

"Hang on," Bosman said. "What for? Ricky confessed, didn't he? About your cold case?"

"Yes, but he's lying."

"He… is?"

Larkin sat again. He placed the Polaroid victims to the far left, the mask to the right, then evenly spaced Jessica's mementos in the middle. "Killers like this, they go through a phase of trial and error, figuring out what they like, what works, etcetera. I'm particularly curious if Polaroids continued to be taken, or if that step was phased out in favor of just the death mask construction as they became more nuanced."

"Suppose CSU doesn't find any," Bosman answered. "Doesn't mean, what were you saying earlier, they were gifts to Ricky? Doesn't mean anything. Maybe LISK—"

"It's not LISK."

"I'm joking."

"A misspoken joke leads to rumors."

"Christ."

"But yes, you are correct," Larkin continued. "Perhaps the perpetrator kept the rest of the photographs to himself. Or he stopped taking a secondary trophy once he grew more confident in his artistic skills. I can't say yet—there's not enough information. But I need confirmation as to whether or not Ricky has more Polaroids."

"Okay, okay. I'll follow up. And the masks?"

"I'm ninety-nine percent certain he has none."

"That one percent?"

"I try not to be overly confident."

Bosman was laughing again.

"Those masks are important. Under no circumstance would the killer part with them. By proving they're not in Ricky's possession, we're heading in the right direction of discrediting his claim."

"This is some serial killer bullshit," Bosman said, but quiet, like he didn't want his voice to carry.

"Yes."

Bosman swore.

"Keep that between us." Larkin provided Bosman with his cell number, asked again to be brought up to date as soon as possible, and hung up.

He stared at the evidence timeline in front of him. Despite not being able to see the faces of the female victims from the early '90s, Larkin could deduce a few physical traits they had in common: petite, small-chested, long hair. He tapped his fingertip across the desk until he reached the photograph of

Jessica and Andrew outside their walk-up. Jessica was also quite small in build, and even when she was in college, she wore her long hair atop her head in a messy bun. A possible type, then. The perpetrator wasn't limited to a race or age so much as stature and aesthetic. And stature could have been also due, in part, to practicality. A hundred-and-twenty-pound woman was easier to take down and dispose of than, say, a hundred-and-sixty. And Ricky had said Jessica was like the others. He would know this based on the Polaroids of earlier murders.

Larkin slid his finger back to the empty space between the evidence bag and the drug-store-developed photos. Were there other murders between 1992 and Andrew's in 1998? Larkin's gut said yes. The perpetrator was just finding his groove. He'd have only stopped if he were caught, which wasn't possible, because Larkin and most other cops would at least be familiar with the story. The only other reason for a period of silence would be if law enforcement had gotten too close. That was also doubtful. It'd be an established open case. Larkin could think of nothing that even closely resembled this situation.

He directed his gaze back to the photograph of Andrew standing outside the theater. A perpetrator with a penchant for small women—possibly focusing his efforts on sex workers simply due to the transient life—suddenly changes course and goes for a college-educated man with a stable lifestyle. And while Andrew wasn't big—he would have stood as tall as Larkin and possibly had the same slender build—he'd still be a more formidable opponent than the three women, if Larkin could judge by the images alone. And it wasn't like Andrew was… beautiful, for lack of better description. He wore his hair short and had very overt masculine features. Ricky had called Andrew pretty—had called Larkin pretty, for that matter. The adjective never suited Larkin, he felt. He'd been called classically handsome, which he felt was code for "you don't look like others," but not pretty, not unless it was meant as an insult. Although Doyle had said so, and while he'd been joking, it'd still felt… sincere.

Anyway. Pretty did not suit Andrew. So it wasn't a matter of the perpetrator transitioning in his taste. Andrew's death was necessary to hide the killer's secret.

Larkin adjusted Jessica's photos. Nathan's hot dog stand was summer. Outside the theater, Andrew had been wearing a coat. Then the apartment perhaps a month or two later. Andrew's nose wasn't broken yet in any of them. Jessica had said that happened after they became roommates. Before graduating college, to be precise. Before meeting the jewelry designer who was, in theory, Andrew's last romantic interest and by default a person of interest.

Larkin looked at Doyle again. Still sketching away.

He still couldn't make complete sense of the nonfatal attacks. The ME suggested domestic assault. Doyle had too. And in the beginning, it had made sense: abuse that'd gone too far and then having to hide the body. But now? With the addition of the three victims earlier in the decade, also left in parks, also with death masks of a sort? It wasn't simple IPV anymore. That wasn't to say Andrew couldn't have been an abuse victim too….

Perhaps the abuser and the killer were two different people and Andrew had been a very, very unlucky young man. Although, Jessica had insisted that Andrew's nose was broken before meeting the jewelry designer, which would suggest he hadn't been behind the assaults. She could have been wrong, though. It was twenty-two years ago, and she couldn't remember the pseudoboyfriend's name, so perhaps her memory of the timeline was off too. After all, only one person on this case had a nearly infallible memory, and it hadn't been Jessica Lopez.

His cell buzzed with an incoming call at 8:32 at night.

Larkin picked it up.

Noah Rider.

Larkin stared at the name. He nearly let it go to voicemail. But he knew Noah. His husband would call his desk next. Larkin tapped Accept, put the phone to his ear, and asked quietly, "What is it."

"Wow, does everyone get that welcoming or just me?"

"I'm working. What do you need."

"I've been texting you all day—"

"I've been working all day," Larkin cut in. Never mind the morning meltdown or foot pursuit of an armed suspect or the rest of the fuckery that'd made up his Tuesday. Noah wouldn't care about any of that.

"Well, you had time to read the messages."

Larkin planted an elbow on the desktop, covered his eyes with his hand, and murmured, "I have to go."

"When are you coming home? It's already eight thirty."

"I don't know."

"*Everett*." And the way Noah said *Everett*, it was like he'd learned how to weaponize Larkin's name, use it against him.

It made Larkin cringe. Made him despise a name he'd once quite liked.

Evie.

Larkin shook his head a little and said, "I'm working a big case, Noah. I don't know when I'm coming home."

"That's great. Our marriage is at a crossroads, but some dead guy is more impor—"

Larkin tapped End and set his phone down. He raised his head in time to see Doyle stand from his chair, eyeing Larkin in open and honest concern. But Doyle didn't say anything, because it wasn't his business and he knew that, respected that. He took his two sketches on a walk to the copy room, which could be found easily without directions—just follow the sound of mechanics and the smell of toner.

Aiko Miyamoto, phone to her ear, spun in her chair to watch Doyle pass her desk and vanish into the closet-sized room. She shuffled her feet, picked up her cell, and then a moment later, Larkin's phone had a text notification.

He opened the app. Miyamoto had sent him a peach emoji. He looked across the bullpen with a frown.

Miyamoto waggled her eyebrows before whoever had her on hold finally answered and she began talking into the receiver.

Larkin's cell buzzed with another incoming call, and this time, he really was going to send Noah to voicemail. He didn't have the time for this—but there was no name on the ID, only a local number. He answered with a brisk, "Detective Larkin."

"Detective, this is Camila Garcia… Marco's mother."

Larkin's mental Rolodex immediately spun to a different case.

Marco Garcia. Pushed in front of an incoming Q train. Tunnel vision. No drugs. Newly reopened twenty-three-year-old cold case. Camila Garcia had refused all attempts at communication thus far.

"Mrs. Garcia. Thank you for calling."

"You were extremely persistent. I thought, if I didn't call you, eventually you'd show up at the salon while I was getting my hair done."

Bit of an exaggeration, Larkin thought with a frown. "I would like to take some time to speak in person."

"Well…." Camila clearly wasn't so keen on that. "Everything I know I told the cops twenty-three years ago. There's nothing new to add."

"I understand. But with all due respect to Detective Kent before me, I'm not him."

"Marco wasn't into drugs." She was firm.

"I agree," Larkin answered. "And so I have different questions to ask, different avenues I'd like to explore. I understand that it's difficult to dredge these memories back up—"

"No, detective. *No.*" Camila laughed a little bitterly, brokenly. "When I wake up, I'm already thinking of Marco. I go shopping and see those Debbie cakes he ate as a boy. I walk my neighborhood and can point out where he scraped his knee riding his bike, the rosebush I made him and his prom date pose in front of for pictures, the exact spot he found a kitten in a cardboard box and took it home because his heart was so big. There is nothing to dredge up, you see. Marco is always with me. My heart is always broken."

Larkin was silent.

Camila sighed, and that single sound conveyed everything. She was certain no one understood this helplessness, this loss, this perpetual unknown, and Larkin had talked a good game, but he was like all the other cops who'd let her down before.

"I know your loss, Mrs. Garcia."

"Do you?" But it was an absent reply. A question she did not expect an answer to.

"Yes. For eighteen years. It never goes away."

Camila's voice hitched.

"I can't promise you that by closing Marco's case, you'll feel any sense of relief. A lot of people don't. I wouldn't."

"Then why bother?"

"Because Marco deserves to be remembered and no one should mourn alone."

Camila began to cry.

Larkin let her.

Doyle returned from the copy room.

Finally, between sniffles and shaky breaths, Camila asked, "Detective?"

"Yes."

"Does anyone mourn with you?"

Larkin grew cold, as if all the blood in his body suddenly stopped pumping. His throat tightened, like a physical barrier had been erected to protect him. *Stop speaking*. He hated this. He hated playing the good cop. No matter how beneficial it could be for a case. "No," he answered, and Larkin could feel Doyle watching him again.

"What was their name?"

Larkin's chin quivered. His eyes stung. He said roughly, "Patrick."

"I'll say a prayer for Patrick."

He raised his head up, stared at the acoustic tiles in the ceiling, and said nothing.

After the seconds stretched into a minute, Camila said, more calmly, "I can see you tomorrow. I'm leaving in the afternoon for California. My sister. Chemo. So… in the morning?"

Larkin hastily said, "Yes. Tomorrow morning works. Nine o'clock. Thank you, Mrs. Garcia." He ended the call, pushed back from the desk, stood, and rolled his shoulders while making a circuit around the bullpen. He needed to move, to shake off the conversation, to tamp down the need to swallow a dozen Xanax and go lie down in the middle of the road.

Larkin walked down the hall toward the Fuck It, turned when he reached the door, then returned to the bullpen. He studied Doyle from across the room—he was still standing, now speaking on Baker's phone and gesturing absently with one hand throughout the conversation. Doyle smiled at something said, laughed, and that smoky baritone had a way of seeping into every nook and cranny of the second floor.

By the time Larkin returned to his desk, Doyle was hanging up the phone. "Your flirting is palpable, Doyle."

"I needed a favor."

Larkin grunted.

Doyle motioned him closer. "Public relations bumped us from the slush pile, so these should be on the app by tomorrow morning." He pointed to the sketches on the desk.

Larkin stared at the images. The unknown person of interest was handsome in his youth, but the aged interpretation suggested a wiser, more dignified man. "He'd be forty-five, right?"

Doyle murmured agreement. "I know he has a daddy vibe going on here, but Jessica had been adamant that he looked older, which of course can, in part, be how an individual acts or presents themselves, but I did want to make some of that physical."

Larkin looked up. "How old are you."

"I say *daddy* and you immediately ask how old I am?"

"*What?* No. I didn't mean—"

Doyle crossed his arms. He was grinning so hard, his face looked about ready to split in two. "Thirty-nine."

Larkin nodded. His cheeks were burning. He looked at the sketch a second time.

Doyle shifted, got closer, and whispered, "Is that a good age?"

"Jesus Christ." Larkin returned to his own desk as Doyle laughed again.

It was 10:41 p.m. when the bullpen emptied for the night.

Ulmer had dropped a printout on Larkin's desk as he passed by it on the way to the stairs. A request had been submitted to Missing Persons to search their archives for any women that fit the dates or known aliases Larkin had, which they'd acknowledged but provided no timeline on the turnaround. A similar request had been sent to Homicide, with the added notation of these women being dumped in Tompkins Square Park. Homicide had not yet acknowledged the inquiry.

Thugs, Larkin thought as he finished scanning the document.

"Hey."

Larkin looked to his left.

Doyle was pulling his suit coat on, obscuring his shoulder holster. He picked up his portfolio bag while asking, "Want to grab something to eat?"

Larkin glanced at his watch. Yes. He hadn't eaten since that morning and still had a headache thumping behind his left eye.

"There's some great Chinese about a block from my place," Doyle continued. "Best egg rolls you've ever had."

Larkin considered the invitation. He didn't want to go home. Wasn't ready to handle whatever inevitable fallout was waiting for him there. But a look around the bullpen told him, if not home with Noah, he'd be sitting in the precinct alone. And for the first time in… he honestly couldn't remember how long, the prospect of *alone* held little appeal. It was disconcerting how quickly Doyle's presence had become routine to Larkin's professional life. He seemed to complement Larkin's job, despite how drastically different their careers were, and he was smart and quick and… just sort of a pleasure to be in the general vicinity of.

"I don't want to impose," Larkin answered.

"It's not imposing if I offered, is it?"

"I suppose not."

Doyle tilted his head in the direction of the stairs.

Larkin quickly collected his casework, returned it all to its accordion folder, put on his suit coat, and followed Doyle to the first floor.

CHAPTER FOURTEEN

Doyle lived on the edge of the Village—West Thirteenth between Seventh and Eighth—in a walk-up painted fire-engine red. Warm tungsten orange glowed in the windows of residents still awake at eleven o'clock on a Tuesday, and the lamps outlined the shape of the fire escape zigzagging all the way up to the fifth floor.

Larkin had asked if he should follow, but Doyle suggested they take his Audi and he'd hop the subway uptown the next morning. While Larkin drove down Lexington, Doyle had called in a takeout order to the restaurant, from a menu he knew by heart, apparently. Sweet-and-sour chicken, lo mein, dumplings, and both egg rolls and vegetable spring rolls. And when they'd reached Doyle's neighborhood, he instructed Larkin on where to park, got out of the car, and said he'd run to the end of the block to pick up dinner and would be right back.

Larkin sat behind the wheel, watching Doyle disappear and reappear in the pools of light cast off by the overhead streetlamps. He checked his phone. No more texts or calls from Noah since he'd hung up on his husband midsentence. Larkin considered phoning, telling Noah he was done with work for the night but was grabbing a quick bite with a colleague before heading home.

A bite at Doyle's apartment, not a restaurant.

But why should it matter where they ate? Larkin had admitted to Doyle just that morning that he sometimes struggled with sensory overload, that it kicked compulsive tendencies into overdrive. And it'd been a long day of *exactly* that. The fact that Doyle suggested somewhere private, quiet, and low-key was really the selling point to eating dinner at all. No competing conversations, bright overheads, or clangs and bangs from a working kitchen.

Not that Noah would see it that way.

"To hell with him." Larkin pulled his key from the ignition and climbed out of the black Audi. He tapped the alarm button, the chirp bouncing off the brick facades, and turned as Doyle came back from the corner. He held a paper bag in one arm and dug his keys out from his trouser pocket with his other hand. "Let me hold that." Larkin took the takeout.

"Thanks. Hope you don't mind hoofing it," Doyle said as he unlocked the front door and held it open. "I'm on the fourth floor."

"I live in a walk-up too," Larkin answered, following Doyle through the vestibule and to the stairs. After rounding the corner on the third floor and starting up the final flight, Larkin asked, "Have you lived here long."

"Hmm… about six years." Doyle stopped at 4A, unlocked it, and stepped inside. He flipped a switch on the wall, held the door with his foot, and took the bag back. "Come in."

Larkin entered the apartment, and the first description he had was: cozy. It was small, although clearly not an issue for someone who lived alone and who worked a lot. The left wall was exposed brick, with a small entertainment stand pushed up against it. Across from that was a couch, coffee table, and bookshelf—nothing particular about the brands or styles of furniture other than comfortable, Larkin thought. The kitchen was toward the end of the one room, fridge, counter, and sink all along the brick wall and a table for two in front of the big windows overlooking the street, although the curtains were drawn. Larkin turned around, and behind him and to the right were a pair of french doors that closed off a very small bedroom, visible through the glass, from the rest of the house. A final door not far from the bookshelf was probably the bathroom. It took an extra second for Larkin to acknowledge the almost fantastical sepia glow wasn't coming from the overhead light, but from all the fairy lights strung throughout the apartment.

"Sorry about the lights," Doyle was saying as if reading Larkin's mind. He put the bag on the kitchen counter, propped his portfolio case against the table, then said, "I can turn them off."

"No. It's okay."

"You sure?"

Larkin nodded. He took off his suit coat and glanced around for a place to set it. Beside the french doors was a wooden ladder—clearly it came with the apartment and provided access to the storage closet overhead of the bedroom entrance, but Doyle appeared to be using it as a coatrack instead. Larkin added to the pile.

Doyle was opening cupboards and taking out plates in the kitchen.

Larkin took a few steps deeper into the room. Doyle had a few framed paintings on the walls of cityscapes, a combination of moody and pensive and boundlessly colorful and joyful. Larkin didn't really know much about art, but he liked these a lot more than the generic landscapes Dr. Myers had on her walls. He stood in front of Doyle's bookshelf. A few fiction titles, but mostly he owned nonfiction. Art books—references, anatomical guides, history—a 2x3 black-framed photo was propped against the book spines. A girl—well, a toddler—her white-blonde hair in two pigtails, was holding up her paint-covered hands to show the camera.

Larkin glanced at Doyle standing at the counter, dishing the food.

He moved away from the bookshelf as Doyle turned and walked across the room with the plates. He set them down on the coffee table, clearly intending to sit at the couch, then quickly grabbed a few stray books, an open sudoku puzzle, which Larkin smiled at, a wireless game controller, and a second framed photo of the same blonde child out of the way. Doyle carried the handful to the bedroom, opened the door, and set the contents on his bed. He took off his suit coat on the way out and shoved it onto one of the ladder rungs without concern for wrinkles.

"*Oh*," he said suddenly, like something had only just occurred to him. Doyle stopped in front of the coffee table. "I don't drink. I, uh—sorry. I have water, Coke, tea—"

Larkin took a seat at the couch as he said, "Water's fine."

Doyle flashed a smile, a rather self-conscious one at that, and returned to the kitchen. He opened the fridge, and the door pointed in Larkin's direction, offering a view of yet another picture of the girl, a bit older, standing outside the steps of an apartment building and grinning from ear to ear. She wore a backpack on her shoulders and held a lunchbox with a unicorn on it.

Doyle shut the door and came back with a glass of ice water for Larkin and a can of Coke for himself. He took a seat and popped the top on his drink.

"Your niece is very cute."

"Hmm?"

Larkin glanced at Doyle, and for a microsecond, there was only confusion on Doyle's face. And then realization.

Then heartbreak. Taken aback, Larkin opened his mouth to apologize, although he didn't know what for, but Doyle spoke first.

"My daughter, actually. Abigail."

Larkin blinked a few times. He didn't need to do a double take of the apartment for proof of a child because he'd already catalogued and memorized everything lying out in the open. There were no toys, no books, no stuffed animals, certainly no separate bedroom for a child. There was absolutely zero evidence of a child in Doyle's life.

Doyle offered a very quiet, reflexive laugh at whatever he read on Larkin's face before picking up one of the forks and absently pushing around the lo mein noodles. "No, she doesn't live here. Abigail… passed away." He set the fork back down and put his hands on his knees, staring at an invisible spot on the bare bricks—at some long-ago memory. "About seven years ago." Doyle turned to Larkin and suddenly sounded panicked as he asked, "What is it?"

Larkin jerked his head and wiped his face with the heel of his hand. "I'm so sorry," he whispered. "I didn't—for you—to relive that." He got to his feet.

Doyle grabbed Larkin's wrist. "Hey. Come on." His thumb brushed the underbelly of Larkin's wrist in a profoundly intimate way before he gave a tug. "Please sit."

Larkin did.

Doyle let go and said, "I can talk about her. But I guess you'd have remembered it differently?"

"As if it'd just happened," Larkin explained, staring at his gold wingtips.

"I don't envy you," Doyle said quietly.

Larkin hastily wiped his face a second time before shaking his head. "Christ. I'm sorry. At work, all that… tragedy is laid out in black-and-white. They know, I know, we can broach the subject together. It's when I'm caught off guard, sometimes I forget not everyone… reacts the way I would." He finally looked at Doyle.

"A knee-jerk reaction to protect me?"

"I guess."

Doyle reached a hand out, caught himself, and returned it to his own knee. "It's okay. *I'm* okay."

Larkin rewound his conversation with Camila Garcia, pushed Play. *My heart is always broken.* Somehow, he doubted Doyle was at all okay.

"I adopted Abigail when she was six months old."

Larkin raised an eyebrow. "By yourself?"

Doyle smiled at the note of interest in Larkin's tone. "Yup. I really wanted to be a dad." He picked up one of the egg rolls and took a bite. In between the crunch of the fried food, he asked, "What about you and Noah? Any children?"

"No." Larkin stabbed some sweet-and-sour chicken with his fork and ate it.

"Don't want any?" Doyle pressed, polite but curious.

Larkin took another bite. "Noah does."

"But not you."

"I'm not parental material." Bitterly, Larkin added, "Just another thing we disagree on." He sipped his water. "You didn't invite me over to hear about how my marriage is falling apart."

"It's all right."

Larkin shook his head. "This must be why you're single."

"I'm single because all the hot guys are married," Doyle corrected as he put a half-eaten egg roll back on the plate. He laughed under his breath and then added, "I really was going to ask you out yesterday. Before I knew you were married, I mean."

Larkin shot him a disbelieving look. "I was an asshole."

Doyle hemmed. "Sort of. But I can spot the difference between sincere and fake assholery. It also helped that you're cute."

Larkin studied Doyle's relaxed and playful expression with a sudden and overwhelming sense of... melancholy.

Larkin had acquaintances.

He had colleagues.

He had a husband.

But he had no friends.

He had no partnership—no day to complement his night. Until now. He'd known Ira Doyle for all of two days and the other man saw, really saw, more of Larkin than Noah did. Saw what Larkin thought he hid so well, because he was odd, he was strange, he was broken, and people *hated* being exposed to that sort of pain. Doyle saw Everett Larkin and took him and all of his complications in stride.

And it broke Larkin's heart.

Broke his heart that he'd been begging for help, dying in front of Noah for a year, and the one who made Larkin eat, who hugged him, who gave that hair tie a tug to make sure he was *okay*, had been an absolutely gorgeous and kind man he wasn't married to.

Larkin took Doyle's face in one hand and kissed him. It was sudden, catching Doyle's parted lips in surprise, but the kiss between them was firm. Certain. Doyle brought his big hands up and cupped just under Larkin's jaw. He opened to Larkin's touch, and Doyle tasted like oil from the egg roll, sugar from the Coke, and something a little like perfection. Larkin slipped his tongue free and kissed Doyle's lips again, relishing the burn of whiskers against his own skin. He leaned back, still holding Doyle's face with one hand. Doyle took a shaky breath, his hands sliding down to rest on Larkin's shoulders.

They stared at each other.

Larkin moved in for a second kiss.

"Wait," Doyle said. He swallowed and his Adam's apple bobbed. "Noah."

Larkin gripped Doyle tighter, rubbed the pad of his thumb against Doyle's stubble, then released him. He stood and took a step around the coffee table. "I have to go."

Doyle jumped to his feet. "Evie, hang on—"

But Larkin opened the front door and left.

CHAPTER FIFTEEN

The kiss had been a catalyst.

It was past one in the morning—Larkin had been sitting on the couch for over two hours in absolute silence, suit coat forgotten at Doyle's, shoulder holster still buckled to his body. He'd turned a lamp on when he'd arrived home, and the light glinted along the polished curve of his wedding band, which sat on the coffee table. Larkin stared at it.

How much did a wedding ring weigh? A few grams, Larkin thought. Not an ounce. Not even half an ounce. More like an eighth. So why did something so delicate feel like an anchor dragging him down, down, down into parts unknown?

Because Larkin was having domestic troubles.

Because his marriage was falling apart.

Because he was dying.

The truth was right there. Out in the open. No way to ignore it anymore.

Larkin's professional career dealt with damaged relationships every day. Abuse led to unhealthy complications with lust, money, and the pursuit of power. This in turn led to death. Every time.

And the victim was always the last to know.

Funny how Larkin knew this—knew all of this—and yet here he was, the last person in the room to realize his relationship had grown toxic as fuck, and he'd, maybe years ago, fallen out of love with Noah.

Maybe shouldn't have ever gotten married.

Maybe should have ended things within the first two years of dating after he sensed Noah's inability to respect Larkin's job commitments or his profound insecurity when Larkin was around other men or his frustration when Larkin didn't spend his free time solely with him.

Damn.

It was a hell of an epiphany. One that hurt a lot.

The bedroom door opened.

Larkin didn't look up.

"Everett?" Noah sounded sleepy. "When'd you get home? It's the middle of the night. Come to—"

Larkin stood and said, like a man who'd finally given up, "I kissed Doyle."

A beat.

Noah asked, "What?"

"Ira Doyle. I kissed him."

"I heard that part."

"I'd have kissed him again if he let me."

Noah said nothing for a long time, his chest heaving in silent rage. Then, as if a part of him managed to be mindful of the time and the fact that they had neighbors above, below, and to the side, Noah hissed, "What the *fuck*, Everett? You—you won't fuck me, but the first chance you get at a new face in the precinct, your dick works again?"

"You're not listening, as usual."

"The hell I'm not!"

Larkin closed his eyes.

Doyle's smile as Larkin corrected the button on his vest.

Sitting together on the back of the ambulance, Doyle tugging the hair tie.

Doyle's whiskey voice reduced to a teasing whisper in Larkin's ear, followed by his larger-than-life laugh.

Being told, "Love and sex can only be used for good."

So much sensory stimulation, and yet, it all had felt right. Like coming home after being lost in the dark woods for a very, very long time.

Larkin looked at Noah—his face red, eyes too bright. "I'm sorry."

"You're not forgiven!"

"No. I'm sorry that we've been unhappy for so long. I'm sorry I didn't see the warning signs sooner. I'm sorry we let it get to this point, because it's going to hurt so much more. But I'm not sorry I kissed him."

Tears spilled down Noah's cheeks, and he asked, "What the fuck are you talking about? Y-you're… are you leaving me? Everett. You just met him! You're throwing away everything we have for a bit of ass?"

Larkin pinched the bridge of his nose and shook his head. "I hope he'll be my friend. I could really use one right now."

"Are you drunk? Or high?"

"No."

"Did you hit your goddamn head? You're out of your mind." Noah wasn't crying anymore. He was incensed. "No, you're fucking insane, is what you are. The years of shit I've had to put up with, and this is the thanks I get?"

Ah. There it was.

People don't want to know.

But I do.

Of course Doyle did. He'd been there. Been to the bottom and kept digging deeper into that darkness. He knew profound loneliness, because what the fuck had people said to a parent mourning a child? They'd said nothing, Larkin was sure. They'd pulled away. Left Doyle devastated and alone. People hadn't wanted to know about Abigail, just like they didn't want to know about Patrick.

Doyle wasn't okay. Larkin understood that now, because he used those same coping tricks. But Doyle had also seen the light. He wasn't afraid of the extremes, of feeling happiness, of being *alive*. He'd been standing in that deep dark hole and thought to look up.

And that was the kind of man Larkin wanted in his life— in whatever capacity Doyle was willing to share himself.

"He was here when I got in." That voice belonged to Porter. "I figure he was working late. Let him sleep a few more minutes—before Connor shows up."

Larkin smelled Doyle before he heard him. Neroli and sandalwood and cardamon.

"Evie?" Fingers touched the back of his head, combing his ash-blond hair into place.

Larkin rolled his chair backward with the momentum of raising his head from the desk. He winced as everything in his back, shoulders, and neck audibly cracked. He looked up, muttering, "Ouch."

Doyle stood in front of his desk, balancing a blue-and-white We Are Happy To Serve You coffee cup and foil-wrapped breakfast sandwich in his other hand. His brows rose, but he set the drink and food where Larkin's head had been just a second before and said, "Good morning."

Larkin stared at the offering. The coffee smelled amazing. The egg and cheese even better. He looked at Doyle again, who smiled lopsidedly—uncertainly, even. Larkin opened the bottom drawer of his desk, removed a small pouch he'd learned after the fact was intended for cosmetics, but really was the perfect size for the handful of travel toiletries he kept on standby, and went downstairs without a word. He washed his face and underarms at the bathroom sink, slapped on fresh deodorant, brushed his teeth, and fixed his hair the best he could without a shower and product.

He returned to the second floor feeling a bit more coherent, put the toiletries away, then noticed that his forgotten suit coat from last night was draped over the back of his chair. He ignored Doyle standing beside Porter's desk, laughing with the older detective and slowly winning over yet another member of Cold Cases with that Academy Award smile. Larkin walked all the way to the opposite end of the bullpen, down the hall with the two interview rooms, and pushed open the door to the Fuck It. He didn't bother with the overheads—watery gray light was trickling in from the window opposite him. Larkin quietly shut the door, took a step to the right, and leaned against the wall. Big fat drops of rain started to splatter the glass. Another storm. He closed his eyes.

Larkin counted to eighty-seven before there was a quiet knock on the door. He glanced to his left as it opened and Doyle stepped inside. "Hi."

"Hey." Doyle shut the door. He took a few steps and sat on the wobbly desk, facing Larkin. He had his long legs stretched out, his hands planted on the desktop at his sides, assuming that now-familiar and welcome pose. "You slept here?"

"It wasn't my intention."

Doyle nodded, waited. No three-piece suit today, which was a real shame. More tweed, in an earthy green that would have washed out Larkin's fair coloring, but suited Doyle surprisingly well.

"I told Noah. About last night."

Again, Doyle nodded, but a cloud of shame darkened his features and lingered in his expression. "I'm sorry. I shouldn't have said any of those things—"

"Please don't apologize. You did nothing wrong."

Doyle was staring at his shoes. "Was Noah upset?"

"I left him."

Doyle's head jerked so quickly, he probably suffered whiplash. "*What*?" He stood, once again that head taller than Larkin. "Oh my God. I didn't—let me talk to him."

Larkin shook his head. "No."

"Larkin—"

"This was a very long time coming." He slid his hands into his trouser pockets and leaned his head back. "I struggled for a long time with the concept of love languages," he said into the quiet. "You know these?"

"Affirmation, quality time, service, gifts, touch."

Larkin nodded. "I'm garbage at all of that. My words are stilted. I like to be by myself. I never know what sort of service wouldn't feel intrusive, and buying gifts is an art unto itself. But I've struggled with touch since—" The words cut off sharply, and Larkin instead raised his hand and tapped the side of his head. "But afterward, when the HSAM started, for lack of better description, I thought: remembrance is the greatest act of love there is. Because… because no one is truly dead and gone, so long as *someone* remembers them."

Doyle touched Larkin's arm and squeezed.

Larkin smiled a little as he said, "And *your* language is touch."

Doyle looked like a kid who was caught red-handed in the cookie jar. "Sorry." A nervous laugh. "I've definitely been accused of being too touchy-feely with people."

"You said something the morning we met," Larkin

continued. "'I can give John Doe back his identity so someone can remember him.' I thought, how incredible it was to meet someone who understood the gravity of remembrance. How incredible it was that you spoke my language, even if it's not your own. And when you hugged me, it was like a shock from a defibrillator. I haven't been touched in a way that's comfortable for me in a long time. Three years, I calculated. Most of my marriage. What marriage is worth holding on to if your partner is resentful of the memories most important to you and can't touch you without wanting something more from it?" Larkin took a breath and wiped a stray tear with the pad of his thumb. "My life feels like wreckage I've only just woken to and I don't even know where to start picking it up… but… whether we only interact as professionals or maybe friends or… *something*… I think you're someone I would be very lucky to continue knowing."

Doyle smiled from ear to ear. "I'd like that too. And I'm not saying this to rush you, because I understand you've got a lot to deal with now, but if someday you want to have that date, let me know?"

Larkin took Doyle's hand to draw him closer, and Doyle leaned down into the hug. Larkin gripped the back of his shirt collar for a minute, soaking up Doyle's warmth, and the promise his embrace spoke: I won't forget you. There was a joy in knowing that if he were to die tomorrow, *someone* would remember Larkin, and fondly. Doyle began to pull back, but Larkin cupped the back of his head and pulled him down into a kiss. Nothing sexual, but not so light as to suggest either of them were standing with feet firmly planted in the friend zone.

Doyle brushed his nose against Larkin's, kissed him again, very lightly, then whispered, "Thank God you brushed your teeth."

Larkin rolled his eyes and gave Doyle a firm shove to the chest as his partner started laughing.

Doyle unbuttoned his cuffs and rolled the sleeves back in what was apparently most comfortable for him if he were to be stuck in a suit for twelve hours a day, and said, "You seem okay right now."

"A combination of exhaustion, relief, and positive associations," Larkin explained. In answer to Doyle's curious expression, he tapped his own lips, referring to their kiss. "But I'll hit a wall once I'm off the clock and don't have work to distract me."

"You can talk to me," Doyle offered. "If you need to vent. All right?"

"All right."

"*Larkin*!" came Miyamoto's muffled shout from the bullpen. She was the only member of the Squad to call him by his real name.

Larkin adjusted his tie, smoothed his shirt, and opened the door. "What."

She stood, tall and thin with a pixie haircut, in the archway of the hall, jutting a thumb over her shoulder. "A Roger Hunt is here to see you."

Larkin spun his Rolodex but came up with nothing. "I don't know a Roger Hunt."

"Something about Local4Locals—that motherfucking piece-of-shit vigilante app."

Larkin drew himself up straighter, looked into the room at Doyle, then asked, "Where is he."

"The lobby." Miyamoto craned her neck. "Who's in there with you?"

"No one."

"Liar. Is it that artist guy? I know you're married, Larkin, but there's no harm in looking. I'd eat a three-course meal off his ass."

Doyle stepped out of the room and joined them in the

hall. "Hey."

"Oh!" she said, surprised. "Hello. Aiko Miyamoto." She offered a hand.

"Ira Doyle."

"I don't regret what I said," Miyamoto stated. "You've got a smashing ass."

"Ah… thank you."

Larkin glanced up. There was definitely a bit of color under Doyle's stubble. Maybe Doyle had met his flirtatious match in Miyamoto. Or a future HR harassment case. It was difficult to tell. Larkin said to Miyamoto, "Could you put Roger Hunt in Interview One for me."

CHAPTER SIXTEEN

At 7:31 a.m., the coffee was lukewarm and the egg and cheese cold, but the breakfast Doyle had grabbed for Larkin on his way in had done wonders to better his mood. It was like that anchor that'd been dragging him down into the crushing, cold blackness of the ocean had finally slipped free of his body and he was kicking upward, the very distant ball of sunlight sparkling overhead, promising warmth and light and oxygen as long as Larkin didn't stop swimming.

He knew this wasn't the end of his troubles with Noah. In fact, it was going to be the beginning of something new and likely awful. But as Larkin entered the interview room with the pressure and taste of Doyle's mouth still on his own, he felt practically… jovial.

Until he saw the man sitting at the table.

"You're not Roger Hunt," Larkin said from where he stood in the doorway.

Not-Roger was practically a kid. Twenty, tops, with a mop of curly brown hair, big doe eyes, a few necklaces, rings on nearly each finger, and piercings. Lots of piercings. Like a pin cushion.

"No shit, Sherlock," he said with an eye roll and attitude that so many of the filthy rich, entitled, just-moved-to-Brooklyn sort possessed.

"Who are you."

"Brian."

"Brian. Why did you say you were Roger Hunt."

That eye roll again. "I told the cop downstairs I *worked* for Roger Hunt. Great to know my taxes pay the salaries of people with listening problems."

"You don't pay taxes. Your parents still claim you as a dependent."

Brian's jaw dropped a little, and he made an offended snort that confirmed Larkin was correct. "I didn't come here to be insulted."

"It's a statement of fact—"

"Okay," Doyle interrupted. He slipped past Larkin and stepped inside the room. "Brian. Detectives Doyle and Larkin. Are you here about the police sketches?"

Brian was quiet, and his snobbish expression softened at Doyle's friendly tone. He picked up his phone from the tabletop, flicked through some open apps, then held it up to display the home page of Local4Locals. "This is my boss, Roger. He called me this morning—*so upset*, mind you—because his face is on a wanted poster."

"It's a composite sketch of someone who is essentially a missing person," Larkin corrected. "Nowhere does it say *wanted*."

Brian actually raised his hand like he was *not* going to communicate further with Larkin. "Do you know how embarrassing this is for him? Roger told me to come sort this out. He's super busy, and this is the last thing he needs before a show."

"Unfortunately this isn't something you can handle for

him," Doyle said, polite but insistent. "We need to speak with Mr. Hunt."

"About *what*?" Brian asked, indignant tone seeping back into his words. "I'm his personal assistant. His life is my life."

Doyle smiled and simply reiterated. "We need to speak with Mr. Hunt."

Brian groaned, loudly. "He's going to *freak out*." But he placed a call and put his cell to his ear.

"Freak out," Doyle repeated amusedly, crossing his arms and leaning against the wall.

"I'm about to freak out," Larkin said dryly, resting his shoulder on the doorjamb.

Brian gave them both a look and then said into the phone, "Hey. The cops won't talk to me. They keep saying… … Yeah, I told them that. They don't care." He pointedly ignored Larkin, stared at Doyle, and added to the conversation, "*Typical*."

"Your people skills are proving to not be infallible," Larkin said.

Doyle hummed in agreement. "I never claimed I was God."

"That's good, because you've called me Jesus a few times, and if you were God, that'd make everything a bit awkward."

"I'll tell them. Okay, bye." Brian drew out the *bye* as if it had four or five extra *e*'s. He stood from the table and unzipped the shimmery gold fanny pack he wore. He removed a business card and offered it to Doyle.

Doyle passed it to Larkin without looking at it.

Larkin stared at it, turned it over, then looked up. "Forges. Beauteous. Distinction. R. Hunt."

"He said he can spare you a few minutes if you show up before three o'clock today. After that is impossible—he'll be crazy with final preparations for the show."

"What show?" Doyle asked.

Brian gave Doyle a pouty face, like he just felt *so terrible* for how utterly naïve this poor cop was. "Roger is one of the world's premiere designers of men's jewelry. It's an untapped market, you know. Jewelry enhances beauty, symbolizes power, wealth, status…." He tucked a bit of curl behind one ear while looking both detectives up and down. "You boys would certainly benefit."

Larkin met Doyle's look, and he was certain his own expression mirrored that of Doyle's skepticism. He held up the business card and said to Brian, "There's no telephone number. No email. No physical address. Does Mr. Hunt conduct his business via telepathy."

"Oh my God," Brian answered with another one of those scoffs, like these police didn't understand *anything*, up to and including fancy business cards. He snatched the card, dug a pen out of his pack, and scribbled on the back.

"Hubris syndrome," Doyle said quietly.

Larkin made a sound of agreement, then took the card when Brian held it out a second time. The studio space Roger Hunt could be found at was located in Williamsburg. "Of course," he muttered.

Larkin stood at the banister that ran behind his and out-of-office Baker's desks in the bullpen, adding his appointment with Roger Hunt to his phone's calendar, then leaning over to watch Brian reach the ground floor and see himself out the precinct door.

"Jewelry designer," Doyle was saying. "At least we can be certain, beyond a reasonable doubt, this Roger Hunt is the right guy."

Larkin's desk phone rang. He turned, picked up the receiver, and said, "Detective Larkin."

"Everett Larkin?"

"Speaking."

"Holly Cooper with *The City*," she said in a rush, the way all journalists introduced themselves and kept talking, perhaps out of a well-founded fear they'd be hung up on. "I'll get right to the point: last October you were involved in a cold case investigation of a dozen sex workers found dead in the Ramble during the late '90s and later again in—"

"Incorrect. I was looking into the unsolved murder of a woman named Daisy O'Callaghan, and a pair of private citizens and wannabe sleuths stumbled their way into the investigation and eventual arrest, which was made by another department."

Holly was momentarily taken aback but recovered quick enough. "But is it true you're now investigating the murder of three, possibly four, sex workers from the '90s in an unrelated case?"

"Where did you hear this," Larkin asked.

"I have my sources, Detective," Holly said with cool confidence. "Can you comment on the ongoing investigation related to the crime scene at Madison Square Park on March 30 and the shooting in Alphabet City on March 31?"

"No," Larkin said. He hung up the phone.

"Who was that?" Doyle asked.

"Press." Larkin glanced at him. "She knew about the victims in the Polaroids."

"That was kept in-house."

"I know." Larkin stared across the bullpen at Ulmer's empty desk. He picked up his phone again, dialed out, and put it to his ear.

"Detective Bosman" came the answer on the second ring.

"Bosman, it's Larkin. Who did you speak to."

"About what?" Bosman asked, his tone that of genuine confusion.

"The Polaroids from Ricky's apartment."

"Besides you and Detective Doyle?"

"Obviously."

"No one beyond confirming with CSU that they didn't find any other Polaroids in the apartment. Which I was going to actually call you about this morning… are we circling back to your 'big cat, gonna attack' attitude?"

"I just got off the phone with a journalist from *The City* who had details of this case."

"*Shit.*" Bosman was quiet for a minute, then came back on the line, saying, "It sure as fuck didn't come from me. I made third-grade six months ago. If a first-grade detective tells me to keep my mouth shut, that's what I'm going to do. Whether or not I like them."

Bosman's words rang true to Larkin. He shot Ulmer's desk a second look before saying, "I believe you."

"Well, there's that," Bosman said with only a hint of sarcasm. "What do you want me to do?"

"Get real good at saying 'no comment.'" Larkin opened the top accordion folder from his stack and removed the photographs from last night. He aligned them with his free hand, saying, "Tell me about the apartment."

"No Polaroids, like I said. No masks either. They've taken all of the kitchen knives in as evidence to test—"

"Not necessary," Larkin interrupted. "None of the victims were stabbed. Photographic and autopsy evidence suggests extreme blunt-force trauma."

"But shouldn't we get them checked out just in case?"

"There is no discernable reason to ask the department to cover unnecessary expenditures and inundate the labs when their time and resources can be put to other cases."

"You've made your point. I'll check with CSU about any potential nonbladed weapons at the scene."

"It won't be there, but go ahead."

"How the fuck does Doyle put up with you?" Bosman asked.

Larkin glanced at Doyle, who was watching and patiently waiting to be filled in. "I don't know," he answered truthfully.

Larkin returned his attention to the Polaroids. Bosman was talking, but Larkin tuned his staticky voice out as he brought the evidence bag up and studied the photos. Brow furrowed, Larkin wedged the phone between his ear and shoulder, opened a desk drawer, and removed a magnifying glass. He raised it to the Polaroids and studied the background all three victims seemed to share—to have in common.

The psychology of place. He had explained to Lieutenant Connor this factor's importance, but then last night, with everything that'd happened.... He'd been admittedly distracted.

Where did the perpetrator hunt and why? What was it about their chosen region that felt safe? He would be familiar with the neighborhood these women came from. He would know where there was ample hiding so he had the time to kill and construct his death mask. No. No that wasn't correct. He wouldn't have done this out in the open. His mask-making was art. It required time, patience, a dedicated workspace.

And with those deaths that'd happened in the Ramble at almost the same time, like Miss Holly Cooper of *The City* said, he'd shy away from Central Park. Those stomping grounds belonged to someone else. Those sex workers belonged to another monster that'd been prowling New York.

Simone, Baby, Nadia.

Larkin had made, at the time, a reasonable assumption that those were street names. But he couldn't imagine every john wanted to know a girl's name, fake or not, before getting down to business. And it struck him as even more off that *Ricky* would have those names. But there was another profession in the '90s that revolved around false identities being publicly advertised, that was deeply frowned upon by society, and could still prove dangerous to the workers, depending on the venue they found themselves in.

"They're all stage names—you're aware of that, right?" That's what Connor had said.

These women had been working as strippers.

The backdrop of the Polaroids was white. Off-white. No, that was a shadow naturally produced by a concave shape. Like a bowl. And there, near the top right, was a nick. Something small and unforgettable, but as unique as a fingerprint.

"Are you even listening to me?" Bosman asked.

Larkin blinked. "Hold on, Bosman." He turned and thrust the bag and glass at Doyle. "What are the women lying on?"

Doyle took the offerings and looked at the pictures. "Table? Tiled floor?"

"No."

"Why don't you just tell me?"

Larkin lowered the phone from his ear and pointed with the receiver. "You're an artist. Look at the shadow."

"I'm going to pretend you said *please*," Doyle murmured without looking up. But then Larkin watched realization dawn in the way Doyle raised his eyebrows. "It's a tub. A clawfoot, maybe, based on the shape."

Larkin smiled when Doyle met his eyes. He raised the phone and asked, "Did CSU get pictures of Ricky's bathroom."

"Uh, yeah, I got them here somewhere. I was going to send you everything—"

"Does Ricky have a clawfoot tub."

"Hang on, Christ… there's, like, three hundred photos to sift through."

"Sift faster."

Bosman swore again, and the clicking of his computer mouse was a constant undercurrent. "I thought you Cold Case guys didn't have to worry about the first forty-eight?"

"We don't. But I'm close to something."

"Yeah? Based on what?"

"Instinct."

Bosman clicked a few more times and then said, "Here we are. What a dumpster fire. Okay, yes, he's got a once-blue now mostly rusted old-fashioned tub."

"The head—top right," Larkin continued. "Is there any kind of nick or gouge in the porcelain."

"Yeah. Hard to say how big; CSU didn't include a scale."

"No. They'd have no reason to."

"Want to tell me what's going on? I thought you said Ricky didn't kill anyone."

"He didn't," Larkin answered. "But he might very well have been complicit in the murders. I believe his apartment was the safe house that allowed the perpetrator the time needed to construct his masks."

"But there's no—"

Line two on Larkin's phone began blinking. "I'll call you later," Larkin said before pushing the phone hook and then tapping line two. "Detective Larkin."

"Detective Larkin, my name is Joe Sinclair. I'm a reporter from *Out in NYC*. We'd like to do a piece on you and the cold case investigation about the body found in Madison Square Park. We understand that he was a young gay man, and you yourself identify as a gay man—"

Larkin ground his molars, his left hand clenching unconsciously into a fist that he had to shake out when his fingernails bit into his palm. "Mr. Sinclair, my homosexuality is not what makes me a good detective."

Porter spun in his chair to stare at Larkin.

"Er—no, I mean, of course not. But we're always looking for members of the community to elevate."

"Which is perfectly reasonable, given that minority groups, by our very nature, are forced to be our own champions. However, are you looking to interview me because I'm a fucking fantastic detective with a track record to prove it, who is also gay, or do you want to interview me because I'm gay. Because being gay does not qualify me to be particularly good at any one thing. Nor does it make me a pleasant person, as you have likely gathered from this conversation."

Doyle rubbed at his stubble and shook his head absently.

"Perhaps I've caught you at a bad time," Joe suggested.

"You haven't, I assure you. And regarding the investigation, no comment." Larkin hung up the phone, turned, and shouted over the banister, "Stop patching the press through to my goddamn phone!"

The phone rang again.

Doyle held a hand up and said, "I'll get this one." He grabbed the receiver before Larkin could. "Detective Larkin's desk." He listened, looked at Larkin, and repeated the message, "There's been a body dump at Madison Square Park."

CHAPTER SEVENTEEN

Traffic was backed up on Fifth Avenue due to the morning commute, and Larkin and Doyle didn't reach Madison until 8:49 a.m. It was still raining, but nothing like the storm on Monday that'd uprooted the crabapple tree and put Larkin on this head-first collision with Noah, with Doyle, with the ghost of Andrew Gorman. He parked the Audi on Twenty-Third Street, popped the trunk, and collected the spare umbrella for Doyle.

"I think it makes sense," Doyle was saying.

"Yes?" Larkin did too, but his line of deduction often lost people, and it honestly felt good to be backed up by someone who perhaps came to conclusions in a different way, but was as equally intelligent as himself.

"Yes," Doyle echoed, opening the borrowed umbrella before they started for the entrance of the park. "The city was already cracking down on the strip clubs in Times Square when I was a kid." He cast Larkin a teasing, sideways look. "Daddy has a few years on you."

"I hate you."

Doyle chuckled. "Anyway. Times Square was the

original den of prostitution, drugs, and decay. I think that's how one of the papers put it. But by the late '90s, most of those places were out of business. Something like three thousand performers were jobless."

"They'd move into any club they could find. They couldn't afford to be picky."

"And that's not to say there weren't women in the industry at the time who weren't content and empowered by their careers. Because there were. It just wasn't the norm," Doyle explained. "After all, if you've been giving lap dances for half a decade and suddenly find yourself unemployed, what's going to happen? Realistically, you're going to wind up giving more lap dances."

They each removed their badges and flashed ID to the uniformed officer standing at the yellow crime scene tape that cordoned off the fountain.

Doyle was still talking. "Most of the clubs these days are in Midtown—prime tourist real estate."

"I'm curious as to your extensive knowledge on the stripping industry."

Doyle stopped. His umbrella bumped Larkin's, and the gentle *thrum* of rain tapped on the plastic overhead. "I only mean, the odds of small, hole-in-the-wall joints existing along the Bowery, East Village, or Alphabet City that are no longer there today are pretty good. They could have very well been the clubs some of these girls moved on to, which would put them in the vicinity of Ricky's apartment, and by your account, our perpetrator's hunting grounds."

"Well, well, well, if it ain't the motherfuckin' Grim Reaper." Detective Ray O'Halloran strode toward them from the fountain. "Did you forget a body on your first pass? Don't worry, it happens. After all, you boys in Cold Cases aren't used to dealing with homicides in real time, are you?"

"No," Larkin admitted. "But I am quite adept at cleaning

up your messes after the fact."

O'Halloran's face colored, and it wasn't due to the chilly air. But whether he wasn't looking for a repeat of what happened the last time he'd insulted Larkin to his face, or O'Halloran simply didn't want a witness, he swallowed his pride and shot Doyle an irritated look. "And who the hell are you?"

"Ira Doyle. I'm with Forensic Artists."

O'Halloran snorted and laughed. He pointed at Doyle while saying to Larkin, "You brought Bob Ross as your backup, Grim?"

Doyle smiled, but it was calculated, cool—a man who had to fight for his title on the regular, even with Larkin. "Happy accidents aside, I'm a detective too."

"Maybe you can draw me a picture of your qualifications sometime."

Doyle's expression didn't waver. "I'd be happy to."

"Detective Doyle was able to put a face to and identify Monday's skeletal remains in less time it takes you to find your ass with a flashlight, O'Halloran," Larkin said dully. "Tell me why we're here."

That ruddy complexion was back, but O'Halloran only gripped the handle of his umbrella tighter, spit at Larkin's feet, then said, "I knew the vic. Well, no, I recognized her name: Danielle Moreno. Park employee called the body in when they opened at six this morning. When I got here, I checked the ID she had in her purse and the name niggled at me. I called it in, had it run, and sure enough, she's got a long history with Vice. Prostitution and drug-dealing at peep shows she worked at back in the '80s and '90s."

Larkin frowned a little. O'Halloran was in his midforties. The math wasn't adding up. Never mind he worked Homicide, not Vice. "Please expound."

O'Halloran cracked his jaw and seemed to struggle with

an inner demon. "You know Charlie? Charlie Stolle."

"Homicide detective, yes."

"Yeah, well, he came up through Vice, back in the day. This is his last year. Fucker's about three hundred years old. Anyway, we've started going through his caseload, you know, what to keep, what to toss to you jackals." O'Halloran paused again, shook his head, then finished with "He's been sitting on a dead stripper since '92. Natasha 'Nadia' Smirnova." Whatever O'Halloran saw on Larkin's face, he said, "Yeah. *That* Nadia. I saw the request come through from Ulmer last night. I was going to fucking ignore it because fuck you, Grim, but it bothered me. I knew I'd just come across that name recently, and it annoyed the piss out of me that you were now asking. It's not a common name, after all. Natasha was your '92 case. I'd done a cursory look at it a few weeks ago with Charlie."

"You said this woman," Larkin began, pointing at the fountain over O'Halloran's shoulder, "was involved in Vice. How is she connected to Natasha."

"Danielle Moreno was Natasha's roommate back then. She was the one to identify Natasha's body after she was found in Tompkins Square Park on April 23, 1992."

"They both worked as strippers?" Doyle asked.

O'Halloran nodded. "That's exactly right. Danielle's stage name was Bettie."

"Bettie," Larkin repeated, raising an eyebrow.

"Like Bettie Page, only with red hair," O'Halloran answered. "That was her schtick. At least, according to her records with Vice." He motioned them to follow as he led the way to the scene.

The fountain, a replica of its 1843 original, wasn't typically turned on until the warmer months, and thank God, Larkin thought, park officials were still holding off, despite that exceptionally warm week they'd had earlier in the month, which had sent sections of the park into early bloom. Rain was bad enough for evidence collection, but a body submerged in water all but promised no results. The fountain was surrounded by massive flower urns and an ornamental fence about waist-high. CSU was already down on the bare brick of the fountain, about two feet lower than the pathway. Larkin was fairly certain it was the same detective from Monday—Millett.

They stopped at the fence and peered down. Danielle Moreno's body was like a broken doll, having likely been tossed over the handrail without a second thought. She'd landed on her side, one arm flung out and partially obscuring her face, one leg twisted back in a pose seen only by professional ballerinas. Her long red hair was wet and plastered to bloated and discolored skin. She was nude from the waist up.

Doyle quickly closed his umbrella, passed it to Larkin, and called down to CSU about joining the scene.

"Not looking for an assistant, thank you." Yeah, that was Millett. Larkin recognized the dry tone, even if he couldn't discern anything about his person, once again due to the full-body PPE.

"Let me check one thing," Doyle said. "Before it gets washed away. If it's even still there."

Squatted beside the body and underneath another makeshift tent, Millett lowered his camera, sighed with enough exasperation that a cloud of white air puffed around his face, then motioned for Doyle with one hand. Doyle hoisted himself over the railing and jumped into the fountain. He accepted a pair of latex gloves from Millett, snapped them on, then crouched beside Danielle.

O'Halloran said, without looking away from the scene below, "I want you to be real with me, Grim. *This*… that request last night… Monday morning." Larkin could feel

O'Halloran turn to study his profile now. "They're all connected, aren't they?"

"I don't know," Larkin said automatically, Connor's threat to keep this on the down-low until they were ready ringing loud in his memory.

"You're full of shit."

Larkin cast O'Halloran a sideways glance but said nothing.

"I don't know who picked up those other cases—Simone and Baby. But I know none of them were ever linked to each other. It'd be common knowledge." O'Halloran worked his jaw again, another audible crack that suggested he held a considerable amount of stress there. "But tell me this: if Charlie hadn't sat on Natasha's case, would Danielle still be alive?"

Larkin considered O'Halloran for a long moment. He didn't like Ray. Didn't pretend to. And O'Halloran felt the exact same about him. But Larkin had to give the Homicide detective credit—he'd put together the scope of their situation very quickly. "Barring an act of God, yes, I believe she would be."

O'Halloran swore. He ran a freckled hand through his strawberry-blond hair. "That lazy fucker. This is turning into what I think it is, isn't it?"

Larkin said nothing.

"He's been roaming free for nearly thirty years?"

Again, Larkin said nothing, which really said everything.

O'Halloran studied the scene again. "Charlie's going to retire and leave the rest of us to clean up the mess he could have prevented if he'd done his fucking job. Goddamn cock-fucker."

"You Irish really do enjoy a good bit of blasphemy in the morning."

"I want you to find this sick bastard, Grim." O'Halloran turned to Larkin again. "And make Charlie eat dirt. Don't let him ride off into the sunset and let the rest of Homicide take the heat for a—" He didn't say *serial killer*, but the words existed between them like a blight.

"I need Natasha's case."

"It's still Charlie's. I don't have that authority."

"Then give me the case number. I need physical evidence to link these murders," Larkin explained. "I've got a man sitting in jail who didn't do it, but he helped. Problem is, he won't admit to who *was* the perpetrator. He wants the credit all to himself. If I can find something in the Property Clerk's warehouse… anything that proves Ricky Goulding wasn't acting alone…. Maybe something that was never tested for DNA."

Releasing a held breath, O'Halloran dug his phone free from his suit coat. "Give me your number." After he inputted Larkin's cell into his address book, O'Halloran said, "I'll text you."

"When you called in Danielle Moreno, you didn't happen to inquire after her current place of employment, did you."

"Why?"

"I need to know if she was working anywhere near Alphabet City."

"Larkin," Doyle called from below.

"It'd be helpful," Larkin continued to O'Halloran. "Since I'm busy cleaning up this mess."

"Fuck you." But after a second, O'Halloran added, "I'll see what I can turn up."

"Thank you."

O'Halloran grinned, said, "Get bent," then walked away from the fountain without another word.

Larkin leaned over the railing, holding his umbrella out

so it covered both his and Doyle's heads. "What."

Doyle raised two fingers to show a watery white residue on the blue latex gloves. "The way she fell, her arm partially covered the hairline. My guess? Plaster of Paris, for making the negative used for casting the mask into another material. There's a bit of something around her right eye too. Of course we need a test to be definitive, but if it were oil—"

"Put on the face to prevent the plaster removing eyebrows or eyelashes," Larkin said, thinking back to the library book's long-winded details on construction methods seen throughout the Victorian era.

"You got it." Doyle lowered his hand. "CSU it taking samples."

"I could kiss you."

"If it turns out I'm right, you're welcome to do more than that." Doyle tugged the gloves off and pointed to the body. "Extensive bruising around her neck."

Larkin's gaze cut to Danielle Moreno. "Like the others."

Doyle hummed agreement under his breath, grabbed the fence, and hoisted himself up and out of the fountain. He took his umbrella back from Larkin.

"Hey!" Millett shouted. "Is evidence going to O'Halloran or you?"

"Me," Larkin called.

Millett gave a wave that conveyed both understanding and dismissal. He returned to snapping photographs and tagging plastic bags.

"We need to send CSU back to Ricky's," Larkin said.

"For what?"

"Based on the current decomposition of Danielle's body, she's been dead between three and… maybe six days, maximum."

"Sometime between last Friday and Sunday."

"Right. And like the other victims, she has very long hair. Women's hair has a way of defying drains."

"So there might be evidence she was in Ricky's tub," Doyle concluded.

Larkin nodded.

Doyle fetched his wallet and removed a business card. "I'll give Bosman a call." He copied the cell number and put his phone to his ear. "We need to ask ourselves: were all the bodies kept for several days, or is this new? And if it's new, where's she been in the interim?"

Larkin had just pulled into traffic when his phone rang. "Who is it," he asked.

Doyle took the cell from the cupholder. "No ID. Local number."

"Put it on speaker."

Doyle did and held the phone up.

"Detective Larkin," Larkin answered as he deftly avoided a taxi who prematurely slammed on their breaks.

"Detective, this is Camila Garcia."

The panic and embarrassment at having forgotten to make a notation in his calendar for his appointment with Camila was immediate and overwhelming. He gripped the steering wheel tight in both hands, swallowed a string of colorful curses, and managed, "Mrs. Garcia, I'm so sorry."

"I should have known better."

"Ma'am, allow me to apologize," Larkin said again, hastily checking his wristwatch to confirm it was 9:22. "I had every intention of honoring our appointment this morning, but—" Offering an excuse made Larkin want to actually vomit, but he'd been trying to get Marco's mother to speak with him for over a month. Anything to save face was necessary at this point. "I was called to a scene this morning involving a homicide victim—"

"My son was a victim of homicide too, Detective."

"Yes, ma'am—"

"I was truly starting to believe you were different from all those other cops. That you actually cared about Marco."

"I do care. With all my heart."

"Save it. I don't want to hear it."

"I can be there in twenty minutes," Larkin tried.

"No. As I said, I'm flying to California today, and I need to finish getting ready."

"Mrs. Garcia—"

"Goodbye." She hung up.

"Fuck," Larkin whispered as Doyle lowered the phone. "Fuck, fuck, *fuck*!" His voice grew with each word until he was shouting inside the car.

"Hey." Doyle put a hand on Larkin's forearm. "Jesus, Evie. You're shaking."

"I forgot. I forgot. I fucking forgot!"

"Pull over. No—right now." Doyle was quiet until Larkin double-parked and put his hazards on. He undid his seat belt and shifted so he could look at Larkin.

"Don't tell me it's okay," Larkin said before Doyle could open his mouth. "It's not. It's not okay at all." He had to blink back the burn in his eyes. "Look at my phone. Open the calendar."

Doyle hesitated before he did as Larkin asked.

Larkin could only imagine how… *insane* it looked to someone on the outside. Every single meeting he'd organized for the dozens of cases he worked had been methodically inputted with a name, date, time, case number. There were reminders for dry cleaning, groceries, gas, even vacuuming.

Everything was color-coordinated. Because nonhabitual engagements or errands were the true Achilles' heel of Larkin's short-term memory issues. He could remember talking to Camila about meeting this morning, could recite the conversation almost verbatim, but being able to recall an appointment plan on its own, as a unique memory unattached to anything else, was like smoke in the wind. He *had* to write dates and times down for appointments if they weren't something worked into his routine. It'd made him obsessive about checking the time, making certain he wasn't overlooking a place to be, someone to speak to, something to pick up.

And he'd blown it with one of the victims who needed him most.

"All right." Doyle closed out of the app and returned the phone to the cup holder. "It's not okay. Is that what you want to hear?"

Larkin leaned forward and set his forehead on the steering wheel.

"You made one mistake," Doyle said. "You forgot to write down an appointment. Will that stop you from investigating the case?"

Larkin brought his head up quickly. "You don't understand. I didn't forget the way other people make a mistake. I forgot because my brain is broken and everyone says I have a gift, that I'm incredible, superhuman, but I'm not! I'm a neurotic, barely functioning nightmare, and if I lost this job, I would have nothing to live for. *Nothing*!" He hit his forehead hard with both wrists out of pent-up rage.

"Stop it," Doyle demanded. He grabbed Larkin's wrists and kept them pinned. "You're not going to lose your job. You're a first-grade detective with more commendations than most captains and deputy inspectors. I've heard your name whispered down at 1PP more than once, and do you want to know why you haven't been promoted? I'm pretty sure it's because people are shit scared of having to take orders from you. Because of your thoroughness and expectations."

"I don't want to be promoted!"

"Evie, that's not the point. You're not going to be fired because one victim decided not to meet with you."

Larkin shoved Doyle off and opened the center console. He grabbed the bottle of Xanax and tried to unscrew the childproof top, but his goddamn hands wouldn't stop shaking.

"What is that?" When Larkin didn't answer, Doyle reached for the prescription bottle and pried it from Larkin's sweating hands.

"It's a legal prescription," Larkin protested.

Doyle nodded as he silently read the label. He cracked the top with his big hand, shook one pill into his palm, then held it out.

"As needed," Larkin said.

Doyle gave him a questioning, suspicious look. "Yeah, I can read. It says one tablet up to twice daily, as needed."

Larkin scoffed, grabbed the pill, and dry-swallowed it. He closed his eyes and leaned his head back against the headrest. As Doyle closed the bottle and returned it to the console, Larkin was struck with an almost overwhelming urge to cry. He covered his face with one hand and took in a shuddering breath.

"Last night," Doyle began, his voice in harmony with the *pat, pat, pat* of rain on the windshield. "I told you I don't drink."

Larkin didn't speak, didn't move.

"I self-medicated after losing Abigail. Hard. Gin was my go-to. It's okay to hurt, but you can't blame yourself."

Larkin lowered his hand and looked at Doyle.

Doyle's eyes were too bright. "You have to be careful

with that stuff, okay? It comes with directions for a reason." He looked out the windshield, shook his head, then opened the passenger door.

Larkin peeled his tongue from the roof of his mouth to… say what, exactly? Apologize for being a pill-popper? Beg Doyle not to scream at him the way Noah had?

Doyle leaned down and motioned Larkin toward him. "Slide over. I'm driving."

"It—it doesn't affect my driving," Larkin said.

"That's great. Slide over."

Larkin awkwardly maneuvered himself from the driver to passenger seat, which he had to pull forward because, Jesus, Doyle was tall. Door still open, rain still falling, Doyle crouched and studied him.

"I'm sorry," Larkin whispered.

Doyle shook his head. He reached across Larkin's lap and tugged the hair tie a few times. "I don't want you to be sorry. I want you to be okay."

"I'm not."

"You had a life-changing night, didn't sleep well, and this case—"

"No. I mean, I haven't been okay for eighteen years." Larkin looked at Doyle, at the raindrops glistening in his dark brown hair like little diamonds. He was beautiful. And so kind. Why the hell was he expelling energy on a hopeless case like Everett Larkin?

Doyle leaned up, pressed his forehead to Larkin's, and carded his fingers briefly through his short hair. "There isn't a finish line in this race. It's not about sprinting—it's about stamina to keep going." He stood, shut the door, and moved around the front bumper to the driver side. Doyle slid in partway, pushed the seat back, then managed to get comfortable. He checked the mirrors before pulling into traffic.

Larkin wasn't riding that hazy high he got from Xanax because one pill wasn't enough for that "don't give a shit" euphoria, but he *was* calm. Well, calmer. When the antianxiety meds wore off, he was going to need another dose just to deal with the fact that Doyle knew he required pharmaceuticals to function, let alone that Doyle had had front-row seats to a memory meltdown, and that, if Doyle were smart, he would run for the fucking hills after this case was closed.

But later. Larkin would worry about all of that later.

In the meantime, Ray O'Halloran had come through with a case number to present to the Property Clerk in order to obtain any physical evidence taken during Natasha's nonexistent investigation. He'd also followed up with employment records for Danielle and had sent Larkin a text:

Strippers fill out W-2s these days. Who knew? Danielle Moreno worked at Full-Flavored. E. 2nd & Ave. A.

"Full-Flavored is Manhattan's premiere club for adult entertainment. Hosted by mature women with skills *and* experience," Doyle read from his phone. "We offer two stages, a full bar, and a dozen big-screen TVs playing all the latest sports—" He put a hand over his mouth to stifle a very uncop-like giggle.

Larkin, hands in his trouser pockets, turned to stare.

"Sorry. It's just so aggressively straight." In an announcer-like style, and dropping his already deep voice another octave, Doyle exclaimed, "Have a beer, eat some meat, catch the game, see some tits."

"Never say tits again."

"That wasn't me. That was my heterosexual, alpha-male persona."

"Jesus Christ." Larkin sighed loudly and directed his exasperation and stare toward the clerk at the front desk who'd been patently ignoring him for twenty minutes now. Manhattan's Property Clerk was located in the basement of 1PP, and this woman, who Larkin felt vaguely resembled and even sounded a bit like Roz from *Monsters, Inc.*, had been "searching" for their case number in her computer system the entire time. "We were the first ones in line."

"It's always like this," Doyle murmured.

Larkin glanced at him again. Doyle was still staring at his phone. "She's purposefully going slow."

"It *is* a case from the '90s. You know what a nightmare these offices were back then."

"Malarkey."

Doyle smiled at his phone. "It's cute when you use dated lingo, especially since I've heard plenty of shits, damns, and fucks from you. Listen to this: Full-Flavored offers VIP business packages, bachelor parties, couples parties—which is interesting, I guess—and divorce parties—which I didn't even know was a thing."

"I'll save my money for the contested divorce Noah's undoubtedly going to drag to court."

Doyle pocketed his cell and looked at Larkin.

Roz's gravelly voice called from the other side of the plexiglass window, "*Larkin.*"

"Thank God." Larkin strode to the window. "What'd you find."

"Nothing."

"Nothing," Larkin repeated as Doyle joined him. "What do you mean, nothing. It's an open and active homicide case."

"I understand, detective," she said, her words dragging like a shovel on sidewalk. "But it's a thirty-year-old—"

"Twenty-eight," Larkin corrected in an almost

absentminded manner.

"You can't round up or down with him," Doyle explained.

Roz did not find this amusing and reiterated in a voice that'd make a cat arch like it were a full moon on Halloween, "A thirty-year-old case. And sometimes things get moved, lost, destroyed—"

"In floods or fires," Larkin finished for her. "Yes, we've heard these excuses before."

"Sorry, detective."

"You need to check again," Larkin said. "You can't lose the only bit of evidence that will bring this woman's killer to justice and then shrug at me."

Roz raised an eyebrow behind the thick cat-eye glasses. "You want to look yourself?" She hit a button out of sight and the lock on the door leading into the caverns of the long-term storage buzzed. "Be my guest."

Larkin met Roz's defiant expression, squared his shoulders, and marched to the door.

CHAPTER EIGHTEEN

Each borough in the city of New York had its own Property Clerk. The warehouses were entrusted to catalogue, store, and safeguard all evidence in criminal investigations, which meant jewels, weapons, drugs, even vehicles, the exception being forensic evidence, such as blood, semen, or other bodily fluids that required special storage and testing. After the case was closed, property was either returned to its owners or disposed of by the department.

It was the *disposal* part that'd really stuck in the craw of Larkin and his fellow Cold Case detectives. Because sometimes the Clerk's office threw illegal gambling machines into the river, and other times they nearly melted down a pair of precious and irreplaceable flintlock hunting pistols that'd once belonged to Empress Catherine the Great. After the various Property Clerks underwent much-needed overhauls in the 1990s, older evidence, as Cold Cases requested them, began turning up as missing. The clerks always cited the same unfortunate reason—floods and fires—but Larkin didn't buy it for a minute. There was no documentation of any natural disasters having damaged evidence beyond salvation. He was certain it was a combination of stealing during the previous decades, disposing of evidence prematurely, and simply never logging those old, old murders into their new system, essentially losing a single envelope or box in the bowels of the building for all time. That last reason in particular was a sore spot for Larkin because he was about ninety percent certain he'd never successfully close his case from 1919 due to evidence still in existence that he literally couldn't *find* on a shelf.

"You've got to be kidding me," Doyle said.

"No."

They stood side by side, staring down a long aisle with cement floors, double-decker shelves on the right, crowded with reinforced cardboard barrels that stood four feet tall each and were spray painted with case numbers, rolling ladders erratically placed throughout the foreboding corridor, and along the left, a line of caged units with more boxes, envelopes, and barrels housed inside them, some elevated on wooden skids.

Larkin removed his cell, checked his calendar, and said, "We have to be in Williamsburg to speak with Roger Hunt no later than two o'clock, ideally. That gives us exactly three hours."

"We can't go through this warehouse in three hours."

"We only need to check this aisle," Larkin corrected. "She said if it were logged in their catalogue system, in theory, it'd be shelved here." He shrugged out of his suit coat and draped it over the steps of the closest ladder.

"Evie…." Doyle said in a desperate tone.

Larkin turned, smiling just a little. "Yes, Ira?" And saying Doyle's first name was… it felt right.

Doyle's face softened. He met Larkin's gaze.

"I like when you call me that—Evie."

"Oh?"

Larkin nodded. He removed latex gloves from his coat and offered Doyle a pair. "Beginning or end." He indicated the entrance and then the dead-end of the aisle with his free hand.

Doyle took off his suit coat before accepting the gloves. "Here. I'll start at the beginning. You really know how to show a guy a good time."

"I'll owe you and your big, capable hands. Of course, I'll probably have to restrain you. You're very touchy, and in theory, we'd be resting your hands after all this work." Larkin finished with perfect sincerity, "Good thing I have handcuffs." He turned on his heel and started for the end of the aisle, daring a glance over his shoulder at the half-mark to see Doyle was doubled over, hands on his knees.

After that, the search was slow, methodical, and tedious. Larkin spent a while digging through the gated section on his end but was able to confirm the evidence all belonged to one large, and recent, investigation. Boxes and barrels were clean, crisp, their labels still bright. Not what he wanted. He wanted the evidence that looked like it'd been punted around the city like a football for a few decades. Larkin turned his attention to the towering shelves instead, and had spent nearly an hour systematically moving back and forth between the ground level and pulling along a ladder to reach the overhead barrels, when Doyle's voice echoed from the other end of the aisle.

"Larkin, I think I found it."

Larkin climbed down from the ladder, watching as Doyle dragged a barrel from one of the gated units, studied the spray-painted information, then worked the top off. He immediately made a gagging sound, dropped the lid, and stumbled away. "Doyle?" Larkin jogged toward him. "What's wrong?"

Doyle held the back of his gloved hand against his mouth and pointed with the other. "Maggots."

Larkin slowed to a walk. "You were pulling plaster of

Paris out of the hair of a decomposing body this morning."

"Yeah, well, there's a certain detachment to that."

"It's just some larvae."

Doyle lowered his hand. "No. That's not just *some*. That evidence is infested."

Larkin raised an eyebrow. His partner looked a little green. "You don't like bugs."

"Nothing that wiggles, squirms, or has an unnecessary number of legs."

"Maggots won't hurt you."

Doyle put his hand to his mouth again and honestly looked about ready to vomit.

"Okay, okay," Larkin said quickly. "I'll look through it." He approached the barrel and noted the back side appeared to have water damage that'd caused a tear in the heavy-duty cardboard. A trail of wriggling maggots led the way back to the unit, like breadcrumbs. Larkin peered inside and, yeah, it was infested. Whoever had collected hard evidence from Natasha's murder scene twenty-eight years ago hadn't properly bagged the items, and *something* in there, something likely with blood evidence, had attracted a fly. Larkin hastily removed his cuff links, pocketed them, and rolled his sleeves back before reaching into the barrel.

"Don't touch—*oh my God*." Doyle took a few steps back as Larkin removed what looked to be a skimpier, sexier version of a cocktail dress. Maggots fell from the folds of material and he made another sound close to blowing chunks.

Larkin set the dress on the floor and reached inside again. "Take my phone," he instructed, removing a stiletto with a broken heel next.

"What?"

Larkin angled himself and said, "Left pocket."

Doyle took a few hesitant steps, got just close enough to

tug the cell from Larkin's trouser pocket, then quickly backed away.

"Call O'Halloran."

"Why?"

Larkin raised a gloved hand covered in squirming maggots and shook them back into the barrel. He reached inside again, saying, "He doesn't have control over Natasha's case file—otherwise this would be easy. Ask him to get a look at the autopsy report. I don't care what he has to do to accomplish that. Find out if the ME had any specific notes about the weapon used to kill her." Larkin found the other shoe. "His contact information is my most recent text."

Doyle swiped on the screen, tapped, and put the cell to his ear. He met Larkin's look and said, "Thanks."

Larkin shrugged. He created a pile on the floor of Natasha's belongings that the perpetrator seemed to have no interest in keeping for himself and tossed with the body when he was done using her face as his mask model. Dress, shoes, purse—everything was covered in maggots. It was difficult to tell without a black light on the dress, but he was pretty sure the crusted surface was old, old blood, and the poor storage, damp floor, and water damage had attracted insects. Larkin didn't have the heart to tell Doyle this wasn't the first barrel of old evidence he'd gone through that had… creepy-crawly friends inside. He half listened to Doyle work his interpersonal magic on O'Halloran while he paced a safe distance away, but otherwise, didn't stop digging through the barrel until he'd found a plastic evidence bag with what appeared to be blood-stained blue and orange threads wrapped around a broken fingernail.

"Appreciate it," Doyle was saying to O'Halloran. "What's that? Oh… I'll tell him." Doyle hung up.

"What'd he say."

"He told me to tell you, fuck you."

"And what about the autopsy report."

Doyle warily returned to Larkin and the barrel. "I can't tell if you're unaware of people's general dislike, or if you truly don't care."

"I don't care." Larkin lowered the evidence bag and stared expectantly.

"Blunt-force trauma," Doyle recited. "Broke her neck. The ME back in '92 had specified the weapon had a curved surface."

"Curved," Larkin repeated. "A bar, a pipe—"

"A hammer?" Doyle suggested. "You use those in working with metal. Rounding hammers, as the name suggests, has a rounded head." He glanced down as Larkin's phone buzzed. "Your—ah, Noah is calling."

"Hang up."

"Larkin."

"Hang up. I'm working."

Doyle obediently tapped the screen.

"Rounding hammers are the same length as a typical hammer."

"Are you asking?"

"Yes."

"I think they come in varying handle lengths and pounds, but to a layman, it's a hammer," Doyle answered.

"Concealable, then."

Doyle nodded.

Larkin frowned, studied the evidence in his hand, then walked a few feet away before returning. "Something isn't adding up."

"I'd say a lot of things aren't adding up," Doyle commented wryly. "Do you know that the build methods of death masks is a relatively undiscussed subject in art history?

Besides the book you borrowed from the library, the only other author I know of who wrote extensively on the matter was Laurence Hutton. He began preserving death masks when a small collection was found in the 1860s in a trash bin in—and we're coming full circle here—the neighborhood of Tompkins Square."

"Really?"

"Yeah, really. He spent the rest of his life hunting down masks in curiosity shops, plaster shops, and studios across America and Europe. He wrote *the book* on death masks because no one else had and it irritated him."

Larkin considered this, then asked, "Could that be used against the perpetrator."

"How do you mean?"

"Mr. Hutton's book—could it be checked out from a library."

Doyle frowned a little and said, "I suppose it could be, but *Portraits in Plaster* is from 1890-something. As far as I know, it's public domain now. It wouldn't be research easily traced back to any one person."

"But you've read it," Larkin clarified.

"I went to art school."

"So did Roger Hunt—designing, literally forging, jewelry. He'd have learned how to use a rounding hammer…. But Natasha was murdered in '92. Roger, according to Jessica, would have graduated in '97 with her and Andrew. He would have been a teenager when the killings began, and while that's certainly not unheard of, most serial killers don't become active until their twenties. And if I'm correct that Ricky was an accomplice—not the killer—and supplied a safe house of sorts, how did they know each other."

"Roger might be a native," Doyle supplied. "Grew up in the city versus moving here for college."

"Maybe."

"Right, maybe," Doyle said suddenly. "Because… what if he pursued Andrew out of sheer convenience? Andrew lived in the same building where Roger and Ricky were busy making masks of dead women in a bathtub. Something goes wrong, Andrew sees Roger in a compromising situation, and now he's gotta go. Plus, Roger never came forward with Jessica. Never helped her with the missing person report. That, in and of itself, is strange."

"People are strange," Larkin supplied. "It's not necessarily suspicious behavior."

"I think it is."

"It's a lot of postulation and little evidence."

"Then let's get to Brooklyn and speak with Mr. Too-Busy-for-a-Murder-Investigation." Doyle pointed and asked, "What'd you find that's not covered in maggots?"

Larkin glanced at the bag and held it up. "She fought her attacker. Blood might be hers, might be his—it's clearly never been tested. She tore at what he was wearing. Fabric with blue and orange threads." He watched a minute shift in Doyle's expression: raised eyebrows, widened eyes—*interest*. "What?"

"Nothing. Just… blue and orange. That's—"

"Gaudy."

"Says the man who coordinates a pink pocket square with gold wingtips."

"They complement."

"Exactly. Blue and orange are complementary on a color wheel. But men's clothing isn't exactly known for such bold palettes, even in the '90s."

"Are you suggesting the perpetrator was a woman," Larkin asked.

"No, no. It's curious, is all."

CHAPTER NINETEEN

Despite his agreement to see Larkin and Doyle before three o'clock that afternoon, Roger Hunt seemed both surprised and irritated by their appearance. Forges was located in a very unassuming, multimillion-dollar warehouse just east of Bedford Avenue, in a neighborhood where residential and mom-and-pop storefronts were at odds with high-end commercial shopping and entertainment. The grit and grime and character of Brooklyn still managed to shine through, even if the chain grocery stores and upscale gyms made it a bit more difficult to see.

Inside, the framework of Forges still screamed of its industrial ancestry, with its brick walls, high-beamed ceilings, and exposed HVAC system. But what had changed with the times and use, was the color. Everything was completely white. From the cement floor to the open staircase leading to the second floor, to the in-process-of-being-set-up art displays and pop-up bars for Roger's "party"....

White, white, white.

"An artist's nightmare," Doyle had whispered after Brian the PA had answered the door, groaned dramatically, and ushered them inside before running off to fetch his boss.

Larkin shrugged. "I like minimalism."

"This isn't minimalism—this is the Twilight Zone. Sneeze on the wall, tack a frame around it, and it'd sell for a million dollars."

Larkin put his hand to his mouth to hide his growing smile. "That's probably true. I prefer cityscapes. There's an organized beauty to them that's pleasing on the eye."

Doyle made a sound under his breath.

"I enjoyed the ones you had hanging in your apartment."

Doyle looked down. "Did you?"

"Yes."

For some reason, Doyle had blushed, and Larkin was going to inquire as to why, but then Roger came down the stairs, with Brian on his heels. Roger Hunt was a well-built man who, as he approached from across the warehouse, stood taller than Larkin. His black hair was going steel-colored, from what was visible under a backward baseball cap, and the powerful cut of his jaw had a well-manicured beard. Per Jessica's description, he certainly looked older than his supposed age. But besides that, if Roger intended to host some sort of cosmopolitan jewelry show that evening, he seemed to be the only one who hadn't gotten the memo. He wore a pair of skinny jeans that were stained below the knees and had clearly seen better days. An apron was still over his front, and a simple, ratty sweatshirt was worn underneath. His hands were stained black. But despite his appearance, Roger spoke like he was born and raised on the Upper East Side.

"Detectives, I had hoped you understood the implication that I simply don't have time for… well, whatever it is that caused you to display my likeness as if I were a common criminal," Roger said before either of them could speak.

"This moment would make for a good argument in favor of frankness, Mr. Hunt," Larkin answered.

"I've been awake for two days," Roger said. "I've got to get these final pieces ready to be modeled tonight. I don't have time for your holier-than-thou attitude, detective."

"Everett Larkin, Cold Cases."

"I don't care."

"Mr. Hunt," Doyle quickly interjected. "What is it exactly that you do for a living?"

"I'm an entrepreneur. A designer. An artist."

"Hm-hm." Doyle made a point of staring at Roger's stained hands.

Roger rolled his eyes, and Larkin could see where Brian's habit must have originated from. "For God's sake. A *moron* would belittle my talents with the overly simplistic label of goldsmith." He held up his hands and added, "It's polish."

"Have you worked with iron?" Doyle continued.

"That's *blacksmithing*," Brian spoke up.

"Brian, please," Roger said, but his tone was placating. To Doyle, he said, "Yes, of course. I've worked with all kinds of materials, although I've favored gold these past few years. Did you honestly come all the way out here to inquire about the ethics of using gold in jewelry or the sustainability of my designs? Again, I don't have time for this. You know where the door is."

"We're here to speak with you about Andrew Gorman," Larkin said.

Roger had already turned toward the stairs but then stopped. He looked over his shoulder, his brow creased in apparent befuddlement before the lightbulb went off. "Andrew… oh, *Andy*? I haven't spoken to him in twenty years."

"Twenty-two," Larkin corrected.

Roger shrugged. "What difference does it make? Is he in some sort of trouble?"

Larkin watched Roger's face carefully as he stated, without any kind of emotional inflection, "Andrew Gorman is dead."

Roger's eyebrows rose and his jaw slackened slightly, an indicator of sincere surprise at the news and not a feigned expression, but what followed was nothing. Roger's face was blank of emotion. There was no anger, no fear, no disgust—nothing that would have indicated to Larkin that this man had something to hide regarding Andrew's murder. And Larkin was… not expecting that. Of course, a common trait shared among those with psychopathic and sociopathic behavior was the inability to feel empathy. And given the methodical planning that went into all of the murders, Larkin was certain they were looking at psychopathic tendencies, which included the ability to pretend, as well as maintain functioning "normal lives" in order to hide dangerous inclinations.

So either Roger truly didn't care about Andrew's death, or he was pretending not to care. Either way, Larkin didn't like it.

"I'm sorry to hear that," Roger said in a detached, WASP-y tone.

"He died in 1998," Larkin added. *Now* he had Roger's attention. "In fact, he disappeared on March 28, 1998, after telling his roommate he was going to visit you."

Roger looked at Brian. He smiled lightly, patted the kid's cheek with the back of his hand, in a manner that suggested some kind of serious age-gap intimacy, and said, "Why don't you make sure Marge has all the champagne she needs for the party? God knows we'll need it." Once Brian had departed, Roger motioned with a stiff nod. "Follow me, gentlemen."

Roger led the way upstairs, the floorplan an echo of the downstairs portion—open, industrial, and white. Although, this area was clearly off-limits to any sort of staff or clientele, as it appeared to house all of Roger's gear and projects. From an expensive Mac computer and 3-D printer setup, to several worktables cluttered with various gizmos and gadgets that Larkin had very little understanding as to their usage in the creation of jewelry, to a pegboard that took up nearly an entire wall, all carefully organized with the tools of Roger's various trades. Lots of hammers, lots of saws, lots of plyers, lots of tongs. Along the opposite wall were a number of retro metal signs, carefully curated so as to imply more than just care in the workplace: Men at Work, Teach Him Safety, Don't Get Wet, and Ask Your Supervisor! The suggestive notices created a rectangle around a number of otherwise entirely innocent and vintage photographs of local baseball teams and events.

Roger leaned back against a worktable and took a defensive posture by crossing his arms. "How did Andy die?"

"He was murdered," Larkin answered.

Roger frowned, took off his ball cap, and scrubbed his going-silver-fox hair with one hand. "I had no idea."

"Jessica Lopez approached you about going to the police with her to fill out a missing person report."

"Who? Oh… his roommate, right? Maybe she did."

"I wasn't suggesting," Larkin answered. "I'm telling you she did."

Roger narrowed his eyes. "All right, well, if she did, I don't remember—"

"That's because you didn't want to be involved. In fact, no one even knew who you were until yesterday." Larkin added after a pause, "That you were Andrew's boyfriend."

Roger offered a dry laugh. "No way. Andy and I weren't dating. It was a casual thing."

"Jessica said Andrew was pretty into you."

"So what if he was? Detective—?"

"Larkin."

"That's right. Well, relationships aren't my cup of tea, as they say."

"You might want to give your PA a heads-up," Larkin commented.

Roger colored. "Brian knows that I—*look*. Andy was a sweet guy, but he was a kid, and this was a lifetime ago. When he stopped calling, I was over it. There were other men. If I had thought for even a moment that something terrible had happened…."

Larkin said, "I'm not interested in hypothetical situations. What's your relationship to Ricky Goulding."

Roger looked confused.

"I'm asking you," Larkin prompted.

"It didn't sound like a question. Ricky Goulding? I have no idea who that is."

He's not lying, Larkin realized in a second of crystalline clarity. "Where did Andrew live."

"East Village?" Roger asked with a shrug. "No, hang on, Alphabet City, I think. I walked him home once or twice but never stayed. He'd take the subway uptown to my place. I didn't have a roommate."

Larkin heard that clue—*I didn't have a roommate*—and glanced at Doyle. The connection between them sparked and ignited the energy in the room. However it was that Doyle understood when to cover Larkin, when to step in and when to give space, and perhaps most importantly, how he approached the same mystery from the opposite end and still met Larkin in the middle—that magic happened again.

"Mr. Hunt," Doyle said, a friendly smile on his face, his posture relaxed with his hands in his pockets. He tilted his head, as if in thought, and asked, "How old are you?"

"Excuse me?"

Doyle shrugged. "College kids usually need roommates

to survive. But you didn't, back then?"

"I'm fifty-two."

"So that'd make you eight years older than Andrew, if he were alive today?" Doyle continued.

"I suppose so."

"Jessica had told us you were all in the same graduating class."

Roger sighed. "Andy was the cutest twink east of the Hudson. A twink is—"

Doyle cut him off with "We're familiar with the term."

"Okay, well, Andy was cute, but he was also wholesome white bread, middle America, and still newly out and just realizing what the scene was like after moving to the city. I didn't want to scare him, being an older man trying to get him in bed. So I lied a little. But I did go to FIT, if you're wondering."

"Noted," Larkin said dryly.

Doyle asked next, "Did you abuse Andrew?"

Roger looked surprised. Surprised and insulted and angry. He asked, in an elite-private-school-upbringing voice, "I beg your pardon?"

"Autopsy reports indicate Andrew suffered from multiple breaks in his fingers, left arm, and within a year of his death, a severely deviated septum."

Roger was breathing hard, trying and barely succeeding to gain control of himself. He managed to spit out, "The broken nose? I didn't do that. I didn't raise a hand to Andy."

"How'd it happen?" Doyle asked.

"I don't know."

"You were fucking him," Larkin pointed out. "He was smitten. He didn't tell his roommate what happened, but I think he'd tell you. He'd tell you because it'd be an act of trust, of vulnerability, the foundations necessary for a healthy, long-term relationship. And while you might not have been interested in that, he was."

Roger looked like if he could breathe the fire used in his kilns and turn Larkin to ash where he stood, he'd have done it. "I asked him one night, after we'd been out partying in the Village. He said some guy had made a pass, or was going to—I don't remember the specifics, but it was in regard to Jessie. Andy was very protective of her. I think she was his only real friend. His family disowned him after he came out—he told me that. And honestly, I think his brothers used to beat the crap out of him. Probably doubled down on it when he came out."

"So Andrew had a history of being abused," Doyle repeated, "but was willing to stand up to a stranger to defend Jessica?"

Roger shrugged his big shoulders. "It wasn't a stranger. He said it was his super's brother… or cousin… something like that. He'd said it was some creep in his building he got real bad vibes from. They ended up in a scrap, which you can imagine Andy lost, with what his nose looked like. But I guess it explained why he'd always want to make sure Jessie got home safe. Or he'd call from my place to check on her, like they were married."

"Why didn't they just move?" Doyle asked.

Roger looked bemused. "The poor kid couldn't afford a hospital bill to fix his busted nose. The last thing they had money for was security and first month's rent for a new place. Like I said, Andy didn't have any family to fall back on, and if memory serves me, Jessie I think only had a grandparent? They were on their own."

Doyle pulled his buzzing phone from his pocket, looked at Larkin, and said, "Bosman." He moved deeper into the workshop before answering with a smoky, "Hey, Bosman, did CSU find anything?"

Larkin studied Roger. The antipathy pouring off him, without Doyle there to act as a buffer, was palpable. "Tell me more about the man who attacked Andrew."

"There's nothing else to tell."

"A brother or a cousin or something like that," Larkin quoted. "Which is it."

"How the hell should I know?" Roger snapped. "It was twenty years ago, and a one-time story a not-so-sober twink told me in between grinding up on my thigh to Bikini Kill."

"You don't remember the specifics of Andrew's story, but you recall the name of a now-obscure feminist punk band from the riot grrrl movement of the '90s playing in the club."

The color was back in Roger's face as he spluttered, "I—I really liked that band, okay? So yes, I remember they'd been playing because Bikini Kill had recently split up and I was still smarting over it." He looked over Larkin's shoulder, likely studying Doyle, who was still on his call. "The guy, whoever it was trying to make a move on Jessie, he didn't live there, I don't think. Andy said something like, the guy had met him and Jessie when they were moving in—I assumed he was hired to move boxes, you know? But honestly, I don't remember more than that. I really don't think Andy *told* me more than that."

Moving in.

A photo from the days of dusty orange exposures, red eyes, and fingertips over lenses. A shared second captured for posterity, like a timestamp of youth and rebellion, and the past lived, and the dreams of the future. Simple in its framing, innocent in its subjects, evil in the clue it left imprinted on the backdrop.

"Do you know why we take photographs, Mr. Hunt."

"What's that?"

"We take photos because we don't want to forget. Even before the advent of such technology, we've always looked for ways to capture our likeness. Not out of egotism—not really. But because we fear being forgotten. We fear forgetting those we loved. But if we have a tangible reminder, a memento mori, there's a kind of relief. A physical connection that still exists. We all die—that is inevitable. What matters is whether or not someone will want to remember you."

"Why are you telling me this?"

Larkin lifted one shoulder in a light shrug. "Only two people remembered Andrew Gorman. Jessica Lopez, who's currently in the hospital, and the man who brutally murdered him."

In a quiet and somber tone, Roger said, "I didn't kill Andy."

"Do you ever construct masks."

"Masks?" Roger frowned, glanced at Doyle as the other detective ended his call and was approaching them again. Then he said, "No. Rings, necklaces, bracelets—headpieces, even. I've never made a mask."

"Can we take a few of your hammers in for testing."

"What? No. Absolutely not. You'll need a warrant and you'll hear from my lawyer if that's our next step."

Doyle reached a hand out, took Larkin's elbow, and steered him away from Roger. He closed the space between them and lowered his head so that he could whisper, "Bosman says CSU pulled a few long hairs from Ricky's tub drain. Red."

"Any with follicles."

"Yeah. They're being sent in to test against Danielle Moreno. What do you think?"

"I think you should make nice with Mr. Hunt on my behalf while I make a call, and then we leave."

Doyle managed to suppress a chuckle, but only barely. He let go of Larkin's arm and moved to Roger.

Larkin pulled out his own phone and dialed Precinct 19. He requested Miyamoto, was put on hold, and heard the tail end of Roger's comment, putting an emphasis on *partner*.

Doyle had answered, "I should be so lucky, Mr. Hunt."

"Detective Miyamoto."

"Good, you're there. I need you to go to my desk and pull a piece of evidence."

"Gosh," she drawled. "I can't imagine who this is."

"It's Larkin."

"I know that, dummy. I'm teasing because if you remembered to say please and thank you even half of the time, you'd have wildly different results with most people."

"Please go to my desk."

"You might even salvage a relationship with Ulmer."

"You must have me confused with someone who gives a fuck. He leaked my case to the press. Please go to my desk."

"Shut the fuck up."

"You give conflicting messages. Do you want me to say please or not."

"I meant about Ulmer. Did he really go to the press?"

"I'm quite certain."

"Why would he do that?"

"I wish I could suggest a more nefarious reason beyond he is an unconscionable prick. Please go to my desk."

"Christ. You're calling a landline. Hold on." She picked up again a minute later at Larkin's desk. "Okay, what did you need?"

"Top folder." Larkin listened to the distant sound of the accordion file being unbound and opened. "There's a photograph of two kids holding up a key on moving day."

"Yeah, found it."

"Take a picture and text it to me."

"Why the fuck didn't you call my cell, then?"

"I wasn't sure if you were in the office."

"All right. Give me a second."

"Thank you."

"Anything for you, Grumpy Gus."

Larkin ended the call. He'd moved toward the wall with the double entendre signs and baseball memories while speaking with Miyamoto. Now, he studied a sepia-colored team photo, complete with collared shirts, ties, and handlebar mustaches. The typeface on the bottom right indicated a copyright of 1882 and an address for the photographer's studio in Union Square. The Metropolitans—a defunct team. Larkin's gaze cut to another team photo, black-and-white, the first season of the newly formed Mets, circa 1962. He was only into baseball in a casual sense, but clearly the Mets found their roots in the Metropolitans? Color began to seep into the photos—that aesthetic unique to the '70s, and then the mustaches of the '80s made themselves known, all the way through just the past few years.

"Ready to go, Larkin?" That was Doyle.

Without looking away from the shrine to America's pastime, Larkin said, "I see you understand the concept I spoke of earlier, Mr. Hunt. You're quite the fan."

"There's something satisfying in rooting for the underdog team," Roger remarked. "They take a beating but keep coming back."

Like Andrew did.

Larkin's phone buzzed. He glanced down, opened the image from Miyamoto, and downloaded it. He touched the screen to expand the picture and study the background—the men who'd been moving the mattress inside the apartment building, unknowingly included in the shared memory of Jessica and Andrew.

Both were big, tough-looking. Manual-labor sort of

guys. One had his back to the subjects, and the other walked backward, his face angled toward the camera, dark hair partially hidden under a baseball cap. *Blue and orange.*

Larkin looked at the wall again. "Did the Mets always wear blue caps." He turned to Roger.

"Blue with orange embroidery. Well, with the exception of one year in the '90s—"

"Which year."

"1997. They tried white but phased it out pretty quick."

"But in 1992, it would have been blue."

"That's right," Roger answered.

Doyle's brows were knit together. "Larkin?"

Larkin looked at the photo again on the phone.

You were there. In the beginning.

Alphabet City had been a home for the wretched.

A haven for the desperate.

A hunting ground for the villain.

You were there.

Surrounded by out-of-work dancers shunned by society, their lives left to collect dust on the desk of a cop without empathy or remorse. You had family who was a little off in the head, who was easy to manipulate, easy to extort.

You were there.

An apartment building no more than fifteen minutes from some of Manhattan's smaller parks. Parks inundated with crime. Parks no one would be surprised to find a body in. Tompkins and Madison. Would there be more cases in the stacks at Homicide of women found in Washington or Union Square during the '90s with the same MO?

You were there.

When you first arrived, you didn't notice the fallen crabapple. You had a body in the trunk—Danielle Moreno.

She was an anniversary kill—Andrew's anniversary. You were going to dump her at Madison like you'd done before.

The night Andrew went missing, he was leaving to visit Roger. Andrew saw you loading a body, perhaps. Andrew had to go. Who that woman was you were loading, she had a name, she had dreams, but you didn't care. You didn't even care about what happened to her mortal remains. Because now you had a problem.

The problem was Andrew.

Because he knew you.

Had threatened you to stay away from Jessica Lopez.

Except you didn't know Andrew had a history of abuse and hadn't told anyone about you. He had the courage to defend Jessica, but the fear of retaliation was too much to shake for a kid still trying to navigate his new life. So he never warned anyone other than a not-quite-boyfriend that you gave off *bad vibes*. That he feared for Jessica's safety whenever you came around to visit your family. Your cousin.

You were there.

You were there because you work for Parks & Recreation and knew how to get in and out of the park before opening hours. But then you saw the crabapple, your secret coming back to haunt you twenty-two years later, and that jogger—*in this storm, the fuckin' douche*—he wouldn't leave until you called police. You couldn't remove Andrew from the crate. You couldn't grab the death mask you'd had the compulsion to make but too much fear to keep.

You were there, wearing a retro Mets cap like a talisman. Wearing the cap Natasha Smirnova had clawed at, the blue and orange threads trapped under caked blood and a broken fingernail.

"Evie?" Doyle grabbed Larkin's shoulder. "What's wrong?"

Looking up, Larkin said, "I know who did it."

CHAPTER TWENTY

It was 4:49 p.m. when Larkin ran up the steep stairs of the Arsenal in Central Park to human resources on the second floor.

"Larkin, come on, slow down," Doyle called.

Larkin reached the landing and turned to watch Doyle coming up from behind. "On Monday, you asked me, point-blank, if I believed the employee who called in Andrew Gorman's body to be responsible. I said, of course not."

Doyle was out of breath as he reached Larkin's side. "You had absolutely no reason to be suspicious of a Parks Department employee *being in a park*."

Larkin's frustration, self-loathing, doubt—it was all peaking again. "If I had put the clues together—"

"*What* clues?" Doyle interrupted, his deep and smoky purr now barely suppressed exasperation. "You had nothing to work with. *I* had nothing to work with. We practically built this case out of thin air."

"Danielle Moreno would still—"

"Stop it," Doyle ordered, now crowding Larkin in the stairwell. "You know that's not true. She was dead twenty-four to seventy-two hours before you were called to Andrew's scene. Short of being psychic, nothing you could have done differently would have saved her life."

"Jessica—"

Doyle grabbed Larkin's shoulders and backed him up against the wall. "You are *not* responsible for the actions of a disturbed mind. Ricky Goulding had been her super since the '90s. Why should you have suspected the man would panic and try to finish her off like one of the original victims before we had any of that evidence?"

"Someone has to take responsibility!" Larkin shouted.

"Harry Regmore will," Doyle said. "He'll rot behind bars for the rest of his miserable life."

"But don't you get it? They're all still *dead*. I can't stop thinking it—it's compulsive. They're dead, they're dead, they're dead."

Doyle raised his hands to hold Larkin's face. "What was it you said on the phone this morning—we have to be our own champions? You remember all of the downtrodden everyday people, right? *All of them*?"

"All of them," Larkin agreed.

"Then they're not dead, Evie."

And then Doyle kissed him. Whether he meant to or not, it was happening now—and it was nothing like their other kisses, which had been gentle, tentative, affectionate. This was hard and aggressive, like Doyle wanted to fight the demons Larkin carried inside by literal tooth and nail. Lips and tongue and hot breath, hands grabbing at suits, chests bumping, middles touching—all of it sparking a flame, a rebirth inside Larkin.

This wasn't how it'd been at the lake, on the dock, with Patrick. There was no hesitation, no shakes, no shivers. This wasn't Larkin's first kiss, and Doyle wasn't a boy; he was confidence, intelligence, and devotion, coalescing in the body of a man whose outer appearance was that of downplayed attraction. A suggestion that he hadn't wanted to be noticed too much. Hadn't wanted to be taken too seriously. But Larkin noticed. And Larkin had eventually seen through the ploy.

For eighteen years, Larkin had been dressing in blues and pinks and greens and golds that no average man would touch with a ten-foot pole, because it seemed like a last-ditch effort to add color to a world that had robbed him of such pleasure. Left in a void after the *boom*, the *squish*, the *crack*—and gray had no home on a color wheel. Then he'd met an artist named Ira Doyle and everything had erupted in a blinding white, a composite of all the colors. And the storm began to move in reverse, the rain and thunder and lightning backtracking into the sky, restoring the watercolor portrait of his life that'd been washed away. The dandelions were yellow again, the campfire orange again, *love* was red again.

But this was better.

This was so much better.

Doyle broke first. His lips were parted, bruised, his breath quick and light. "I don't regret that," he whispered.

Larkin mentally replayed what he'd said to Noah the night before. "I'd kiss you again if you let me."

Doyle smiled, his entire face a beam of sunshine, radiant and unadulterated as he leaned in to allow just that.

"*Oh!*" called the startled voice of a young woman from behind Doyle. "Geez. I'm sor—hang on—it's Stabler and Benson!"

Doyle let go of Larkin and turned while smoothing his rumpled shirt.

Larkin cleared his throat and wiped his mouth on the back of his hand.

It was the same blonde, alt-reality fashionista from Monday—Kelly. Currently donned in another pair of mom jeans and a tucked-in button-down with a floral print pattern about two sizes too big, she smirked and said, "I don't remember *that* episode."

Doyle at least had the good graces to look chagrined.

Larkin reached into his suit coat and produced a folded piece of paper. "I have a warrant for all employment records pertaining to a Harry Regmore."

Kelly pursed her lips. "Okay, but we're closed for the night."

Larkin looked at his watch. "It's 4:56."

"Yeah."

"And you close at 5:00." He extended the warrant.

Kelly blew out a breath, took the form, and motioned them to follow. She unlocked the HR office, flicked the overheads, and said, "Let me check the filing cabinets." With that, she deposited her coat and purse onto her computer chair and disappeared around the corner.

Larkin and Doyle stood at the same front desk with its high countertop. The room was quiet but for the hum of the fluorescents overhead.

Larkin's even tone broke the stillness. "You inappropriately manhandled me, and now we're in HR."

Doyle chuckled, deep and rich and thoroughly amused. "Worth it." He gave the hair tie on Larkin's wrist a gentle snap.

Larkin didn't answer, but he caught Doyle's hand, gave it a brief squeeze, then let go.

Kelly returned, by Larkin's count, two minutes and seventeen seconds later. She was carrying a hanging folder that'd clearly been hanging the better part of a decade, now bent and warped in on its four inches worth of paperwork. "Sorry that took so long." She plopped the file on the countertop with a touch of over-the-top dramatics. "Mr. Regmore has worked here a *long* time, apparently."

"When did he start," Larkin asked, already grabbing the file and opening to the most recent document.

"1991."

Larkin glanced up, stared.

"May," Kelly quickly clarified.

He grunted and returned to digging through the mass.

"So are you two, like, crime-fighting boyfriends?" Kelly asked.

"No," Doyle answered quickly.

Larkin lifted several years' worth of performance reviews and set them to the side.

"When a guy kisses me like that," Kelly continued, "I better get either lobster for dinner or new sweatshirts to borrow."

Larkin heard the smile in Doyle's voice when he asked, "What's the outcome been so far?"

"Two lobster dinners and one cheapskate who ordered the chicken."

"Tough break."

"Tell me about it."

"What department within Parks and Recreation does Mr. Regmore work for," Larkin asked, looking up. "I see training certificates for half a dozen unrelated skills."

Kelly reached out, spun the folder around so she could study the contents, and then said after a minute of searching herself, "He was hired originally as part of the restoration crew at Tompkins Square Park. Oh my God." She slapped the folder with both hands and looked up with an eager smile. "You guys are so smart. Remember that OSHA stuff you were talking about on Monday? It looks like that's why he transferred in 1998—some accident with insecticide when he was working the restoration at Madison…."

"Good call," Larkin murmured to Doyle.

"Wasn't helpful until after the fact, but thank you."

Kelly bobbed her head absently while digging toward the bottom of the folder. "Here it is." She handed Larkin a printout that was older than her. "He's been the Parks Department's official blacksmith since June of 1998. Isn't that crazy? We have a blacksmith like ye olden times or something."

"I appreciate you looking into that." Doyle ended his call before saying, "Harry's supervisor—if you can call it that, he's left to his own devices pretty much at all times—confirmed he called out sick this morning. She said there was nothing strange in the request, other than he's not taken sick leave or a vacation in years. By her account, Harry's a stellar employee. Hardworking, on-time, personable, talented."

Larkin pressed down on the gas, and the Audi accelerated north on Grand Concourse in the Bronx. "He had said he was there to remove the crabapple."

"Let's not do this while you're driving. It's rush hour and school's out."

"I meant, if that had been true, he would have had a reflective safety vest on. A hardhat at minimum."

"Sure, I mean, I'm not a lumberjack—"

"But he didn't. He had blackened jeans, but the grime abruptly cut off at the knees."

"What's that mean?" Doyle asked.

"An apron. Roger wore one. You wear one. Artists wear aprons. He had UV protective glasses. I suppose I didn't think twice about eye protection. Of course you'd need that when taking a chainsaw to a tree. But you'd also need that if you're working in front of a forge all day."

Doyle made a sound of agreement.

"I was so caught up... making myself feel better, after

the start of a shit morning, by poking holes in his timeline that I overlooked why those holes really existed. His nerves weren't because he'd gotten stoned out of his mind and feared being reprimanded by his boss. He was nervous because he had Danielle Moreno's body in his car and had never come so close to being caught in his entire career."

Larkin sped past the Franz Sigel Park, a corner bodega with a bright yellow awning and a gaggle of preteen boys on bikes, all drinking sodas and laughing, and a barber shop with an older gentleman sitting outside the front door in a plastic lawn chair. He drove by blocks of hundred-year-old walk-ups in the classic shapes of H's and E's, early-evening sunlight gleaming off brick and green fire escapes like they were about to catch fire.

"You think he's running scared?" Doyle asked into the lull between them.

"I do. He held on to Danielle's body as long as he could, waiting for the police presence to die down, because compulsion wouldn't let him dump her anywhere but where it mattered to him—the park. But she was beginning to bloat and smell and decompose, and he learned of Ricky's arrest yesterday and panicked. His panic is good in the sense that it proves Ricky couldn't have been involved with the dumping, but problematic in that I believe he might try to get rid of other evidence now."

"The death masks."

"Yes."

Larkin made a left on East 165th Street and turned down Walton Avenue. He'd passed a high school and a ninety-nine-cent store when his GPS pinged their arrival. He pulled to the side of the road, parked, and turned off the engine. They both checked their holstered pistols without a word, then climbed out of the car. Larkin moved to the front door of another H-shaped building as Doyle trailed, on his phone again, calling for backup—no lights, no sirens. A posted notice beside the intercom indicated there was to be absolutely no loitering, littering, ball-playing, or sitting on the property. Perhaps ironically, an older black woman sat in a camping chair to the left of the sign, wearing big sunglasses, and reading what Larkin surmised to be a romance novel, based on the dated but nonetheless appealing cover featuring a bare-chested man.

"Ma'am," he said.

"Sir," she answered, without looking up from her page.

"Do you live in this building."

"I do."

Larkin removed his badge and displayed it, despite still not having gained her attention. "Detective Larkin with the NYPD."

"I didn't think you were with the LAPD, sir."

"We're obligated to identify ourselves regardless."

She hummed absently in reply, turned the page.

"Will you buzz us inside." He recalled his earlier conversation with Miyamoto and added, "Please."

"You got a warrant?" She asked, but was still mostly focused on her book.

Larkin tucked his badge away and then removed his second warrant. "I have an arrest warrant for Harold Regmore."

"He goes by Harry."

"Fantastic. Buzz me in, ma'am."

She finally looked away from her book, lowered the sunglasses, and studied Larkin over the rims. "I know I said his apartment stank, but arresting him for not taking out the trash seems excessive." She leaned forward in her chair to study Doyle standing a foot or two behind Larkin before saying with obvious appreciation, "Mm… just like Duke

Simon." She bookmarked her page, stood from the chair, and tapped a code on the intercom panel.

The lock disengaged and Larkin grabbed the door handle. He and Doyle moved quickly through the lobby, the *tip-tap* of their oxfords bouncing off the tiled floor and vaulted ceiling. They went to the staircase on the left, drew their weapons, and cautiously began to ascend. The second floor echoed with televisions and voices behind closed doors, but otherwise the hall was empty. Larkin turned the corner and kept moving to the third floor. When he reached the landing, the smell hit him. Maybe to an untrained nose, that smell was sour milk and rotting leftovers kept to warm in the sun for a few days. But to a cop who'd experienced death in all its various stages?

"Decomp," Doyle whispered from behind.

Larkin only nodded as he moved slowly down the third-floor hallway. Ahead of him, a door opened and a woman his age, her hair done in two long pigtail braids so as not to catch on her hoop earrings, stepped into the hall. Larkin trained his pistol on the floor and jerked his head, whispering, "NYPD. Back inside."

She immediately backtracked, slammed the door shut, and threw the deadbolt.

Larkin waited, listened, then crept closer to 3G. The door wasn't open, but it wasn't closed and locked either. Larkin pressed himself to one side of the threshold, Doyle mirroring the motion, and then he tapped the door with his shoe. It creaked open. Light filtered into the hall. No movement came from inside.

Doyle whispered, "Backup."

They'd come this close. No reason to make stupid mistakes now. Harry might still be home—he might not be. And whether he was destroying evidence that very second or was going to be caught red-handed, the stink of putrefaction told Larkin that Harry was accelerating out of control, and they'd be next if they went in balls-first. But before Larkin could nod in agreement, the light inside went out.

Larkin heard a very quiet *thwiiick* and his brain's Rolodex spun out of control to place the sound. *Cupboard or drawer—no. Cocked firearm—no. Lock—maybe. What kind? Door—no. Window—*Larkin turned, studied the layout of the hall, the stairwell, then whispered, "Fire escape."

Doyle mouthed, "Fuck," with all of the facial grammar of a scream, which would have been funny at a different place and time.

Larkin reached a hand out, pushed the door, and let it fall open the rest of the way. "Harry Regmore, this is Everett Larkin with the NYPD. I have a warrant for your arrest." He listened but heard nothing again. The smell of rot wafted into the hall. "Make yourself known at once."

Poking his head around the corner, Larkin took in a very quick assessment of the dim interior. A hall led to what he suspected was a living room on the right. Directly ahead was an empty kitchen. The hall continued on the left side with two closed doors—bedroom and bathroom, most likely. Looking at Doyle, Larkin nodded, raised his SIG P226, and slipped inside.

The living room wasn't exactly tidy—a shared space that'd been haphazardly converted into a bedroom. A balled-up blanket and pile of pillows lay on the couch, an overflowing laundry basket of men's clothing sat on the floor, and a few empty plates and beer bottles were on the coffee table beside a stack of what looked like dubious-consent skin magazines. The curtains were drawn on the right window, the faint shadow of security bars visible in the setting sun. The left was partially drawn back, the lock undone, but no obvious sign it'd been opened to utilize the fire escape. Larkin shot the walls a quick look, and in the dimness, was able to count one… two… eleven… *thirteen* total picture hanging hooks. No prize for correctly guessing what had been so blatantly displayed prior to their arrival.

Motioning to the hall, Larkin left Doyle so as to clear the rest of the apartment. The first door was unlocked and opened onto the bedroom. The bed was unmade, blankets and sheets yanked to the floor like someone had gotten tangled and struggled to free themselves. Nearby was a walker, and the nightstand held a number of prescription bottles, as well as a discarded mask attached to a portable oxygen tank. The room had the vague appearance of a nursing home suite. Had Harry taken in an elderly family member? *No*, Larkin thought. That wasn't right. This had been the parent's home and Harry was the one crashing, hence the impromptu setup in the living room.

Larkin cleared the corners before backing out. He moved to the last door, the stench even stronger now, and he knew this wouldn't bode well for whoever usually laid their head down in the master bedroom. Trying the doorknob, he found it locked. "Harry Regmore," he called loudly. "NYPD. Open the door."

Stillness. Silence.

Larkin glanced down the hall. Doyle stood there, weapon raised and waiting. So he took a step back, elevated his leg, and slammed the heel of his shoe against the lock plate. The flimsy interior door immediately shattered and crashed inward. He trained his weapon on the empty room, but was nearly bowled over by the rancid stink of decay. Larkin put the bend of his elbow to his nose and mouth, took a deep breath, then held it as he stepped inside. No one behind the door. He yanked back the shower curtain.

She had been old and frail and who Larkin could only presume was Harry's mother. She lay dead in the tub, the side of her skull caved in. The blood was dry and rigor appeared to have dissipated from her limbs.

He swore and stepped out. "She's probably been dead

since Monday."

"He's panicking and spiraling," Doyle said as he holstered his weapon.

Larkin nodded as he pulled shut the broken door as best as he could. He looked at Doyle and said, "The hooks."

Doyle nodded. "I saw them. Backup should be here any minute. Let's take a look around for the masks." He returned to the living room.

Larkin took another breath through the bend of his elbow. The smell of death was stuck in his nose and had probably permeated his suit. He'd smell it when they'd leave, smell it in the car, smell it at home—well, no, probably not home. He shook himself. That was a problem for a later time. Larkin adjusted the grip on his SIG and returned to the bedroom to do a more thorough check for Harry's collection.

Larkin heard a closet door open in the living room, and then a sudden scream. Like an animal, like rage, like seeing only red. It seemed to fill every corner of the apartment. The crash of bodies followed, a shout of protest, the *thump* and *whack* of two full-grown men knocking into drywall. Larkin ran into the hall in time to see Doyle heaved from the living room like he was a sack of potatoes. He crashed against the hallway wall to the right of the front door before raising both hands and grabbing onto a baseball bat that took a swing at his body. Harry Regmore stepped into view, shoving Doyle against the wall a second time with the force of the bat they both struggled to maintain control of. He heaved, and the momentum cracked the back of Doyle's head against the wall. Doyle cried out, lost his grip, and Harry was able to yank the bat free. Spinning it around, Harry raised the knob of the bat and struck Doyle across the head. Blood spurted in an arc and Doyle was knocked to the floor.

Harry turned his attention on Larkin. He looked fanatical, incensed, *no, say it—insane*. He didn't say anything. There was no villain monologue. He just spun the bat to hold properly, hollered at the top of his lungs, and charged.

Larkin saw only the bat.

It was night again. It was raining again. Thunder *boomed* so loud, it rattled the teeth in his skull. Boots *squished* in the thick, sloppy mud as that man entered their campsite.

Disgusting.

Immoral.

Hell.

Larkin had been seventeen and terrified. Because that monster had raised his bat, swung, and he'd heard his own skull *crack* before everything had gone black. And when he'd woken up, Patrick was dead.

Patrick's dead.

Patrick's dead.

Dead.

Doyle.

Doyle's dead.

Doyle's dead.

Larkin was thirty-five, and he was still terrified. He couldn't breathe, couldn't scream, couldn't cry. All he could do was raise his left arm with the SIG, and it didn't even feel like he was in control—it felt like his spirit wasn't even attached to his body anymore.

Harry swung the bat against Larkin's left forearm.

Snap.

Larkin dropped the SIG and lurched forward, instinctively cradling his arm to his chest. His vision doubled, blackened, seemed to narrow to a pinpoint. Then Harry bellowed. He raised the bat and took another swing, but Larkin dropped to one knee, narrowly avoiding having his head lopped clean off. Instead, Harry slammed the barrel of the bat into the drywall and flecks of white rained down on the old wooden floorboards. Undeterred, Harry raised the bat high overhead and brought it down. Larkin fell backward on his ass to avoid the next assault, and he watched as Harry ended up beating the floor with the bat instead, the reverb going through his hands and arms making him grunt in pain.

Larkin scrambled to his knees, pushed himself up with one hand, went for the SIG. Harry gave another feverish cry and kicked Larkin in the ribs. Larkin let out a *whoosh* of air and dropped, curling into a ball.

"Are you certain it was seven o'clock?" Harry leaned over Larkin, repeating back one of his statements from their conversation Monday morning. "You arrogant little fucking cocksucker! I knew then I was going to *love* bashing your brains in!" He grabbed a handful of Larkin's blond hair, yanked his head up, and shoved it against the wall. He pinned Larkin in place with the bat's endcap against his neck and spat in Larkin's face.

The sound of a gunshot consumed the small apartment space, caused it to warp inward and then expand out again like a bubble that refused to pop. Blood spurted across Larkin's face, and for a brief second, he thought he'd been shot and his body simply hadn't yet acknowledged the pain, with all of the adrenaline pumping through his veins. But Harry sagged forward, then slowly back, released his grip on Larkin, and collapsed to the floor.

Larkin looked down. A clean shot to Harry's chest. It looked like it'd shattered his collarbone. Harry was bleeding, still breathing, but clearly without considerable labor. In contrast, Larkin could feel his own chest rising and falling in a mess of sharps and flats and impromptu rests. He couldn't hear anything except that high-pitched ringing left in the aftermath of gunfire, but he was alive. Larkin looked down the hall.

Doyle, breathing hard, his right eye nearly swollen

shut and a nasty gash across his forehead bleeding all over, lowered his Glock from firing stance.

CHAPTER TWENTY-ONE

Larkin sat on the side of an emergency room bed in nothing but a pale blue hospital gown. His forearm had been given a temporary splint in the time between him being divested of his clothing and the operating room being prepped for his visit. His left flank hurt like a motherfucker, but the X-ray technician had sworn up and down he'd only been on the receiving end of two bruised ribs. Larkin's forearm hadn't been so lucky. Harry had fractured both the radius and ulna with his goddamn baseball bat, and apparently it was the kind of break that needed surgical correction before they'd slap a cast on and send Larkin on his way.

He studied the granular patterns in the tile floor and listened to the murmur of emergency room nurses nearby and the constant drone of various machines beeping. The room smelled like recycled air and harsh cleaning products, but it was better than a bloated body in a bathtub. Larkin closed his eyes and massaged his forehead with his good hand. The curtain rings rattled on the overhead metal railing around his bed. He raised his head, expecting staff arriving to whisk him off for surgery. But it wasn't hospital personnel.

It was Doyle. He did a double check over his shoulder,

like he damn well knew he wasn't allowed back here but was going to break the rules anyway, then moved into the space. He smiled, but the black eye and bandage across his forehead had a way of muddling the effect that killer look usually had. Still, though, it buoyed Larkin.

"Hey," Doyle said in a low murmur.

"Hi." Larkin pointed. "How's…? Are you…?"

"I'm fine," Doyle insisted. "Looks worse than it is. A nick in the bat sliced me open, but after a few stitches, I'm good to go." He studied Larkin for a long moment. "How're you?"

"Physically, I need surgery. Probably won't lie comfortably for a few days either." The recycled air suddenly felt stronger, like an Arctic gale. Gooseflesh broke out across his exposed legs. Larkin studied the tiles again as he said, "I saw that baseball bat and froze."

Doyle took a few more steps before his wingtips came into view.

Larkin shook his head, cleared his throat, and looked up. "I don't want to talk about it." He had to work his mouth so Doyle wouldn't see his chin quiver, but there wasn't a way to hide the tears welling in his eyes. "I'm sorry I let you down."

"You didn't. Harry was hiding in the closet, and it was my fault for holstering my weapon before properly clearing it."

"But I froze. If I hadn't—"

Doyle leaned down a bit awkwardly, given his height, in order to press their foreheads together. "I'm alive. You're alive. And better still, I didn't blow that human-sized piece of shit into next week, so they're gonna patch him up and then we can question him to our hearts' content. Ask him why he stopped with the Polaroids. Why he transitioned to cast iron when it meant forging the mask at work and taking a huge chance with his safety. How many victims, where he left them, what their names were…. Evie, you caught this sick son-of-a-bitch red-handed." Doyle straightened his posture a bit. "In the closet there was a gym bag full of the cast-iron masks. I think he didn't go out the window when you heard the lock, because the first cruiser had already pulled up. He was a caged animal."

Larkin quietly considered this.

Doyle drew his fingers through Larkin's hair a few times. "Jessica Lopez is still alive. That bat is likely the original murder weapon used against all those women *and* Andrew. Three days ago, no one knew who Andrew Gorman even was, now he's going to get the justice he deserves. Please tell me you understand that you've done something incredible?"

Larkin nodded. He looked up when Doyle dropped his hand. "I wouldn't have been able to without you."

Doyle sighed and rolled his shoulders. "Listen."

"Nothing good ever begins with *listen*."

"I came back here because on my way out, I saw Noah in the waiting room. Obviously, the hospital gave him a ring. But I thought, maybe you'd appreciate knowing in advance. And that…." Doyle rubbed a hand over his mouth, tugged his lower lip, bit his thumbnail. "Given the circumstances, I'd understand if you went home. With him. I mean, he's your husband, right?"

"On paper."

"Well, you're going to be out of commission for a bit, so I'm not entirely sure that sticking it to Noah right now is the best thing."

"I'll rent a hotel room when they discharge me."

"Evie—"

"No," Larkin interrupted. "I broke my arm. I'll be fine. I don't need a caretaker who'll, in the next forty-eight hours, find a way to twist this whole situation on its head and convince me *everything* is my fault. It took me years to come to last night's realization about our relationship, and I know… I know right now, up here," he said, tapping his forehead with his good hand, "I'm too fragile for whatever he's going to throw at me."

"All right." Doyle appeared to have nothing else to say about Noah. He finished fixing Larkin's part with his fingers. "Can I make a suggestion? One that I want you to say no to, if that's what you need."

Larkin raised his head. "Okay."

"If you call me when you're ready to leave tomorrow, I won't ask you any questions. You don't need to say anything. I'll be here to pick you up and we'll… figure this out together."

Larkin studied Doyle's face for a long time, but for the first time in maybe eighteen years, his brain was paralyzed. No cataloguing, no memorizing. Larkin just had one simple thought repeating over and over as they stared at each other: *He's such a good man.* Larkin motioned to his pile of folded clothes. "The hair tie."

Confused, Doyle turned, collected the black tie from atop the pile, and raised an eyebrow. "What about it?"

"Can you hold on to that for me, so it's not lost."

Doyle tugged it down over his bigger hand and wrist, then gave it a pat. "It's safe with me, work husband." He kissed Larkin's cheek. "Don't pick a fight with any nurses." He walked to the curtain and pulled it aside to leave.

"Ira." Larkin smiled when Doyle looked back. "How're you going to pick me up when your eye is swollen shut?"

A wicked grin split Doyle's face, and he laughed while saying, "I'll call an Uber."

Larkin was left alone in the makeshift room once again, this time with the smallest skip in his heartbeat, like someone—*Doyle*—had finally found his pulse. He looked back down at the floor, studied the Rorschach-like patterns, and counted the passing minutes.

And when the curtain rings jingled a second time, a female nurse in green scrubs appeared on the other side. "Detective Larkin?"

Larkin nodded and asked, "Are they ready for me."

She shook her head faintly and raised an envelope. "This was dropped off at the intake desk." The nurse stepped forward and held it out.

Larkin reached for it with his good hand and asked with a curious spike in his tone, "By who?"

"Some man? I don't know. I didn't really get a look at him. I'll be right back to bring you to the OR."

Larkin waited until she departed, until the curtain was pulled taut again, then studied the plain, greeting-card-sized envelope. A bit awkwardly, he clasped it between his knees, flipped the unsecured flap, and carefully drew out a folded piece of thick cardstock. Larkin set it on the bed beside his thigh and flattened it to reveal a message spelled out in cut and pasted letters:

HAPPY APRIL FOOLS' DAY, LARKIN

The *o*'s in "fools" were created with the circular logo of the Parks Department's green maple leaf.

DEATH MASKS ARE "HORRIBLE THINGS"

The quotation was a reference, but Larkin was unsure of its origin.

I HAVE A BETTER MEMENTO FOR YOU

Resting in the crease of the fold was an old MTA token with the slogan: Good for one fare.

COME FIND ME

Everett Larkin and Ira Doyle return in:

Subway Slayings
(Memento Mori: Book Two)

C.S. Poe is a Lambda Literary and two-time EPIC award finalist, and a FAPA award-winning author of gay mystery, romance, and speculative fiction.

She resides in New York City, but has also called Key West and Ibaraki, Japan, home in the past. She has an affinity for all things cute and colorful and a major weakness for toys. C.S. is an avid fan of coffee, reading, and cats. She's rescued two cats—Milo and Kasper do their best to distract her from work on a daily basis.

C.S. is an alumna of the School of Visual Arts.

Her debut novel, *The Mystery of Nevermore*, was published 2016.

cspoe.com

ALSO BY C.S. POE

SERIES:
Snow & Winter
The Mystery of Nevermore
The Mystery of the Curiosities
The Mystery of the Moving Image
The Mystery of the Bones

Snow & Winter Collection
Interlude

Magic & Steam
The Engineer
The Gangster

A Lancaster Story
Kneading You
Joy
Color of You

The Silver Screen
Lights. Camera. Murder.

Memento Mori
Madison Square Murders

An Auden & O'Callaghan Mystery
(co-written with Gregory Ashe)
A Friend in the Dark
A Friend in the Fire

NOVELS:
Southernmost Murder

NOVELLAS:
11:59

SHORT STORIES:
Love in 24 Frames
That Turtle Story
New Game, Start
Love Has No Expiration

Visit cspoe.com for free slice-of-life codas, titles in audio, and available foreign translations.

Join C.S. Poe's mailing list to stay updated on upcoming releases, sales, conventions, and more!
bit.ly/CSPoeNewsletter